PRAISE FOR ERIQ LA SALLE'S
MARTYR MAKER SERIES

"Eriq La Salle's *Laws of Wrath* is all thriller; no filler—a white-knuckled treat."

—James Patterson

"Raw and gritty, with a careening plot and brisk dialogue, Eriq LaSalle's satisfying new novel will especially appeal to fans of serial killer thrillers."

—Wendy Corsi Staub, *New York Times* bestselling suspense author

"A brilliant and bloody cop thriller from Eriq La Salle that Ed McBain himself would have been proud to have penned."

—Adrian McKinty, *New York Times* bestselling author of *The Chain*

"*Laws of Depravity* by Eriq La Salle should be on a fast track to Best Seller status. It is the story of good vs. evil where it's not always clear who are the good, and who are the evil. *Laws of Depravity* may be the most engrossing book you read this year, bar none."

—Lee Ashford, *Reader's Favorites*

"Eriq La Salle, in *Laws of Depravity*, has written an utterly compelling and riveting thriller with echoes of the dark master, Thomas Harris. Here, La Salle also adds a surprising twist by weaving in a spiritual component that raises the narrative to lofty and thought-provoking levels. It's a wonderful accomplishment."

—Leonard Chang, author of *Over the Shoulder* and *Crossings*

"Actor and director Eriq La Salle's intense debut is a modern day parable cleverly masquerading as a crime novel. A muscular, gritty, and spiritual thriller."

—John Shors, bestselling author of *Beneath a Marble Sky*, *Beside a Burning Sea*, *Dragon House*, *The Wishing Trees*, and *Cross Currents*

"*Laws of Depravity* will take you on a heart-pounding ride of vengeance, murder, and atonement, never letting you rest until you've reached the final page. Eriq La Salle deftly draws unforgettable characters who tangle with good and evil and seek spiritual understanding and forgiveness for some of the most dastardly deeds human beings are capable of committing. Drawing on his talent as an acclaimed actor and director, Mr. La Salle digs deep into his characters' psyches, delivering a group of bruised and tarnished individuals you won't soon forget."

—Neal Baer, coauthor of *Kill Switch* and former Executive Producer of *Law and Order SVU*

"The surprises keep coming in La Salle's twisting debut thriller, in which good and evil aren't always black and white. In addition to the absorbing, fast-paced plot that will keep readers guessing until the end, each wonderfully sculpted character has a distinct, lifelike personality. The plot offers catalysts for change while raising spiritual questions and blurring the line between good and evil, which propels the story upward from being merely a solid, entertaining thriller to being a gripping must read that could have readers pondering right and wrong long after they've finished."

—*Kirkus Reviews*, Starred Review for *Laws of Depravity*

"A serial killer known as the Martyr Maker is on his final round of murdering 12 clergymen once every 10 years. Two New York City detectives and the FBI are on his trail, but maybe the dead clergy aren't as innocent as they appear. A gritty crime thriller, spiritual quest, and love story all woven into one compelling tale."

—*Publishers Weekly*

"Fast-paced… Characters are richly textured [and] none is without faults. Sets the hook for the captivating series."

—*Kirkus Reviews*

ALSO BY ERIQ LA SALLE

Laws of Depravity

COMING SOON

Laws of Annihilation

LAWS
OF
WRATH

ERIQ LA SALLE

Lavette
Books

 sourcebooks

Published by Poisoned Pen Press, an imprint of Sourcebooks,
in association with Lavette Books
P.O. Box 4410, Naperville, Illinois 60567-4410
(630) 961-3900
sourcebooks.com

Originally published in 2014 in the United States by 4 Clay Productions.

Cataloging-in-Publication Data is on file with the Library of Congress.

Printed and bound in the United States of America.
VP 10 9 8 7 6 5 4 3 2 1

"It is mine to avenge; I will repay. In due time their foot will slip;

Their day of disaster is near and their doom rushes upon them."

DEUTERONOMY 32:35 (NIV)

Dr. Zibik didn't believe in hell. She was much too learned to subscribe to the existence of such mundane things as God, heaven, or damnation. If anything, she endorsed the concept that one created their own variations of heaven and hell, not in some made-up afterlife, but rather here on earth. The minute she stepped off the bus, handcuffed and shackled with the other female prisoners, she knew she had arrived at the closest thing to hell that she would ever endure. The stone walls of Bedford Hills stood as an intimidating monolith before her and the nervous fresh meat that accompanied her. Bedford Hills was a women's maximum-security facility, considered one of the toughest in the country. Zibik was an average woman; average height and average weight, with an average, forgettable face. She had short dark hair that was neatly parted down the center. Based on her appearance, her chances of survival as an inmate were slim to none. Zibik was the nerdy type that would be easy pickings for the more hardened prisoners. Female inmates were often just as brutal as their male counterparts. They pimped, raped, and sold weaker inmates, with little to no regard. The new prisoners, or puppies as they were often called, were greeted and quickly sized up by the hawks. By the time the puppies were processed and led to their cells, some of the more amorous predators had already selected their dates for the night.

Queenie loved it when they called her a big bad bitch. Even in whispers it was the ultimate compliment that only reconfirmed her position as the leader of the pack. She stood at 5'10", weighed north of 220 and was a red boned, freckle faced bruiser from a long line of Mississippi Choctows. Much to her mother's dismay, Queenie managed to spend more time in prison than out. She was comfortable with the fact that she had found a place in the world where her life had meaning, influence even. She made both the guards and cons respect and fear her. It was accepted by all parties that she ran her wing hard and pretty much did and got what she wanted. From the minute the puppies made it into the general population, Queenie decided she wanted the nerdy white woman with the short dark hair that was parted down the center. In prison, pussy was often much more than just pussy. It was taken, given, bartered, and even rented. It was everything from power and currency to a desperate attempt at reclaiming what little human-ity survived in less than humane circumstances. To prisoners like Queenie, it was the confirmation of her status as the undisputed head of the ruling class. One of the perks of being in such a position was that the spoils of war were hers to choose from according to her whims or predilections. Queenie definitely had a thing for the white, intellectual types. They reminded her of the ones that made her feel stupid the majority of her life; the ones that mistreated her mother and grandmother because they were only the hired help and, therefore, viewed as less than human. Queenie adopted the philosophy that whites had been screwing her her entire life, so why not return the favor. She loved turning out the straightlaced conservative types, and then using them to recycle her harem from time to time. Queenie already had six bitches that she alternated fucking. They were all easily identifiable by her branding: white bookworms with shaved heads and a tattoo of a queen bee on the side of their necks.

Zibik was put to work right away. She requested and was granted a sanitation job. Her main duty was to dump the leftover food and disposable utensils into industrial garbage bags. She was intercepted by Queenie on one of her trips back to the kitchen.

"Lunch is over at 1:30. Make sure you have your ass in my cell no later than 1:45. Ask around. I'm not the kinda bitch that you wanna keep waiting. And you damn sure don't want me comin' lookin' for you. You feel me?" Queenie said, threateningly.

"Uh, I uh… Yes, I feel you," Zibik muttered back.

Queenie liked relaxing right after lunch. That was when all the other prisoners went outside for their two hours in the yard. The guards knew not to question her on the days she decided to stay in or commanded one of the other prisoners to join her. They turned a blind eye to her many rendezvous, not just because they were afraid of her but also because she made sure the other prisoners paid the guards tariffs from the various illegal enterprises that were being run behind the walls of Bedford Hills. The warden may have held the title, but everyone knew who was really in charge. Running the prison certainly had its various advantages, but it was also demanding as hell. Fortunately, Queenie knew how to pace herself and refuel. The only thing that she liked more than the peace and quiet after lunch was the company of fresh meat. She had a good feeling about the new puppy.

Zibik showed up on time. The entire wing felt desolate. Queenie was completely naked, sitting on the toilet taking a piss, when her date arrived. The large woman stood without bothering to wipe herself, because part of her method in breaking a bitch was making them learn to cherish the taste of her no matter what. She was surprised to see Zibik wearing nothing but a garbage bag that she had fashioned into a tunic. She'd cut out a hole for her head and arms, and used the drawstring from the bag as an improvised belt. At first Queenie was confused, but then burst into laughter.

"What the f… What, this the best you could do for a dress?" Queenie said laughing.

Her feeling about the puppy was right. She wouldn't need much training. Using the garbage bag thing as a dress didn't really work for Queenie, but at the same time she had to give the nerd some 'props.' She was showing obedience, initiative, and creativity.

"Get on your knees, crawl over here, and show me what you're workin' with," Queenie demanded as she sat down on the bed and opened her beefy legs.

Zibik slowly crawled across the cell, knelt between the large woman's knees, wet her fingertip, and began rubbing the lips of her master's vagina. Queenie's pussy was wet and pungent with the scent of leftover piss that hung in the air like newly marked territory. When Zibik inserted her finger, Queenie closed her eyes and leaned her head back as she started getting more and more turned on. She never saw it coming. Dr. Zibik knew the weakest points of the human body. She reached behind her with her free hand, and pulled the knife that she had stolen from the kitchen. Zibik stuck the knife into the fleshy dimple in the front of the base of Queenie's neck, completely rupturing her trachea. Queenie bolted up, but quickly fell backward, as red liquid and air, rushed through the breach in her windpipe, and she began suffocating on her own blood. Zibik stood over Queenie to make sure the dying woman saw her. She had no idea, and really didn't care, what religious views, if any, Queenie may have entertained. She neither knew, nor cared, whether or not Queenie believed in heaven or hell. The only thing that mattered to Zibik in that moment was that wherever the large woman was on her way to, the very last image she saw was Zibik looking down on her, smiling. Zibik had chosen to wear the garbage bag for what came next.

1

AJ started trickin' at seventeen. His warm-up came in the summer of '86 when he was sixteen, and interning for one of his father's colleagues.

He graduated from giving the married attorney hand jobs and head to a full-blown "sex for pay" relationship. AJ never saw himself as a victim because he was the one who initiated the arrangement. His motivation and reward was neither the pleasure nor the perks, but rather the sense of power derived from the trysts. Despite their innumerable differences, his father Clay had taught him the importance of power, no matter what the situation.

In AJ's eyes he wasn't just the black sheep of the family but a different species altogether. Although he was the firstborn, his every move was compared to, and defeated by, his younger brother Phee. He loved, envied, respected, admired, and even at times resented his brother. Phee succeeded in all the things at which AJ had failed. Phee was smarter, more athletically gifted, charismatic, and the apple of their father's eye. Although AJ was close to his mother Dolicia, her overcompensation of love inevitably began to feel more conciliatory than anything else. She tried as best she could to bridge the divide that existed between him and his father. AJ spent the better part of his childhood and adolescence doing all that he could to win his father's heart. At fourteen, he conceded the fact that he would never have the type of relationship that he desired with the man who gave him life. At fifteen, he stopped trying, and at sixteen, he left home in pursuit of more achievable goals.

When AJ left home, he had no idea that it would be almost twenty years before he saw his family again. Dolicia died of a heart attack in '09, the same year that AJ's HIV status was upgraded to full-blown AIDS.

AJ attended his mother's funeral in stilettos, a black Donna Karan dress, and a platinum blonde pageboy wig. His father never acknowledged him at the funeral, neither with a word nor even a glance. The years of estrangement, and AJ's cross-dressing, had rendered him persona non grata in the eyes of Clay. Phee was another story. He rarely took his eyes off his brother throughout the funeral. The long, hard stares made it clear to AJ, in no uncertain terms, the vitriol directed at him from his younger brother. In the years following the funeral as he was turning tricks on 38th Street, AJ often saw Phee spying on him from a distance in his car. A few weeks ago when Shay DeVane, his roommate and fellow cross-dressing sex worker, went missing, AJ went to see his brother.

Even though Phee was a cop, and it was his duty and responsibility to serve and protect the people of New York, he made no attempt to mask the fact that such services were in no way extended to the likes of AJ, or the "freaks" he associated with. From the time his doctor gave him his death sentence, AJ began to think a lot about his splintered relationship with his brother and father. He had long ago released the anger that had defined him most of his life. The thing he longed for most was, at the very least, some semblance of closure from the two men who still mattered to him. He thought he would have time to make reparations before his disease killed him. He was wrong on both counts. Not only would the closure not come, but it also never occurred to him that the horror of AIDS would have been far more merciful than the brutal and unexpected death he would soon endure.

Branches high and low tore at AJ's skin as he ran naked and bleeding through the woods. The hard, cold November earth cut his feet and compromised his attempted escape even more. AJ was running on pure fear. A mile or so away, he could see the taillights of a car disappearing over a ridge. He ran as best he could to make it to the road. If he could hold on for another three minutes, then it was possible he might escape the lunatic that pursued him. As he got closer to the road, AJ saw a truck coming in his direction. As he ran faster to head off the truck, he heard the crumpling sound of dry leaves not far behind. His heart was beating like a war drum. He tried to ignore the feeling of nausea and the stale taste of warm bile in his mouth as he ran toward an opening in the barbed wire fence that encircled the property. Five feet from the opening, he stepped awkwardly on a rock and felt the violent snap of his Achilles tendon. He could feel the tendon separate and painfully roll up the back of his leg, like a tightly wound window shade. AJ cried out loudly as he hit the ground face-first. He tried unsuccessfully to get up and move on, but the second he put his weight on the injured foot, he collapsed once again in pain. He crawled as fast as humanly possible, but over the sound of his labored breathing, AJ heard the approach of heavy footsteps just behind him. The bright moon projected enough light to cast a shadow over AJ as his pursuer hovered over him. Even though he knew pleading was useless, AJ still begged for mercy. There was very little question whether or not AJ would die on this cold, November night. It was no longer his life that he begged for. At this point, the best he could hope for was that his death would come quickly and that he would be spared the type of slow torture his tormentor threatened him with.

2

Phee and Quincy were both noticeably more relaxed than they had been in years. Even though it had only been a few weeks since they'd killed Abraham Deggler and stopped his rampant murders of New York clergy, it felt like much more time had passed. Their leave of absence from the force seemed to agree with them. The Deggler case had certainly taken its toll on the both of them in ways they wouldn't have imagined. The case had so thoroughly challenged them physically, emotionally, psychologically, and even spiritually that the two of them thought about early retirement. Both the police chief and the mayor campaigned aggressively to convince them otherwise. Although Deggler almost destroyed them, he inadvertently ended up making them heroes. The partners had already enjoyed somewhat of a rock star status amongst their brothers and sisters in blue, but the notoriety from the Deggler case catapulted them even higher, not just in the eyes of their fellow officers but the brass as well. Between accumulated vacation time, disability, and some string pulling from the chief of police, the two of them were looking forward to two months of paid leave. The mayor had made it very clear to give them whatever they needed to get them to stay on the force. After some negotiating and soul searching, their only demand was downtime, which, ironically, took considerable effort for them to begin to enjoy. It was quite possible that soon they would miss the job. It was likely that they would even be bored without their former routines. Only time would tell. For now, they were content with some of the more simple things in life. Quincy had finally started sleeping consistently, peacefully—a feat more attributed to him having fallen in love with Elena than anything else. And although he was reluctant to admit it, Phee wasn't far behind Quincy and Elena in his own burgeoning love affair with Brenda, one of his closest friends, and occasional, lover for years. It was ironic, and somewhat apropos, that the two men who had accumulated shared experiences of violence and crime had finally stumbled into love at the same time in their lives. For now, both men lived for the moment and enjoyed the possibilities that each day brought.

Phee and Brenda decided to bring Quincy and Elena to a popular soul food joint up in Harlem for Sunday brunch. As a surprise, Phee got Quincy's brother Liam to meet them there as well. They were all celebrating Quincy's birthday two days early, because Phee and Brenda were scheduled to leave from JFK that night on a flight to Nice. There was certainly no shortage of fancier restaurants that they could have chosen for their celebration, but Phee knew what mattered most to his best friend and partner. He got Quincy hooked on soul food within two months of them meeting. Shortly afterwards, Quincy got his brother addicted as well. Elena was the only virgin at the table. She had never had the majority of dishes that the waitress brought to them. Smothered pork chops with grits and gravy, homemade buttered biscuits, and salmon croquettes. It was only 11 o'clock in the morning, and Quincy was recommending that she order the fried catfish and scrambled eggs, while he ordered the honey fried chicken and waffles. Having grown up in Colombia with a father who was an amazing cook, Elena knew how to appreciate food. She inhaled her meal and part of Quincy's, both literally and figuratively. Phee discreetly got the attention of Brenda, Liam, and Quincy as Elena cleaned her plate and looked as though she wanted more.

"The next time we go out, hopefully we'll choose a spot with food that you actually like," Brenda teased. As the five of them burst out laughing, Phee was happy about how easily the two women hit it off. From snippets of conversations that he overheard, he felt that Brenda and Elena could have very easily been friends independent of him and Quincy. Men loved it when their women genuinely got along. It just made everything so much easier. They laughed and drank mimosas as the waitress brought out sweet potato pie and warm peach cobbler. Even though technically it was Quincy's celebration, Phee often found himself smiling broadly, as though the special day was for him as much as his partner. He loved Quincy even more than his own brother, and he was finally learning to submit to the love from Brenda that he had long suppressed. He was looking forward to their trip to the South of France. He was excited about exploring, and figuring out the next step in, this new chapter of his life. He couldn't remember ever being this happy as an adult.

The Deggler case had somehow given him a new perspective on life. It gave him hope, fragile and uncertain, but hope nonetheless. It was the first time he could remember entertaining the thought that somehow the universe had forgiven him for committing a crime for which he'd never forgiven himself. Phee accepted long ago that true happiness was for other people, others more deserving than himself. The admiration and respect from Quincy, and the unconditional love from Brenda, left him thinking that maybe somehow he had cheated his fate. Maybe it was possible that true and long-lasting happiness was somehow still attainable, even for someone like him.

At fourteen, Phee had murdered a man. He'd never told anyone, not Brenda, or even Quincy, but hardly a day went by that he didn't think of the life that he callously took.

Three waitresses and half of the restaurant, along with Phee, Brenda, Liam, and Elena, sang "Happy Birthday" to Quincy. Elena didn't know that in America there were two versions of the song. There was the traditional version and the unofficial soul version à la Stevie Wonder. Elena liked the latter version better. Right after the song was sung and wrapped presents were placed in front of Quincy, his phone rang. As he checked his caller ID, he saw that the call was from Ira Kravitz, the medical examiner.

"Kravitz, either you miss me already or you're calling to wish me an early happy birthday," Quincy said smiling. As he listened to the voice on the other end, Quincy's smile quickly faded. Everyone at the table knew immediately that there was something wrong. Quincy hung up the phone and asked Phee to step outside.

3

Deep down, Kravitz was afraid of Phee. Over the years they had enjoyed friendly banter, and there was certainly a healthy dose of mutual respect. And even though Phee had never said or done anything directly that gave Kravitz cause to fear him, he was afraid of him nonetheless. Part of the reason was that Kravitz knew Phee's father long before Clay had purportedly put his life of crime behind him. Phee reminded Kravitz too much of Clay when he was younger. The father and son shared the same intensity, the same fearlessness, and the same temper and potential for violence. Kravitz called Quincy because he was too afraid to call Phee directly.

"There was no ID, but when I ran the prints, we found out that he was in the system on a couple of old solicitation charges. Phee, I don't mean any kind of offense, but I don't think you should see this. It's bad, real bad," Kravitz warned.

"Just show him to me," Phee said flatly.

Kravitz looked to Quincy for some type of support but had to settle for a quick nod. As the M.E. led the two men down the narrow hallway to the morgue, he nervously glanced back over his shoulder at Phee. The two morgue assistants that stood near the covered body avoided Phee's eyes when he entered the room. Of all the times they had been here, and of all the bodies they had viewed, Quincy never remembered Kravitz feeling a need to have his assistants present. Knowing Phee as well as he did, Quincy sympathized with Kravitz and understood his reasoning quite clearly.

"They found his body in a dumpster in Chinatown. We haven't touched him yet. Everything you're about to see is exactly the way he was when they brought him in," Kravitz said.

"Just show him to me," Phee snapped.

As Kravitz nodded, one of his assistants pulled the sheet off of AJ's corpse. Quincy released an involuntary sigh at the gruesome sight. AJ's eyelids had been cut off, causing him to look up in an eerie fixed stare. The skin on the front of his torso was butterflied and crudely pinned to his sides. Every internal organ had been removed, like the gutted carcass of a cow.

Quincy, Kravitz, and his assistants stood by silently and waited for Phee's reaction. The only thing that scared Quincy more than Phee freaking out was the complete indifference he was presently exhibiting. If Phee released the rage that Quincy imagined he was experiencing, at least he had a chance of helping and possibly protecting him in some way. The longer Phee waited and the more he held it in, Quincy was convinced, the more detrimental it would be upon its release. Quincy nodded to Kravitz, signaling him and his assistants to leave.

"I'm sorry, Phee," Kravitz said before exiting.

As one of the assistants tried to place the sheet back over the body, Phee stopped him with a hard look. The three men exited, leaving Phee and Quincy alone with AJ's body.

The sight of his older brother made him equal parts angry and sad. The last few times that Phee saw AJ alive, he was camouflaged under the makeup and wigs of his streetwalking alter ego. Ironically, it was in death that Phee saw his brother closer to what he had resembled in their childhood. Despite the violence done to AJ, Phee couldn't help but notice the physical similarities they shared. They both had their father's features. Deep-set eyes, thick lips, and a strong jawline. AJ had also inherited his mother's high cheekbones and hazel eyes, which Phee had always secretly envied, because he felt those two things made his brother slightly more exotic looking. As Phee looked at the body of his dead brother, he saw evidence of not only both of his parents but himself as well. Phee thought that they looked more alike now than they did when they were younger. Of course, the years and life on the streets had taken their toll, but it was still surprising how well AJ had ultimately preserved himself. Phee felt his entire body begin to tremble as AJ's lidless eyes stared back at him. Regardless of the alienation and animosity that defined the two men's relationship in the past several years, looking at his brother's corpse wounded him deeply. Quincy put a comforting hand on his shoulder.

"I got no idea what to say, Phee. You just gotta tell me what you need. We talk to the captain and get him to put Alvarez on this right away. If there's anybody that can close this thing, it'll be him," Quincy offered.

"I've gotta go see my father," Phee said as he continued staring at his brother.

4

Quincy eventually convinced Phee to let him drive him to his father's estate in Connecticut. Even though they made it to Greenwich in forty-five minutes, Quincy was painfully aware of every long, silent, awkward moment. As they entered the massive gates and pulled up to the house, Phee sat silently for a while, blankly staring at the front door. Quincy saw his partner take deep breaths to steady himself—trying to prepare for the most difficult moment of his life. The partners had on several occasions knocked on the doors of unsuspecting parents to tell them that their children had been killed. Each knock presented its own host of painful possibilities. Losing a child was never easy. Losing a child to murder was unbearable. Of all the speeches that Phee had offered to victims' families, nothing had come close to preparing him for this moment. He inhaled deeply, and then opened the car door. Just before getting out, he turned back toward Quincy.

"I'm gonna stay the night with the old man. I'll get his driver to take me back first thing in the morning."

"If you don't mind, I can just crash in the guesthouse and we can go back together."

"You don't need to do that."

"I know, but I want to."

Phee looked at his partner and made the choice not to protest. "Alright. Hey, do me a favor."

"Anything."

"Call Brenda and…"

"I already did, before we left the morgue. She canceled the flight and hotel. She's worried about you and your father. I asked Elena to keep an eye on her so she wouldn't be alone."

"Thanks, Quincy, I'll call her later. I gotta take care of my father, but I'm just not in the mood to do much else right now."

"You don't have to explain anything. Listen, I know your mother was Catholic; if you want I'll ask my brother to hold the funeral at St. Augustine's. One less thing you and your father have to sort out."

"Hadn't even thought that far ahead. Yeah, that would be a big help," Phee said as he exited the car.

Quincy stayed inside the car while Phee made the dreaded trek to the front door. A few minutes after Phee disappeared into the house, a dark-skinned man approached Quincy, tapped on the car window, and escorted him to the guesthouse. Quincy recognized the man from having met him once through Phee, when the partners needed unregistered guns to kill Deggler. He originally thought the man's was name was Azuma Debekko only to later learn from Phee that the name was one of the aliases the man sometimes used. His real name was Solomon Nangobi. Aside from Clay and Phee, most people that knew him or knew of him simply referred to him as The African.

The African was lean, sturdy, and graceful. Built for hunting. His skin had undertones of blue and purple and glistened like a wet eggplant. He was so dark that "brothas" in the 'hood called him "blue-black." He had big cheekbones and a wide nose that looked like a small hut with twin entrances. He had a sloping forehead that hung over a pair of deep-set eyes that were the color of black stones. The man had big, thick hands that were heavily scarred and missing two fingers. Despite the twelve hundred dollar suit and Gucci boots, there was something undeniably primordial about him.

Phee had mentioned a few things about the man in passing. Quincy knew that he was a former Ugandan child soldier who was now Clay's all-around fixer and right-hand man. If any heavy lifting or dirty deed needed to be done, this was Clay's go-to person. Supposedly he owed his life to Clay and paid his debt with his undying loyalty. It was widely known in the streets of New York that The African had threatened, beat, and killed and was willing to die on Clay's behalf.

After The African left Quincy alone in the guesthouse, Quincy found it impossible to relax, because he knew there would be more bloodshed in response to AJ's murder. Between Clay, Phee, and The African man with the scarred hands, something very bad would more than likely happen. Quincy tried to imagine the situation being reversed. What if someone had done to his brother Liam what he had seen done to AJ? He and Phee were similar enough for him to fear the answer to that question. Both men believed in a life for a life. Case after case, Quincy had seen Phee move mountains on behalf of anonymous victims. Estranged or not, blood ran much deeper. Regardless of how much Phee may have tried to mask it, Quincy knew his partner still loved his brother. Hidden beneath his anger, hurt, and disappointment over the choices AJ made, they were still connected—not like Quincy and Liam, but connected nonetheless. Men like Phee and his father valued family and honor above all things. Sooner or later, someone would have to pay for the crime committed against the Freeman family. Quincy knew this, because if someone had murdered his brother, he would go to hell to find them and make the Devil pay personally, if necessary.

"They found him down in Chinatown," Phee said.

"How was he killed?" Clay asked.

"Pop, at this point, that doesn't really…"

"How was he killed?" Clay demanded.

"A blow to the back of the head. He probably never even saw it coming. The coroner hasn't made an official ruling yet, but that's what it's looking like," Phee lied.

The only other time Phee saw his father cry was when Dolicia died. As he held his father, Phee made peace with the lies he told him. The second that Clay pushed back from him, Phee saw the rage swell in his father and boil over, bursting like a broken dam. Clay violently kicked his chair and then overturned his desk. He attacked and broke the seven-foot mirror by the doorway as though his very reflection were somehow responsible for AJ's death. As quickly as the violent outburst started, it suddenly stopped. Phee watched his father pacing in a corner like a caged panther. His stare was cold and vacuous. The only sound in the room was the short, staccato breaths that Clay flicked out. As Phee watched his father seething, he knew that Clay no longer saw him or anything else around him. Clay was gone, at least temporarily. He disappeared deep into a black hole, and all his son could do was watch and hope for his return. The majority of people who ever had the opportunity to witness Clay's ire this close didn't survive to tell about it. Phee had heard more about Clay's famous temper than he had ever witnessed or experienced. Clay was a completely different man when pushed to his darkness. At that moment, even Phee feared Clay as he watched him continue to pace in the corner. Phee was afraid, because he didn't recognize his father. As he continued to stare at Clay, all he saw was a dark, wounded stranger, inconsolable and dangerous.

Even if Phee wanted to tell the truth now, he wasn't about to risk a potential apocalypse by fueling his father's fury. As much as it cost him, Phee was willing to live with the lie at least for a little while. He was sixteen the last time he lied to his father. It was over something insignificant and unmemorable, but the look of hurt and disappointment on Clay's face at the time made Phee vow on the spot that, no matter what, he would always tell his father the truth. The minute Phee saw his brother in the morgue, he knew he would have to break that vow. How could he tell the man who he worshipped that some sick bastard decided one of the lives that Clay brought into this world was of so little value it could be shredded and discarded, like the piles of garbage in which it was found? How could he accurately describe the level of wickedness and violence that was directed at his own flesh and blood? All Phee could think about was how much he had failed both of his parents. His mother, Dolicia, pleaded with him for years to reconcile with his brother. Each time, he simply appeased her with vague and empty promises. Phee let his mother die, knowing that he hadn't honored his word to her. He now lied to his father because he lacked the courage to tell him the truth—not just the details of how AJ was murdered but how cruel he had been the last time he saw his brother. When AJ came to him in need just a few weeks earlier, Phee had treated him like shit and turned him away. He wondered if his brother might somehow still be alive if only he had extended to him a fraction of the humanity that he so readily offered to total strangers. He knew the truth would come out eventually, but hopefully by then Phee would have found whoever was responsible and made them suffer as much as possible. Even though he wouldn't be able to kill them in the same fashion AJ was killed, he was nonetheless determined to make them feel intolerable anguish and suffering before killing them. He owed at least that much to his father, mother, and brother.

5

Phee sat in his father's office until two a.m. He watched Clay throw back shots of offensively expensive liquor as though it were water. There was very little conversation between the two. Phee just wanted Clay to know that he wasn't alone. After Clay finally convinced his son to go to bed, he sat alone in his office for the rest of the night. The mahogany walls were filled with awards and plaques of various sizes. There were many photos of Clay and famous public figures from the upper echelon of politics, sports, and entertainment. As he looked around at his opulent surroundings, and the various reminders of his success, he thought only of his failures. Clay thought back to the beginning and how he had failed AJ from the start. His mind wandered but always returned to the death of his firstborn.

The comforts of apathy had long ago afforded Clay the luxury of losing count of the various men he killed or the copious number of deaths he'd commanded. For the most part, his victims remained blurs and faceless memories that rarely crossed his mind. Now that AJ had been murdered, Clay thought about the grieving parents and orphans that his actions had created, along with the innumerable lives he'd destroyed.

AJ's murder granted Clay admittance into an exclusive network into which every member lamented their induction.

Experiencing his own personal tragedy left Clay thinking of some of the deadly crimes he'd committed decades ago and the karmic debt that he owed to either an angry God or delighted Devil. Little did he know that the consequences of blood he'd shed forty years earlier was finally coming back to claim payment in full…and then some.

In 1972, Harlem was at war with itself. It had become a microcosm of the "Negro" experience in America. Only four years removed from the death of King and the height of the Civil Rights era, Black America was in the midst of an identity crisis. The nonviolent teachings of King were rejected in large part by a rebellious generation that leaned more toward Malcolm than Martin. "Brothas" from Harlem only turned the other cheek when they were rearing back to counterpunch. Like most inner cities, Harlem had a lot on her plate: the Vietnam War, Black radicalism, the devastating influx of "heron," along with the ever-growing population of pimps and "hustlas." The post-Civil Rights era had brought with it many opportunities for empowerment and economic advancement, both legit and illicit. Clay Freeman got his start with the latter but wisely decided with a new wife and son on the way that the early '70s was the right time to venture down more lawful avenues. By the time his wife Dolicia was in her ninth month, Clay had divested all of his illegal earnings into real estate and legitimate businesses. His mentor, Alton James Slopes, unsuccessfully tried on numerous occasions to dissuade him from totally leaving the small criminal empire that they had built together. "I'm just saying, you keep enough of an interest in the business to keep your presence felt. You could still bring in 40-50k a month, without even having to do anything," Slopes urged.

"I got more than enough money, Slopes; so do you. Gotta know when it's time to leave the game," Clay responded.

"I'm fifty-two years old and been hustlin' my whole life. The game is all I got, little brotha'."

"You ever want out, just let me know. Cats like me and you could run this whole city, legally."

"That's the difference between me and you, Clay; I ain't tryin' to run the whole city. I'm cool with just a piece of it."

As the two men continued eating at the small spot on Lenox Avenue, a muscular, dark skinned Puerto Rican named Blue Morales approached them at the table. Blue was a pretty boy and a flashy dresser.

"We gotta meet Honey Boy Jones in twenty minutes," Blue said.

"Alright. Grab the car. I'll be out in five," Slopes responded. Blue threw a nod in Clay's direction and then turned and left.

"Who's the young buck?" Clay asked.

"Some Puerto Rican muscle out of the Bronx. Been groomin' him for a month now. Eventually, somebody's gotta take your place."

"You think he's ready?"

"He ain't you yet. A little young, dumb, and full of cum, but he's got real heart. He grew up on the street. Kid doesn't know fear. Reminds me of you."

"I've been seeing a lot of new faces around the way. What are you gearing up for?"

"Once word gets out that you're no longer runnin' things for me, I might get fools comin' out the woodwork to test me."

"Is that why you're meeting with Honey Boy?"

"Yeah, tryin' to squash some shit before it gets out of control. Sure you don't wanna ride along with me for old time's sake?"

"I told you, I'm officially retired. Besides, I gotta stay near Dolicia. The baby's coming any day now."

"You pick out a name yet?"

"It's supposed to be a surprise, but we're naming him after you. We'll call him AJ for short. Tonight Dolicia is gonna ask you to be godfather."

"Wow, of course. I'm honored, and don't worry, I'll act surprised. For the record, I'm real proud of you, Youngblood."

"Having this kid is the only thing I've ever been scared of. What if I don't know how to be a good father? I mean what if I fail AJ?"

"You'll be fine. Just keep doing what you've already started doing, puttin' your son above everything else. You do that, and you can't fail him."

6

As the television played in the background, Michael Jackson was on the Ed Sullivan show, crooning about a rat named Ben. Clay, Slopes, and Dolicia were just finishing up dinner. Dolicia was a stunning Dominican, with long black hair, hazel eyes, and a café au lait complexion. She was the most beautiful woman Clay had ever seen, a fact he confirmed with her every time he looked at her. As Dolicia served the two men caramel and coconut flan for dessert, Clay gently grabbed her and rubbed her pregnant stomach.

"You know she's carrying a future NFL Hall of Famer," Clay said proudly to Slopes.

"What if he doesn't even like football?" Dolicia asked teasingly.

"Then I'll know you been makin' it with the milkman, 'cause if he's a son of mine, he's NFL all the way."

"As tall as the two of you are, don't be surprised if you end up with a basketball player," Slopes chimed in.

"Basketball don't count, it ain't a contact sport. She give me a basketball player, I'm sending him back," Clay teased.

Dolicia affectionately hit Clay with a dish towel as he pulled her in and kissed her. Slopes looked on and smiled at the newly-weds' playful exchange.

"Slopes, did Clay tell you that we're gonna name our son AJ after you?" Dolicia asked.

"Really? No, he didn't mention it. I'm flattered," Slopes responded.

"You two are the worst liars in Harlem," Dolicia laughed. "Next, you're gonna pretend that he didn't tell you that we want you to be godfather as well."

The two men looked at each other and started laughing.

"I'd be honored to be AJ's godfather," Slopes said smiling.

Clay drove Slopes home around midnight. They pulled up to one of the beautiful brownstones in the high-end enclave of Striver's Row. As Clay killed the engine and the two men sat in the car, Slopes pulled out a silver flask, toasted his friend, took a swig, and then passed it to Clay. Clay took a sip and winced as the bitter alcohol burned his lungs.

"Never could understand how you drink this shit," Clay said.

"Scotch is like a good woman: takes a little time and a few hiccups to learn how to truly appreciate."

"Well then, I guess I'm halfway there," Clay laughed.

"You got a real good situation, Youngblood. I'm glad you got what I never found. Just make sure you always take care of them, 'cause a man ain't a man if he's not willing to do whatever he has to do to take care of his family. Maybe if I had ever found a good woman to come home to, I wouldn't be still runnin' these streets the way I do."

"It's never too late."

"I keep tellin' you, I been in the game so long I only know how to play it one way, even when they keep tryin' to change the rules on me."

"So how did your meeting go today?" Clay asked.

"Honey Boy claims he can run six keys of smack a week. Wants me to give him 110th Street for a 30 percent cut. I told him to kiss my ass; there's no way he could push that kind of weight. I'm sure there'll be some kind of fallout from it."

"Yeah, but Honey Boy ain't gonna be the one you have to worry about."

"What do you mean?" Slopes asked.

"He ain't got the brains or means to put that kind of shit on the street. The cat that you're gonna have to worry about is the one who's backing him. My guess is that it's Varelli."

"Fuckin' Guineas, been tryin' to take back Harlem for years now."

"For what it's worth, I think you should cut some kind of deal with Varelli directly. It's just a matter of time before someone besides him makes a play for 110th Street. Better the devil you know than the one you don't."

"Fuck all them faggot-ass Wops. They go anywhere near 110th, I'll kill 'em all."

"What kind of example as a godfather are you gonna be to my son with that kind of attitude?"

"Shit, Man, with you gettin' all soft, Little AJ is gonna need some balance. Alton James is a helluva name to live up to. I'm just tryin' to protect my mother-fuckin' legacy."

Slopes laughed, took another quick swig from his flask, and got out of the car. After watching Clay drive off, he climbed the stairs to his brownstone.

Even though Slopes was already a little tipsy, he entered his dark parlor for a nightcap. Sensing the presence of someone else in the room, he pulled out a chrome .38 snub nose and flipped on the light switch. Three large men in various parts of the room stood frozen with their guns trained on Slopes. A well-dressed man sat reclining in a leather chaise lounge. Calvin "Honey Boy" Jones was black, 5'6" and wiry—an up-and-coming gangster with a Napoleon complex.

"If I wanted to kill you, you wouldn't have made it into the house," Honey Boy said.

Slopes knowing that he was heavily outgunned, lowered his pistol and stared at Honey Boy. One of the men crossed to Slopes and took his gun as he patted him down for more weapons. The large man removed a second gun from the small of Slope's back. As Slopes stepped forward, he noticed that his iron and ironing board were set up near the middle of the room.

"What the hell is this, and what the fuck are you and these fleas doing in my house?" Slopes barked out.

"Relax, Slopes. I was hoping that you and I could iron out any differences that we had earlier," Honey Boy said smiling.

"I already told you what I thought, and you showing up like this ain't gonna change nothin'."

"For your sake, I hope it does. I got orders to leave here either with your cooperation or your life. Choice is yours. It's all just business. So you really need to think about this. Come on, Slopes, Harlem has enough to make sure we all get a taste and not step on each other's toes in the process. You gotta accept that shit is changin' up here."

"That's because brothas like you are willin' to sell it out to the first white devil that comes along, but it ain't gonna happen as long as I'm alive."

"Well then, that might only be a temporary problem," Honey Boy responded.

"Is that supposed to scare me or make me laugh?"

"You think I'm fuckin' with you?"

"I think you're severely confused about who you are versus who I am, so let me clear it up for you. I'm the nigga that's been runnin' this game while you were crawlin' around pissin' on yourself and smilin' about it. You don't get to do business on 110th Street, not just 'cause you're some corny motherfucker tryin' to play gangster but because you're stupid. Sooner or later stupid people fuck the game up for everybody. So now that we understand who we are, you need to get the hell outta my crib."

As one of the henchmen punched Slopes in the face, Honey Boy jumped up red hot.

"That's the problem with old-ass niggas like you. You're too shortsighted for your own good. I come up here to talk to you man-to-man, and all you do is insult me."

"A real man don't need three dogs to do his talkin'."

As the 300-pound man who punched Slopes moved in for another blow, Slopes quickly and surreptitiously pulled a pearl handle straight razor from the inside of his shirt cuff and swung for the man's jugular. The blood spraying from the man's neck distracted everyone, which gave Slopes the opportunity to lunge for Honey Boy, just making contact with the right side of his face. The two remaining henchmen both tackled Slopes and punched him repeatedly. Honey Boy looked on in disbelief as his man lay choking on the blood still gushing from his throat. After a minute or two, the man stopped moving altogether. As Honey Boy turned his focus back to Slopes, he used a silk handkerchief to dab at the four-inch cut from his cheek to his chin. Honey Boy crossed and plugged in the iron…

"You stupid son of a bitch. You wanna see who I am. I'll show you. Gene, Freddy, pick him up. Open his mouth. You shoulda' tried talkin' to me, Slopes, when you had the chance," Honey Boy said.

Honey Boy broke off the three-inch pearl handle of the razor, and forced it vertically into Slopes mouth to prevent him from closing it.

Once he had successfully propped Slopes' mouth open, he used the blade to cut his tongue.

"Strip him and bring him to the board," Honey Boy commanded. Gene held Slopes as Freddy used the razor to cut off his clothes.

As they crossed to the ironing board, Honey Boy spit on the hot iron for Slopes' benefit. The loss of his tongue had cost Slopes some of his hubris and defiance, but he still struggled as Honey Boy's men restrained him. Honey Boy placed the iron on Slope's chest and left it there as it seared the skin and filled the room with a sickening sound and scent of charring human flesh. Slopes thrashed about in muted agony. As Honey Boy took off his jacket and raised the iron to Slopes' face, he spoke to him very casually.

"We should both get real comfortable, 'cause we've got a long-ass night ahead of us."

7

Blue Morales woke up Clay and Dolicia when he frantically called around seven a.m. As was his duty, Blue arrived at the brownstone at seven a.m. to bring Slopes the four different newspapers with which he started each day before going to Sylvia's restaurant for breakfast. No matter what happened the night before, good or bad, Slopes started every day the same. When Clay's phone rang earlier, he'd assumed it was Slopes, because he was the only person in the world who would dare call him at such a time. Clay was so caught off guard by Blue's ranting, that he inadvertently allowed Dolicia to overhear enough of the conversation to know that something horrible had happened to Slopes. Clay, as a steadfast rule, never discussed his business and dealings around his woman. Dolicia immediately became hysterical. Both she and Clay loved Slopes as though he were blood. It took some doing, but after he finally got her to calm down for their baby's sake, Clay took Dolicia upstairs to her parents' apartment. As he and Dolicia dealt with the tragic news in their own way, he did everything he could to make sure that the stress didn't jeopardize the welfare of his wife and unborn son.

Clay rushed through the front door of Slopes' brownstone, to find Blue sitting on the stairs with puffy, red eyes. Blue fidgeted with his clothing in an effort to make himself more presentable. His grief left him sniffling and uncertain of himself.

"Where is he?" Clay demanded.

"They fucked him up, Man," Blue spurted out.

"Where is he?"

Blue awkwardly stood and led Clay to the sliding cedar doors of the parlor. As he slid the doors open, Clay saw Slopes hanging from a ceiling beam. He was completely nude, and his face and body were covered with at least a dozen black imprints from a hot iron. His lips and chin were covered with dark, plum-colored blood, and his tongue lay on the floor beneath him.

Clay had never lost anyone he loved. Certainly there were a few associates that he had rolled with over the years whose deaths had saddened him, but he had never grown to love them. The streets and the game never left much room for deep, emotional attachments. Slopes had taught him years ago that the less he had to lose, the more he stood to gain. Although he never said it directly, Clay got the feeling early on in their relationship that Slopes saw love as a handicap. Despite Slopes' hustla's creed, the two men grew to love each other very much. Slopes was a big brother, favorite uncle, and father figure all rolled into one. Clay was, for better or worse, the man that he was because of Slopes.

"Cut him down," Clay said flatly.

"You know this was Honey Boy Jones," Blue said as he grabbed a chair and pulled out his knife, and the two men lowered Slopes. "Things got heated at the meeting yesterday. Honey Boy tried threatening Slopes after Slopes turned down his offer to let him run 110th Street. Son of a bitch. When do we hit 'em?"

"We don't."

"What do you mean we don't?"

"Just what I said. Slopes knew the game. This kind of shit is the life we chose. I got a family now. I can't get back into this. I'll tell you the same thing that I told Slopes he should have done. Go to Honey Boy and Varelli and make peace, then cut a deal with them."

"What the fuck are you talking about?"

"You go after Honey Boy, you're gonna get into a war with Varelli that you can't win."

"Can't be a war if only one side is standing."

"Don't underestimate Varelli. He might not be mob now, but he will be soon. You go after him, and I promise you, when all the smoke settles, they'll completely own Harlem, and you and everyone that you know will be dead. And everything that Slopes built up will be gone. That's not what he would have wanted."

"You wanna pussy up, then go ahead and do that, but don't try to sell it as what Slopes would have wanted."

Clay was quick and precise. By the time he slammed Blue up

against the wall, he had his .45 firmly pressed against the surprised man's forehead.

"I know you got grief in your heart right now, but if you ever call me out of my name again, Honey Boy and Varelli will be the least of your worries," Clay said firmly.

"Go ahead; makes no difference which one of you pulls the trigger today. I go down, at least it's gonna be for the one cat that taught us both the real meaning of family."

Clay lowered his gun and walked away.

It was just after nine in the morning when Clay made it back home. He immediately went to his in-laws' apartment to check on Dolicia. Her face was swollen, and she looked like she had been crying the entire time he was gone. Clay held her and refused to talk to her about any details surrounding Slopes' murder. The most he said was simply that Slopes was gone. He gently rocked her until she fell asleep. After her mother came to take over, Clay went downstairs to make arrangements for Slopes' funeral. He called the best funeral parlor in Harlem and gave them very specific instructions on how he wanted Slopes' funeral to be the best that Harlem had ever seen. He wanted his mentor to be presented and remembered as royalty. Clay made it clear that there would be no expense spared. It made no difference whether or not God accepted or rejected him, or even if the Devil laid claim, Clay needed to make sure that Slopes was going to his final destination in style.

As soon as he hung up the phone, he broke down. He had

been able to suppress things for Dolicia's sake. He'd even managed somehow to hold it together when he saw the horrible things that had been done to Slopes. As long as he was moving and doing things, he succeeded in staying a half step ahead of the myriad emotions he was feeling, but now, alone in his apartment, the thin façade crumbled and fell apart. Blue had touched on it earlier. Slopes was as much a definition of family to Clay as Dolicia and her parents had become to him. The simple truth was if anyone did harm to one of them, Clay's reaction would be swift and merciless. Surely the man who had been the most influential in his life deserved the same considerations. Forty-five minutes after hanging up the phone, Clay went back upstairs with a large envelope containing account numbers and instructions for Dolicia's father, telling him what to do in the event that he was killed. Clay left the envelope at the front door, knocked, turned, and left as he heard footsteps approaching from inside. Slopes was right: a man was nothing if he wasn't willing to do whatever was necessary to take care of his family; as such, his murder, most certainly demanded retaliation. By the time Clay grabbed his gun and headed out, the only thing on his mind was blood for blood.

8

Honey Boy Jones was a preemie that wasn't expected to live, but he proved them all wrong. Because of his size, people often made the mistake of underestimating him. Honey Boy thought big, talked big, and dreamed big; and there was no way he was gonna let a narrow-minded nigga like Slopes hold him back.

Varelli was down to back him and supply him with six keys a week of the best heroin that was being smuggled back to the states from Vietnam in the body bags of dead vets. The only way he was going to consistently move that much weight was if he controlled a major avenue like 110th Street. Cats like Slopes were dinosaurs. Honey Boy Jones saw himself as the future of the game. Once he was certain that Slopes' right-hand man, Clay, was no longer in the picture, he knew it was time to make his move. He could handle Slope's new boy, Blue Morales, but everybody knew that

Clay Freeman was not the kind of man you wanted to have a beef with. Now that Clay was a civilian, he had to respect the moves that Honey Boy was making. Slopes' murder was business, nothing more, nothing less. If Blue Morales didn't go into hiding, the same would soon happen to him.

Honey Boy ran a few whores and numbers out of a joint on 121st near 7th Avenue. Sunday afternoons were pretty quiet. He was checking his books and cash from all of his spots to make sure all the week's numbers were on the up-and-up. Gene sat at a nearby table, counting money as a pretty, high-yella' whore named Dee Dee, changed the gauze covering the gash that Honey Boy received from Slopes the night before.

"Where the hell is Freddy with my fish sandwich?" Honey Boy said with obvious irritation.

"He shoulda' been back by now. You want me to go look for him?" Gene asked.

"Finish counting the money first. If he's not back by..."

There were three quick knocks at the door, followed by a pause and then two more knocks.

"That's him now," Gene said, as he grabbed his gun and crossed to the thick speakeasy door and opened the small window to confirm it was Freddy.

"What took you so long?" Gene demanded.

"I ran into some trouble," Freddy responded nervously.

"Get his ass in here," Honey Boy barked in the background.

As soon as Gene unlocked the door and opened it, Freddy was shoved into him by Blue, who rushed into the room and put several bullets into both men. As Honey Boy reached for his gun on the nearby desk, Clay appeared and shot him in the hand. Dee Dee was hysterical, until Clay calmly pointed his gun at her and convinced her to calm down. Even though the two henchmen showed every sign of being dead, Blue put an extra bullet in both of them... Honey Boy remained seated at the desk, holding his bloodied hand.

"This ain't got nothin' to do with you no more, Clay. Let it go. I offered Slopes a good deal. One that a cat like you woulda jumped all over. You and me both know it was just business. I didn't do nothin' that you wouldn't have done. Ain't too late for you to walk away from this. We killed Slopes, and now you killed my boys for him. We can just let it go at that."

"Is Varelli backing you?" Clay asked.

"Does it really make a difference?"

"It did to Slopes."

"Yeah, Varelli's backing me. Look, brotha', I was just following orders."

"Where's Varelli now?"

"You don't wanna mess with Varelli."

"Where is he?" Clay said as he moved in closer with his gun still trained on Honey Boy.

"He lives out on Long Island, a yellow house, at the end of Lake Edge Way."

"Cool. Listen, don't worry, your mother will keep it closed."

"My mother... Keep what closed?"

"Your casket," Clay said as he thumbed back the hammer of his .45 and pointed it directly at Honey Boy's face.

Honey Boy pleaded, "Please Clay, don't do this. Slopes was just business."

"Naw, he was family."

Clay placed the barrel of his gun on the front of Honey Boy's forehead and fired. As the man fell back in his chair, Clay stood over him and shot him again twice in what was left of his face. Blue heard stories of how calm and collected Clay was when he killed, but seeing him up close was much better than anything he had heard. Dee Dee went into shock and was still seated in her chair hyperventilating.

"What about her?" Blue asked.

"What about her?"

"You want me to do her, or do you want to? Can't just leave her. She knows who we are."

"She knows not to talk."

"Why take the chance?"

"Because I don't do women."

"Yeah, well, I do," Blue said as he turned and shot Dee Dee.

9

Clay sat across the street from Varelli's house, with Blue Morales next to him in the passenger seat. They waited until dark, because back in '72, black men stood out in Nassau County, Long Island like pepper on rice. Varelli lived on a quiet street, on a large lot, with the nearest neighbor being a hundred or so yards away. Blue reached in the back seat and grabbed the double-barrel shotgun that he brought along for the occasion. Clay never regretted killing anyone. In one way or another, it always boiled down to necessity and survival. Aside from the first time when he was nine and killed his abusive stepfather, today was only one of two times that he killed solely based on emotion. He was a controlled and calculating strategist who always looked at least four steps ahead. His survival and success was predicated on the very things that he was now ignoring. Clay defied odds his entire life. There was the childhood that he should have never survived, the criminal life he should have never succeeded at, and the love of a good woman that he never truly felt worthy of. As he reloaded his gun and looked at Blue, he knew that he was jeopardizing everything he had, everything he wanted, and everything he cherished. Just as he was on the verge of putting his past life behind him, vengeance reared its ugly head.

Varelli's wife Leona, a round woman with thick ankles, was cooking dinner when her son Joseph darted into the kitchen, in search of a place to hide. As he beckoned her silence, she broke a piece of warm cannoli crust, fed it to him, and then nodded in the direction of the kitchen table. Joseph scurried under the table and hid under the long tablecloth that covered it. Joseph, who was seven, was her second born and had almost died at birth. On the day he was born, Leona was at Mass when she suddenly started bleeding profusely as her placenta prematurely detached. The priest rushed her to the hospital personally, and by the time doctors cut her open and removed her son, he had been deprived of oxygen for several minutes. He was delivered blue and lifeless. Even as the doctors desperately worked on him, they made it clear from the start that the baby had very little chance of survival. If by some miracle he did survive, it would more than likely be in a vegetative state. She flat-out rejected any dire prognosis, because in the deepest reaches of her heart, Leona believed in the power of prayer. Even when her own husband started trying to prepare her for the inevitable death of their newborn son and tried to comfort her with the promise of other children, she held steady to her faith and prayed incessantly. Her faith was rewarded when, against all odds, she heard baby Joseph cry. In fact, the entire ward heard him cry. His voice bellowed throughout the halls of the hospital, defiantly announcing his survival. Leona joyously cried at the voice that was clearly touched by God. When Joseph grew into a young boy, he sang like an angel, which constantly reminded his mother of the miracles received the day he was born.

Leona enrolled him in choirs and even got him a private singing instructor. Like most little boys, his priorities were much simpler. He thought playing hide-and-go-seek with his brother was a much better use of his time than the hours he was forced to dedicate to piano lessons and singing exercises. He sang for one reason and one reason only. He sang because somehow, even at his age, he knew nothing in the world brought his mother more joy.

After finishing up his scales for the day, Joseph played his favorite game with his older brother Anthony. Anthony rushed into the kitchen slightly out of breath a few seconds after Joseph hid.

"Mama, have you seen Joseph?" the boy whispered.

"I suspect he's around here somewhere. When you find him, tell him it's time for the two of you to wash up and get ready for dinner. I'm frying cannolis for dessert now."

To Anthony's delight, she dipped her finger in the bowl of sweet ricotta cream and put it in his mouth. As he smiled and turned to leave, he suddenly saw Clay and Blue blocking his path. He rushed back to his mother's side.

"Mama…" the boy said nervously.

Leona turned around just in time to see the two dark men casually walk into the kitchen. She instinctively pulled her son in closer.

"Who are you? What are you doing here?" she demanded.

"We're here to see your husband," Clay said.

"He's not here," Leona replied.

Clay nodded to Blue, who left the kitchen to go check out the rest of the house.

"We just need to talk to your husband for a few minutes, and then we'll be gone and you can get on with your dinner. Smells good; what are you cooking?"

She and her son just looked at the imposing man, terrified.

"You and your son got no reason to fear me. I told you; I'm just here to talk to your husband," Clay said.

"I'm making some veal and pasta. And some cannolis for dessert," she said.

"Your oil is burning."

"Excuse me?"

"Behind you, your oil is burning."

Leona quickly turned around and turned off the bubbling oil, just as Blue reentered the room.

"He ain't here," Blue announced.

"Where's your husband?" Clay asked calmly.

"I don't know," she said.

"She's lying," Blue raised his voice.

"No, I'm not. I don't know," Leona said emphatically.

Blue revealed the shotgun as he stepped in her direction. She flinched and held her son tighter.

"I bet if I told you I was about to unload one of these barrels into your boy, you'd tell us," Blue threatened.

"Take it easy, brotha'," Clay said.

"Fuck easy, I say we do 'em all," Blue spit out.

"We're not touching them, you hear me?" Clay yelled.

"She knows where he is. If I gotta pop this brat to get her to tell us, then that's what I'm gonna do. I ain't askin' your permission," Blue responded.

Just as he made a slight turn in Clay's direction, Leona seized the opportunity, grabbed the pan of hot oil, and threw it on Blue. As the oil burned the left side of his face, Blue half turned and reflexively pulled the trigger of the shotgun, which unloaded both barrels into the mother and son. Leona took the brunt of the load and was killed right away. Anthony lay nearby, with heavy buckshot in his chest and face, his blood pouring freely over the white linoleum floor. His lungs were failing, as evidenced by the horrible wheezing sound he was making. Blue writhed on the floor in unbearable pain, yelling loudly. Clay rushed to the sink, ran cold water on a nearby dishtowel, and placed the dripping cloth on Blue's face.

"Clay, you gotta get me to a hospital man. Please, Clay."

"Listen to me, Blue; you gotta be cool while I figure this out. If I take you to the hospital, cops will know you were here. Just trust me. I'm gonna get you taken care of, but we gotta do it my way."

As he helped Blue to his feet, Clay tried to ignore Anthony, who continued to struggle with his breathing, his condition worsening with each painful moment. Clay propped Blue up against the doorway and pounded the wall out of frustration. An overhead clock fell and broke; its time was frozen at 7:38 when Clay turned around and walked back toward the dying boy. Clay didn't think or hesitate as he picked up Blue's shotgun, trained it on Anthony, and put him out of his misery.

As Joseph hid under the table in the kitchen, he saw the legs and feet of two strangers. He lifted the tablecloth slightly and saw two scary black men arguing with his mother. The boy was frightened by the gestures one of the men made when he talked to his mother and brother. Joseph could only see glimpses as he looked up from underneath the tablecloth. He was terrified when the scary man pointed a long gun at his mother and yelled at her. Joseph wanted to do something, anything. He wanted to scream, to make the men go away, but when he opened his mouth nothing came out. His voice, his strong, beautiful voice, was somehow lost to him. His fear kept him curled on his knees under the table. Joseph heard the blast and felt a strong vibration as a flash came from the gun. The flash terrified him and made him pee on himself. The loud sound was the last thing he heard. No matter how hard he tried, he could no longer hear anything, not even the sound of his own breathing or the heavy footsteps of the bad men. His voice was muted and his hearing deafened when he saw his mother fall to the ground, bloodied and deathly still. The best he could manage was to silently cry as he saw all signs of life leave his mother's still opened eyes. A few minutes later, there was another flash and vibration, and he saw his brother stop moving. He got a better view of one of the scary men after he fell to the ground with half of his face burned. When the other man kneeled to help him, he got a good look at both of their faces. They were faces that seven-year-old Joseph would never forget.

Doctors would eventually diagnose him as having had a post-traumatic psychosomatic episode. He would never speak again. He would never hear another sound. Hate came early to Joseph Varelli. As he watched the two men leave, he vowed no matter how long, or whatever it took, one day he would kill them and avenge his family.

10

After Varelli's wife and son were killed, Clay loaded Blue into the back of the car and took off. About four blocks away, he saw a late-model El Dorado coming around the corner. The El Dorado or "El Dog" as it was often called, floated down the street like a metallic canoe. Clay recognized Varelli right away, but Varelli was too busy belting out Sinatra's "The Best Is yet to Come" to notice Clay. Clay hooked a U-turn and sped after him. He cut off Varelli just before he made it to his house. Clay grabbed Blue's shotgun, jumped out of his car, and went after the El Dorado. By the time Varelli reached for his gun in the glove compartment, Clay unloaded two shots through the driver side window, killing him on the spot. He jumped back in his car and sped away.

Back in 1972, Ira Kravitz was burning the candle at both ends. The young intern doubled four times a week as a paramedic. He was struggling to put himself through med school, and the extra money he made was worth the sacrificed summers he drove med rigs to make ends meet. His financial troubles aside, he knew this was the part of his career where he had dues to pay. That never bothered him, because Kravitz had big plans. Most interns and students obsessed over being the protectors of the living. Kravitz preferred the dead. Scientifically speaking, he found them much more fascinating, less likely to be assholes, plus the dead never lied. In the spring, when he finished his final rotation, he would be free to pursue what he really wanted to do, which was pathology. He dreamed of being the best coroner New York had ever seen. He constantly reminded himself that all the temp jobs and positions he currently held would help him toward that end.

After dropping his partner off at a girlfriend's, Kravitz drove the rig back to the hospital. Just as he was backing into the bay, he looked in the mirror and saw an imposing black man approaching him. He was surprised, because he wasn't exactly used to seeing many black men in or around Nassau County. As he was rolling up the window, the black man stuck a .45 pistol in the passenger side and got in the rig's cab. Kravitz assumed it was a desperate junkie looking to score any kind of drugs he could, until he noticed how well groomed and dressed the man was. As the man ordered him to drive off, Kravitz, who had no interest in being a hero, complied. They drove three blocks to an abandoned paper mill, where Kravitz found another man, Hispanic, who was unconscious in the back seat of a car. As they loaded him into the back of the rig, the tall man kept the gun pointed on Kravitz and ordered him to work on the Hispanic with the severely burned face.

"He needs to be in the hospital," Kravitz pleaded. "I'm just an intern for Christ sakes."

"Tonight you're a doctor. If he doesn't make it, you don't make it. You dig?"

"Yeah, I got it. I'll do the best I can."

"You'd better hope that's good enough."

Kravitz immediately hooked up an IV, then assessed the extent of damage to the airways. He had seen burn victims before, but nothing like this. Half the man's face was cooked, and his left eye was singed shut. Kravitz worked on the man for an hour and a half before he thought he was out of immediate danger of dying. He didn't know if the man would ultimately survive; his only real concern was that he lived right now, because Kravitz knew his own life depended on it.

"Okay, I've got him stabilized as best I can and gave him what I could for the pain. You gotta get him to a hospital though." Kravitz said.

"I told you that's not an option. Give me your driver's license," Clay demanded.

Kravitz looked at Clay with terror in his eyes.

"If I was gonna kill you, I wouldn't be asking for your license," Clay added.

Kravitz pulled out his wallet and handed his driver's license over to him. Clay read the name and address.

"Okay, Ira Kravitz at 120 Bennett Avenue, it's in both our

interests if you forget any of this ever went down. As a matter of fact, I think you should find another job," Clay warned.

"No problem, I never saw you or anybody else. The job was just a way of me paying for med school—definitely ain't worth dying over."

"Good. I meant what I said. Don't give me a reason to kill you Ira, okay?"

Kravitz nodded nervously. "Yes, sir."

There was no doubt in Kravitz' mind that the man pointing the gun in his direction would kill him if he crossed him. Kravitz never consider himself racist, although at times he had to admit that black people as a whole left him feeling a little ill at ease. The well dressed black man that pocketed his driver's license absolutely terrified him.

Little did Kravitz know how fortuitous their chance encounter would prove to be. Two days later, he discovered that his entire tuition and every loan he had ever taken out had been mysteriously paid for by an anonymous donor.

It was after one in the morning when Clay dropped Blue off at his old lady's spot. Their two kids woke up crying when they saw their heavily bandaged father. The doctor that Clay used to use in case of emergencies had moved to Philly but would be down first thing in the morning to look after Blue. By the time Clay pulled up in front of his apartment building, he decided to let Dolicia stay upstairs at her parents for the night. It wasn't so much that he didn't want to disturb them; he just didn't want to face anyone. He still had blood on his hands from the day's carnage. He was much more concerned with what was in him than what was on him. There was no way he could look at his wife tonight and hide the things he had done or the lines he had crossed. He hoped in the morning he would be able to put all that had happened behind him and focus on the important things that lay ahead.

As he walked into the vestibule, Clay saw a note with his name taped to his front door. The note was from Dolicia's father, letting him know that she had gone into labor and been rushed to the hospital. Clay bolted out and drove as fast as he could to Harlem Hospital. He would never forgive himself if anything happened to his wife and child in his absence. As he rushed down the hall to Dolicia's room, he prayed that his son had not been born without him being there. Dolicia's parents were huddled over her when Clay entered the room. All he could see was their backs. As the father turned to face him, Clay saw Dolicia holding their newborn son. He stood at the door frozen by the wide range of feelings he was experiencing, shame, fear, relief, and pride. Dolicia burst into tears at the sight of his safe arrival. Her father took AJ from her arms and carried him over to Clay.

"Are you done?" her father asked as he stared at Clay.

"I'm done," Clay said as he stared back.

"This is the only thing that matters now."

"I know. I'll never 'not' be there for my family again."

From the first day they met, the two men had a very clear understanding of each other's character and will. The old man made no judgment of Clay's past, because when he was young, he too had made questionable choices that poor and desperate men often made when plagued with ambition beyond their means. The day that Clay asked him for his daughter's hand, he gave his consent under the condition that Clay allowed him to mentor him in the ways of politics and legitimate business ventures. The first lesson he ever taught Clay was that the only three things in the world that really mattered were God, Family, and Power, but not always in that order.

"Say hello to your son," Dolicia's father said as he handed over his grandson to Clay, making no mention of the dried blood on his son-in-law's hands and cuffs.

"Hello, AJ," Clay said as he looked down at the tiny life in his arms. "What time was he born?" he asked.

"7:38," Dolicia's father said as he took out his Polaroid camera.

Clay crossed to Dolicia, kissed her, and begged her forgiveness. He silently thanked God for the well-being of his family. Holding his son, he grew solemn as he thought about the irony of time. One life was born at the exact moment another was lost. In the span of just a few minutes, Clay had effectively killed not just both father and son, but for the first time in his life, he thought about how he had also murdered the possibility of generations to come. On what should have been the happiest night of his life, Clay was tormented by thoughts of the dead boy and how he would never grow to welcome children of his own into the world. Those were the things on his mind when the first photos of him holding AJ were taken.

11

Phee couldn't stop thinking about Clay. His father's pain and anger scared him. As Quincy drove, Phee looked out the window at the beautiful New England foliage that jetted by as they cruised down I-84 toward New York. When they were kids, this was his and AJ's favorite time of the year to make the drive to and from Connecticut. Phee knew that the storms of winter were coming early this year. It was only late November, but the brooding, gray skies were constantly threatening the downpour of rain or snow. He felt it in his gut: there were miserable days ahead.

As the partners sped down the highway, there was very little conversation between them. Phee restlessly played with the radio, until he settled on a sports talk show. He appreciated the sound of voices in the car as long as they weren't his or Quincy's. There was too much potential exposure in talking to the man that knew him better than anyone. There were decisions that Phee had already made that he didn't want to be talked out of. Quincy may have thought that Phee was just ignoring him or shutting him out in his period of mourning, but the truth was he was protecting him. Quincy couldn't be compromised by what he didn't know.

"I need to tell you something," Quincy said.

"What's that?" Phee asked.

Quincy reached out, turned down the radio, and took a beat before he spoke.

"I'm back on the job as of today. Whedon called me last night and asked me to come back and run lead on your brother's case. Maybe he'll be open to breaking protocol and let you work this thing with me, since technically, I would be the lead," Quincy added.

Cops who happened to be related to, or otherwise connected to, victims of violent crimes were, as a policy, forbidden from being a lead investigator in the case. Quincy had a couple of things working to his advantage in what would be his request to get the captain to make an exception. First, it was the captain who had called him to personally ask him to cut short his leave. The other thing was that he and Phee were fresh off bringing down Deggler and solving one of the worst series of murders in New York's history. The mayor, and even the head of the FBI was hailing the two partners as heroes. Quincy was prepared to call in all favors and play whatever hand he felt necessary to have Phee join him. There was definitely no such thing as controlling Phee, but he needed to keep a close eye on him to make sure he didn't go off half-cocked and do something he would later regret. Getting Phee involved with the case was a good move toward that end. Quincy needed Phee to be constantly reminded that he was still a cop. Of all the policemen Quincy had ever known, Phee honored and respected the badge the most. Quincy was counting on those principles to, at the very least, help temper any violent thoughts of revenge that Phee may have been entertaining. The two men were similar in many ways. Quincy was afraid of what Phee might be capable of, because he himself had come close to committing cold-blooded murder recently when he went to see the priest who had molested Elena's son. Ultimately, Quincy's faithfulness to the badge was what had saved him. He hoped the same would be true for his partner. Quincy was afraid of what Phee might do on his own, because in his darkest moment, Quincy understood firsthand the power of hate. Phee thought about the pros and cons of being able to legitimately work AJ's case whether it was ultimately his choice or not. It was obvious that he would have access to many more resources, not to mention the sanction of the law. Even though he was determined to use any and all things available to him, he knew at some point it would come at a cost. In avenging his brother's death, Phee accepted the fact that he would ultimately dishonor everything he held sacred as a cop. There would be lying, cheating, and eventually murder. The only thing that came close to bothering him was his indifference to all of those things.

12

The minute they made it back to the station, Phee and Quincy headed toward Captain Whedon's office. Whedon was in a meeting with another police captain from Jamaica Queens. Quincy was summoned in right away as Phee waited at his desk. It had only been a few weeks since he left, but some of the cops and staff seemed different to him. More specifically, their interaction with him seemed different. Even as some offered their sympathy and condolences, it all felt awkward and forced. Phee was well aware of the bawdy and politically incorrect sense of humor that most homicide cops shared as a means of coping. Very few things were off-limits, including the victims that they investigated. Crude jokes and tasteless teasing was nothing more than a way of life in the department. Phee had been as culpable as any of his peers. The irony was, now as he waited for Quincy, he could only wonder which jokes about his dead, cross-dressing brother had gotten the most laughs.

Phee was acutely aware of all of his colleagues and the different energy that he felt from the squad. The death of AJ had slightly shifted both the professional and social paradigms throughout the department. For all of the cops' collective strength and fearlessness, AJ's murder struck much too close to home. Everyone went through the motions of going about their usual business, but beneath the surface, there was a definite uneasiness. Phee wasn't sure what was expected of him, and neither were the people whom he worked with. None of them had ever been in the unfortunate position of having to investigate the murder of someone closely related to their fraternity. Everyone felt a need to be more serious and formal out of respect for Phee. He, on the other hand, felt an unspoken pressure to try and be as normal as possible.

After ten minutes or so, Quincy stuck his head out of Whedon's door and invited Phee in. As he walked into the office, Whedon intercepted him with a comforting hand on Phee's back.

"None of us can adequately express to you how sorry we are for your loss," Whedon said. "I left a message for your father about an hour ago and told him that we're gonna do everything humanly possible to find whoever is responsible," he added.

"Thank you, Captain," Phee responded.

"How are you holding up?"

"I'm fine, sir."

"Look, Phee, I'm not gonna sugarcoat this. We're in a hell of a cluster-fuck here. Quite honestly, this whole thing scares the bejeezus out of all of us. The mayor's already flippin' out, because this city can't deal with something like this so soon after the Deggler case. Even though Quincy wants you to work this one with him, you know that goes against department policy. On the other hand, the mayor's been yelling 'Fuck policy' all morning, because everybody knows you two are the fastest closers we have." Whedon sighed, and then walked back to his desk.

"Lawyers for the department said that, technically, the policy is more protocol than any actual law. The chief thinks it's a bad idea to have you anywhere near this case, but if you honestly think you're up to it, I'll back you, since he's leaving the call up to me. We don't have the luxury of doing everything by the book here. We can't run the risk of anything resembling a Deggler repeat. We'll deal with whatever consequences as long as the two of you shut this thing down as soon as possible. If I'm about to put my ass on the line for you, Phee, I gotta at least know where your head is."

"Let me make this easy for all of you, Captain. Everybody knows that my brother and I weren't close. Whoever killed him in the way that they did needs to be stopped—pure and simple. That's my job. That's what I do. This case is ultimately no different. You don't have to worry about me freaking out or anything; I'm good."

"I hope that's true, because we're not in a position to exclude you on this case, especially since there's a good chance things will only get worse." Whedon sighed heavily.

"What are you talking about?" Phee asked.

"He means your brother's murder is not an isolated incident."

Phee turned to face the tall, thin captain from the 187th

precinct. The man's name was Martin Gronkowski, a Polish lifer-in-blue from Queens. He looked to be in his early sixties, despite his attempts to look younger with a bad dye job.

"We caught a couple of similar cases like this a few years ago in Queens," Gronkowski continued.

"Three years ago? I don't remember ever hearing anything like this going down," Quincy jumped in.

"It was right around the time New York was bidding to host the Olympics. The mayor got the press to squash it. When it finally did come out, they wrote 'em up as random unconnected murders. No gory details or anything that would put the city in a panic or jeopardize our chances of bringing in over a hundred million in revenue."

"You said a couple of cases. Exactly how many vics are we talking?" Phee asked.

"Three. They were killed at different times over a five-week period," Gronkowski answered.

"Were they all like…my brother? Lifestyle I mean," Phee pressed.

"No, not at all. One was a retired male college professor, one was a married electrician, and the other was a female banker. No connection whatsoever. Here's the kicker, the perp was a female nut job by the name of Dr. Daria Zibik. She was one of those Doogie Howser kids that got both her medical and psych degree from Harvard by the time she was twenty. Now she's doing twenty-five to life at Bedford Hills. We never got enough evidence to convict her on the actual murders, but fortunately, we caught her on a hit-and-run homicide the night the banker was killed. At the time, it wasn't in the best interest of the city to divulge the full details of the murders, so we settled for the charges that we knew could stick."

"So now we're looking at a copycat?" Quincy asked.

"Maybe. Maybe something worse," Whedon joined in.

Quincy and Phee looked at the two captains confused. Gronkowski stood for the first time, crossed directly to Phee, and addressed him.

"Dr. Zibik headed a cult. We thought they either disbanded or went underground after her arrest. Your brother and the three prior vics were killed on some sacrificial, devil-worshipping shit, which is right up Zibik's alley. The reason they were all cut open the way they were was because Zibik and the rest of her nuts actually believed that they could capture the souls of their victims."

13

It was almost four when Phee and Quincy stepped through the gates at Bedford Hills. They reported to the warden and spoke to her for twenty minutes before she had a guard escort them to the prison's D-wing. D-wing at Bedford Hills in the last few years had been nicknamed TMZ because the majority of high- profile female cases that had been tabloid fodder and mainstays on the covers of the New York papers ended up here. Ninety-five percent of the inmates that occupied D-wing were doing twenty-five to life. These were women who had committed the most serious of crimes: drug dealing, robbery, assault, kidnapping, murder, and some a combination of all of the above. Some had killed husbands, lovers, and even their own children. The guards simply referred to the inmates of D-wing as the "depraved." If Bedford Hills was considered one of the toughest women's prisons in America, then the ladies that lived in D-wing prided themselves on being the baddest of the bad. Everyone in D-wing, cons and guards alike, steered clear of Dr. Daria Zibik, because not even the most hardened amongst them were foolish enough to fuck with the Devil.

Zibik was raised just outside of Montreal near Rougemont, a small town known primarily for its apple and apple cider production and sugar shacks. Both of her parents were intellectuals and former educators who moved from the big city after Zibik's father was fired from the university over his controversial teachings on atheism. Daria Zibik was an odd child who was homeschooled on a farm in the middle of nowhere. At nine years old, she started exhibiting classic telltale signs of a budding sociopath. Her obsession with the torture and mutilation of small animals grew more rabid each year. She was addicted not just to the rush of the kill but even more so to the awesome power she held over life. By the time she was twelve, her father had successfully drilled into her the intellectual improbability of God's existence. They diligently studied the Bible to point out its contradictions and the fallibilities of its teachings. Young Zibik was taught by both of her parents that true intellectualism had no room for belief in God. The entire foundation and the acceptance of an omnipotent being, particularly in terms of Judeo-Christian belief, was completely predicated on fear, control, and ignorance. When she was sixteen, Zibik discovered the satanic teachings of Anton LaVey, who was widely regarded as the father of modern-day Satanism. One of the first quotes that she remembered reading was that according to LaVey, "God was a psychological manifestation of the ideal human state, able to kill without mercy or explanation and free to do as he/she wishes because he/she is responsible to no one." Zibik was much too smart to believe in God in the traditional sense, but at sixteen, she had found a religion that was worthy of her allegiance.

As Phee and Quincy sat in a sterile holding room, Quincy glanced at Phee. "You sure you're up for this, the case I mean?"

"I'm good. I already told you that, and I'll tell you the same thing the next time you ask."

"I'm the one that's on your side, remember?"

"Yeah, I know, and it's appreciated."

"If you ever need to…"

The heavy metal door opened, and two burly guards escorted a shackled Zibik into the room. After seating her, one guard left and one stayed. Both Phee and Quincy had read and heard things about Zibik that made each of them expect a monster that was much more imposing than the nebbish-looking figure that sat before them.

"Dr. Zibik, I'm Detective Cavanaugh, and this is my partner Detective Freeman. We're investigating a murder that we wanted to talk to you about," Quincy said.

"I make it a practice not to speak with the police unless I have an attorney present. Let's just say I had a bad experience in the past," Zibik said.

"You're gonna have a much worse experience in the present and future, if you don't tell us what we want to know," Phee said calmly.

"I've never really been one to respond to empty threats, Detective."

"That's cool, because I've never been the type to give one," Phee responded.

"A murder that was committed two days ago has quite a few similarities to the three murders that you were accused of committing three years ago," Quincy joined in.

"Accused but never convicted of," Zibik said smiling. "I'm in here for a hit-and-run misunderstanding, not some premeditated murder."

"We all know you're in here because some sorry-ass prosecutor felt he could convict you on a hit-and-run quicker than the murders. As long as you're doing twenty-five to life, nobody really cared what the reason was," Phee said. "Things are different with this case. People actually care this time."

"And is this newfound concern based on the fact that the victim was your brother, Detective Freeman?" Zibik said coolly.

Because the case hadn't gone public yet, Phee and Quincy were equally surprised at Zibik's admitted knowledge of it. Phee crossed to the guard who stood by the door and spoke to him.

"The warden said we could talk to her in private. I need you to wait outside," Phee said.

"Nobody told me that," the guard responded.

"I'm telling you now," Phee shot back.

"Well, it's not procedure," the guard said.

"It is today. We need privacy with the prisoner, and I told you we have the warden's permission. Now you can go call her or do whatever you feel you need to do, but one way or another, you're leaving this room right now. How you do that is really up to you."

Being a correctional officer, it was imperative for their own survival for the guards to know who were the posers and bull-shitters and who were the bona fide threats. The vacant stare of a person with nothing to lose was the most threatening of all. As the guard looked at Phee, there was no questioning that the detective was bona fide.

"You got five minutes before I call for support," the guard said as he opened the door.

Quincy kept his eyes trained on Phee as he crossed back to the table, roughly pulled Zibik to her feet, and pressed her up against the wall. "Let's drop all the bullshit. What do you know about my brother's killing?" Phee demanded.

Quincy and Phee had done the "good cop, bad cop" routine several times over the years. This was the first time in all of those years that Quincy was uncertain whether Phee was in character or not.

"You're here because you think that I, or someone associated with my following, had something to do with all of this. I can assure you that neither case is true," Zibik responded.

"And we're just supposed to believe that?" Phee asked, still holding Zibik.

"I'm not responsible for what you choose to believe or not. You asked me a question and I gave you an answer. Maybe if you did your homework, you would know that I was telling the truth," Zibik said.

"What the hell is that supposed to mean?" Phee demanded.

"The timing alone doesn't support the theory that I would have anything to do with this."

"What do you mean by timing?" Quincy asked.

"Last week, the Appellate court decided that it would finally hear my appeal. Why would I wait three years for that to happen and then turn around a week later and be involved with anything that would hurt my chances of getting out of here?" Zibik said smugly.

Phee released her and took two steps back.

"We haven't made any information public on the murder. How did you hear about it in here, and how did you know it was Detective Freeman's brother?" Quincy asked.

"Let's just say I have a few supporters that I consider family who keep me up to speed on all things bizarre," Zibik said.

"This is some kind of game to you? You think this is funny?" Phee snapped.

"The only thing that's funny is the obvious fact that the two of you keep overlooking."

"And what would that be?" Quincy asked as he stepped closer to Zibik.

"Whoever is responsible for this murder has you doing exactly what they want you to do, looking in the wrong direction and suspecting the wrong party. You want to find out whoever's behind this, then the first thing the two of you need to do is to educate yourselves on what you're dealing with here. There's a website called True Light Believers. It's a good primer for you. It'll lead you to a couple of chat rooms that you might find interesting. In my circles, people tend to share details of their conquests and conversions." Quincy put a hand on Phee's shoulder as he felt Phee's anger rising. "Look, you came here for information, and I'm giving you an intro to my world. That's the best I can do," Zibik added.

"So how do we know this isn't all just bullshit?" Quincy asked.

"You don't, but that's because you're not appreciating my motives here. My only reason for helping you is self-serving. Not all enemies of my enemies are friends. Whoever destroyed Detective Freeman's family is ultimately trying to do the same to me and mine by making us look guilty."

"I find out that you're dicking us around, I will come back here and I will hurt you," Phee said very matter-of-fact.

"Homework, Detective. If you knew anything about me, you'd know that I would actually enjoy that very much."

Zibik smiled at the two detectives and watched them carefully as they walked to the door and exited.

14

After he and Phee got back from the prison, Quincy drove up to the Bronx to see his mother, because the day happened to be their shared birthday. When he was a child, his mother Colette bragged about how Quincy was the greatest birthday present in the world. Of her two sons, Quincy was her favorite. Even though now they were no longer close, Quincy still had a soft spot in his heart for the woman who had turned her back on him and Liam when they needed her most.

Even though they rarely visited her, both brothers still had their own set of keys to come and go as they pleased. When Quincy unlocked the door, he was pleasantly surprised that Liam had arrived before him. "Hey, I'm glad you made it," Quincy said to Liam as he walked in and discovered his brother sitting uncomfortably on the plastic slipcover of the oversized sofa in the cramped living room.

"Have I ever broken my word to you?" Liam shot back as he pushed aside a pile of clothes to make room on the sofa.

"No, never. Where is she?"

"In the kitchen; I think she made a cake or something."

Their mother was a hoarder. Stacks of books, vinyl records, and newspapers were in boxes and milk crates piled floor to ceiling. Clothes and odd knickknacks formed false walls and hallways in the overcrowded space. The difficulty of navigating their mother's obsessive disorder was always very challenging to her sons. The space naturally left both of them feeling claustrophobic. The air reeked of old cigarette smoke and mildewed carpeting, which consequently always left both men racing for a shower the minute they left. Quincy tried to ignore the scent of the stale air that burned his nostrils and irritated his eyes. He tried to pretend that he had grown used to the offending scents. He lied to himself when necessary that the apartment and his mother's condition were improving. He downplayed his discomfort, because he knew whatever he was feeling, Liam was feeling it twice as much. Quincy didn't want in any way to encourage his brother's overall distaste for their mother. In general, he was much more tolerant of Colette than Liam.

Liam's visits never lasted for more than thirty minutes. Not only was he not close to his mother, he was actually afraid of her or, more specifically, he feared his similarities to her. Like her, Liam had long suffered depressions and mood swings. Ironically, he was more afraid of his chances of inheriting his mother's mental state than he was of inheriting the cancer that took his father's life. Liam was actually scared when he was forced to endure the same type of "blue phases" that he had witnessed Colette having, which came often with no particular pattern or reason. His greatest fear was the possibility that he had inherited a recessive gene from his mother and that it was rearing its ugly head more and more, with the intent of destroying his life. He managed to hide his depressions from Quincy, mainly by avoiding him, when he felt the gloominess approaching. Deggler on the other hand had shown Liam how to direct his darkness and free himself from the debilitating helplessness that plagued him the majority of his life.

Returning to the home that he grew up in presented a range of emotional challenges for Liam. The three-bedroom apartment harbored many difficult memories for him. Each time he returned, he felt small and angry. He hated what this place meant to him. In his youth he was a victim, both he and his brother. His childhood home brought back horrible memories of the times that he and Quincy were molested by the priest that Colette entrusted them to. Although the offenses perpetrated against the brothers happened far beyond the walls of the small apartment, this place had come to represent the crimes of his mother's complicity.

Despite the fact that Liam was a devoted priest, he was incapable of forgiveness when it came to Colette. Unlike Liam, Quincy still loved his mother, regardless of all that she had or hadn't done. And even though some days, like today, were harder than others, he still made the necessary efforts to connect with her. He was sometimes surprised how laborious the simple act of visiting her could be. Although it was both his and Colette's birthday, Quincy found that he had to work a little harder to keep feelings of bitterness in check. Whereas Liam resented what he saw in his mother, Quincy regretted it. She was irreparably broken, and there was nothing he could do but pretend otherwise, for her sake. On the best of days, the truth was suppressed, made invisible by superficial conversation from seasoned actors, making the most of their respective roles. They were each guilty in their own way of varying offenses that prevented them from ever having an honest and healthy relationship.

Although it took a certain amount of both effort and agility, Quincy, Liam, and their mother were able to avoid the proverbial "elephant" that accompanied them throughout the better part of their lives. Quincy got Liam to laugh at Colette's jokes and smile at the appropriate times. They both managed to give her the outward appearance of caring and thoughtful sons. On the rare occasions that the three of them got together, Colette got what she needed most, the lies and delusion of a happy family unit.

"The Knicks are finally playing like they want to win," Colette said, with her customary cigarette dangling from her lips as she smiled at Quincy and Liam.

"We go through this every year, Ma. I keep telling you, they're only setting you up to break your heart at the end of the season," Quincy lobbed back.

Colette was a huge sports fan, just like both of her sons. Although she genuinely loved the competitive aspects of all types of games and matches, she also knew on some level that it gave her neutral ground on which to communicate with her boys. On a day like today, when she felt them struggling to be in her presence, she played the card that consistently allowed the three of them to engage each other much more effortlessly.

"Mark my words, things are going to be different this year. Carmello was the missing piece. He scored thirty-eight last night," she added.

"Yeah, but they still lost, Ma," Liam said.

"Sometimes, you just gotta have a little faith," she looked at her sons and smiled even more broadly. As the three of them debated the probability, or more accurately, the improbability, of the Knicks winning a championship, Quincy found himself letting go. The uneasiness that he had when he first arrived was slowly disappearing. Liam however was another story.

15

When Phee left the station, he called Brenda from the car to let her know he was finally on his way home. Their exchange was short, flat even, but he at least managed to end the conversation with a "me too" in response to her telling him that she loved him. Brenda was gentle and supportive with him, possibly what he needed most, but unfortunately the very thing that irritated him to no end. The indictment wasn't specifically aimed at her as much as it was at everyone. Phee hated pity and anything remotely resembling it. Maybe it wasn't their collective intention, but everyone's deep concern for him left him feeling that way, regardless. He knew he was being completely irrational, that Quincy, Brenda, and even his fellow cops were all just expressing their support for him in his time of loss. He shunned their sympathy, because deep down, he felt their concern and outpouring was better suited to someone much more deserving than himself. Phee didn't feel worthy of their compassion, because he'd written his brother off for dead long before AJ was actually murdered.

Even though Brenda was expecting him, Phee was in a funk and didn't want to risk bringing his foul mood home. He felt the darkness moving through him, like slowly digesting syrup stuck in the center of his chest, thick and insalubrious. He drove around, trying to clear his head and lift the veil that dimmed his view. He cruised to the section of the city where his brother used to sell himself. Phee parked up the block and watched the cross-dressing sex workers walking the dirty asphalt, like a catwalk for curious spectators and horny suitors. He wondered which of the T-walkers had known or befriended AJ. Were any of them mourning his death? It was the first time that he saw them as other than carica-tures or seedy acts from a freak show. He saw alienated, scared sons and brothers. Each one of them, at least at some point in their lives, had had someone who cared for and loved them. Phee thought of the times that he spied on his brother from this very spot and how he had loathed the sight of him. As he sat in his car on the corner of W. 39th Street and 10th Avenue, he thought of his brother and lamented the reconciliation that they never got around to having.

After she greeted him at the door with a kiss and lengthy hug, Brenda promised herself that she would give Phee as much space and time as he required. Being there for him unconditionally was the thing that mattered most. Even though he didn't arrive home until two hours after she spoke with him on the phone, she didn't have the luxury of expressing her worry or irritation. She walked on eggshells in fear that the slightest thing might harken his all-too-familiar retreat. Brenda hated the fact that Phee's MO was to disconnect from her in times of vulnerability or emotional upheaval. She often felt that the closer he got to her, the more he tried to push her away.

"I wasn't sure that you'd be hungry, but I made some bluefish just in case," Brenda said as Phee made his way to the couch.

"Maybe a little later," he mumbled.

Phee never looked at her directly. He acted as though eye contact with her would cost him. Brenda was careful not to press him, because she would only risk losing him more. The most she could hope for was to keep him aboveground, resisting his usual pattern of introversion.

Unfortunately, she knew his routine better than she wanted to. It was one of the hardest things in the world for her, waiting and watching as he grew moody and disappeared to a place that was far from her reach. All she wanted to do was love and care for Phee and let that carry him through the difficult times, but she could feel the walls that he erected to keep her at a distance. He pretended to be present. He pretended to be engaged, but from the moment that she greeted him, she could feel his desertion. It had left her frustrated over the years that as close as she felt to him, there were many times he left her feeling like a stranger, hopelessly on the outside peering in. She suspected, but never confirmed, that there were things that haunted Phee, that in turn, prevented him from completely giving or receiving love.

"How's your father?"

"He hasn't killed anybody yet, so I guess that's something," he responded with a wry smile.

Brenda smiled back and appreciated his attempt at levity, because whatever lightness he offered, she assumed it was much more for her sake than his.

"How about a long, hot shower followed by an even longer back rub," she suggested. "I'm sure that's exactly what you want about now."

"Am I that easy to read?"

Brenda nodded and smiled.

"Don't worry, your reputation of invincibility is still safe with me," she joked as she kissed him, and headed toward the bathroom to turn the water on.

As Brenda entered the bathroom, she looked in the mirror and inhaled and exhaled a heavy breath. She was increasingly more emotional and had to fight a sudden urge to cry. It took effort to quell the growing frustration of biting her tongue. There were conversations that she wanted to have with Phee, things that needed to be discussed, but she knew that he was unavailable. He might go through the motions or even feign interest in the things that were weighing heavily on her, but there was no real chance of truly connecting with him. The most she could do was suppress her feelings until a more convenient time.

Just as the steam from the shower started filling the bathroom, Brenda watched Phee enter. After he took off his clothes and dropped them on the floor, he encouraged her to do the same. No matter the good times or bad, Phee standing naked before her always did things to Brenda. She was happily weakened by his chocolate skin and muscular frame. He was built like he still played in the NFL. His body was tight, cut, and powerfully sculpted. After all the years of knowing him, she still found herself stealing glances at his body as though he were something taboo and slightly out of her league. Although she intended to give him his needed space, once he extended the invite for her to undress, all bets were off. It wasn't until she got into the shower with him that she started second-guessing her every move and his every gesture toward her. Everything she did had a potential misinterpretation. She didn't know if the situation was supposed to be sexual or if he just wanted a warm body next to him. As she washed his back and tried to otherwise comfort him, she was insecure about making him feel pitied and childlike. It was important to her that he knew she was there for him, but she didn't want to make him feel patronized in any possible way.

After they got out of the shower, Phee lay naked on his stomach, while Brenda rubbed the musk-scented oil on his back that she'd bought from a Cuban vendor in Brooklyn. She gently ran her fingers over the healed edge of a bullet wound, taking the time to appreciate the contrast of his dark, shiny skin against the white cotton sheets. When he turned over and kissed her, she was pleased by the tempting erection that greeted her. She had bragged to her girlfriends for years that he had the "prettiest dick" she'd ever seen. Her initial instinct was to at the very least stroke and taste him, but she forced herself to wait and let him dictate the level of intimacy that he felt he needed.

Phee never had control over how his body reacted to Brenda. Although he was fully aroused, his mind was at war with invading thoughts that had nothing to do with her. He kept seeing his brother and the horrible things that had been done to him. As the darkness came, Phee fought hard to control his focus. Like a series of discontinued dreams, his mind raced to and fro in search of something less toxic to think about. He fought his submersion as best he could by holding on to Brenda in hopes of her being the buoy that kept him afloat.

Phee didn't know until that moment just how much he needed Brenda. He needed the connection and peace she offered. He wanted her to take his thoughts to a better place. He fought to keep his mind on her, partly as a means of reprieve from the vivid images that held him captive. If she couldn't fully transport him, then he at least needed her to be a temporary distraction.

Phee gave her an obligatory kiss, put her on her back, and straddled her. The heavy, ruminating thoughts continued tugging at his concentration until his mind started drifting from her. Phee had never been with Brenda and had challenges focusing. Her mind, body, and beauty both commanded and rewarded his full attention. Even now as she lay naked beneath him, still damp from the shower, he thought about how erotic she was and how under normal circumstances, he would have by now been buried deep inside of her, where he belonged. Even though they had been lovers off and on for almost twenty years, there had never been another woman who consistently turned him on quite the way she did. She may have often declared that he was the only man that had the skill and power to make her come multiple times, but it was Phee who secretly regarded her as the one who taught him how to truly please a woman.

By the time he graduated high school, Phee had already been with several girls who were fascinated by him, for all the wrong reasons. When it came to females, he proudly mistook quantity for quality. The extent of his pleasing them was his assumption that his being with them was enough. Like most boys, he was thoroughly impressed by the things he thought he knew. Even though he was just out of high school, he thought he had somehow magically figured out the greatest mystery in the world that no man before him had been able to unravel. At eighteen Phee thought he knew women. When he met Brenda as a freshman in college, she changed all of that. The first thing she schooled him on was that carnality for a woman was at least 60 percent mental and 40 percent physical. She converted him and taught him that not all temples were made of stone and mortar. By the time she finally gave herself to him, she slowed him down and taught him not only how to explore a woman's body but also how to read, please, and serve it. She taught him how to go down and enjoy it. Brenda disarmed him and redirected his ego, until he bought into the notion that the commitment to being unselfish and pleasing his lover elevated him above most men.

Brenda had no doubt that Phee loved her, even when that love seemed to scare the hell out of him. Sex with her was the time when he was the least guarded. She tried using everything she had to keep him connected and present. As he roughly flipped her over and mounted her from behind, it was the first time she felt that he was somewhere far beyond her grasp. Tonight, unlike their usual routine, there was no foreplay or buildup; he was just robotically implanted inside of her, pumping away as though he were either chasing or being chased by some unseen force. Long ago, Phee had grown to become Brenda's greatest lover, as considerate as he was passionate, but now, there was very little evidence of either trait. He was simply selfish and distant.

16

When Quincy left his mother's house, he stopped by Elena's and had dinner with her and her father Romero. Romero had only been home from the hospital for two weeks, after suffering a frightening stroke. Quincy accredited the surprising rate at which Romero was recovering more to the repaired relationship with Elena than anything else. He watched the exchanges between the father and daughter and saw firsthand the power of forgiveness. Elena no longer blamed Romero for her son's suicide. Even though they had a long way to go to get back to being anywhere near how close they used to be, Quincy appreciated witnessing the beginning steps toward that end. After Romero went to bed, Quincy and Elena lay on the sofa and talked about everything from Phee and his brother's murder to the walk she and her father took after his checkup. Just before midnight, Elena brought Quincy a warm slice of sweet potato pie with a lit candle and the wrapped presents from the restaurant.

"Before the day officially ends, we have to properly celebrate your birthday. Since you ran out before you got to finish your pie and open your presents, I thought now would be a good time," she said.

With all that had happened in the last day and a half, had it not been for his mother calling him to come over, Quincy might have actually forgotten all about his birthday. After blowing out his candle, Elena fed him pie and urged him to open his gifts. The first gift she handed him was hers.

"I kind of stole the idea from Phee and Brenda, but I know it's something you'll love. It'll be for when things calm down," she said.

Quincy unwrapped the small flat present and found two elaborate mock-ups of airline tickets to Cartagena, Colombia. He was genuinely surprised. He cupped Elena's face and kissed her. Elena opened and read her card to him.

"My Dearest Papi, I want you to see and know where I come from. At the very least, it might help you better understand my insanity."

As Quincy laughed, he thought about all the things he wanted to know about her. He had never met another woman like her or felt the things that she brought out in him. Even though they met under the tragic circumstances of him investigating her son's suicide, he suspected from the first time he laid eyes on her that she would be the first and last woman whom he ever loved. Watching her now and how her eyes lit up when he smiled, he knew he had suspected correctly. Quincy thanked her with a kiss and a forkful of pie. Elena handed him another card and a long and narrow object.

"This one is from Brenda," she said as she opened the card and read. "To Quincy, the only person I know whose golf game sucks more than Phee's. Hopefully this will help."

Quincy pulled the wrapping paper off to find a TaylorMade Corza Ghost Putter. He stood up and took a practice putt. "As soon as this case is over, I'll be using this thing a lot," Quincy said.

"I hope so. I already bet Brenda twenty dollars that in three months you'd beat Phee."

"Only twenty? O ye of little faith."

"Calm down, Tiger, you know I believe in you. Okay, come on, this one is from Phee," she said as she handed him a jeweler's box with a white ribbon on top. Elena read the card.

"To my brotha' from another motha', badge or no badge, always know that there is someone in this world that wouldn't hesitate to take another one for you."

When Quincy removed the ribbon and opened the box, he found a 14-karat gold chain with a dented bullet attached. He was quiet and reflective for a moment, obviously touched by the gesture. Elena thought she briefly saw his eyes get a little wetter than normal. Quincy looked at Elena and explained the meaning of the gift.

"Two years ago, Phee and I were working a case. Guy kills two people because he wants to know if the real thing feels any different from the video games he played. We track him down to a crack house over in Alphabet City. As soon as I cuff him, his girlfriend comes out of nowhere with a gun pointed at me. I don't have time to draw back on her, but Phee pushes me out of the way and takes a shot square in the chest for me. I didn't know he saved the bullet."

"You're so blessed to have two brothers that love you as much as they do. That's because you're a good man, Quincy."

"Not really, I just have a good publicist," he said smiling.

Elena playfully pushed him as she reached for the final card and present. "Last but not least, this is from your other brother." Elena opened the card and read:

> *Quincy, knowing how much you're already surrounded by love, my only other wish would be if somehow it were possible for Papa to be here on your special day to see the man that you've become. I could never adequately express how proud of you I am. Think of this present as a small token from both me and Papa.*

Quincy took the card from Elena and read it again. He smiled brightly as he let his brother's words resonate through him. Liam had always been Quincy's hero, even before they lost their father to leukemia. Quincy idolized his brother for so many reasons. Liam had always been his protector, supporter, and most consistent example of goodness. Having his brother's respect meant the world to him. Of all the gifts that he opened, Liam's was the one Quincy was the most animated and excited about opening. He tore the wrapping paper off like a kid at Christmas. He opened up the beautifully carved mahogany box and discovered a very rare, autographed Babe Ruth baseball with a familiar looking nick in the stitch and a small wine stain just above the last name. Quincy stopped breathing. Every voluntary or involuntary function locked up on him and froze. It felt like he was suspended in some weird, dreamlike state, where he was conscious of being in part of a nightmare but was completely incapable of waking himself from it. The thing that he saw and held in his hand made no sense to him whatsoever. As his brain slowly started functioning again, he did the math. What were the odds of there being two rare Babe Ruth autographed baseballs with an identical nick in the stitch and wine stain in the same places. Two weeks ago, just minutes before Father Conner was butchered, Quincy sat in the priest's office and held in his hands the very same baseball that had mysteriously gone missing after the murder. Since he assumed that the murderer had taken the ball, he was completely confused about how his brother ended up with it.

17

Joseph "Jelly" Varelli got his nickname when he was seven and was placed in Saint Paul's orphanage after both his parents and brother were murdered. The other kids teased him mercilessly and called him a deaf-mute. At first they called him "Jelly Brains," because it was widely assumed at Saint Paul's that children with special needs were simply stupid. Once they found out his last name was Varelli, he was permanently saddled with the nursery rhyme nickname. The life he led was anything but fairy tale or nursery rhyme status. He was at the orphanage for two years. Just as he began to believe that life couldn't get worse, he started what felt like an endless cycle of foster care. The constant physical and emotional abuse that he endured at the orphanage was a tragic precursor of things to come. To most of the foster parents that took him in, Jelly was nothing more than an inconvenient means to a paycheck. A stupid mute brought in more money than the usual delinquent misfits. Before he reached the age of fourteen, Jelly had been beaten, burned, choked, caged, hospitalized, and nearly killed twice. At seventeen, he began to give as good as he got. It was around that time that he did his first stint in prison, after nearly beating a man to death for kicking a dog. His many stays in New York prisons allowed him to hone his fighting skills. He went undefeated in the prison boxing league under the moniker "The Silent Assassin." Jelly had no technique; he just knew how to hurt people. Every opponent that stood before him fell, because very few men carried at their core the pain and hatred that he did. He consistently motivated himself with the one thing that released his demons. Every time Jelly fought, he pictured his opponents as the two men who killed his family.

Jelly was a new convert to Satanism. He turned to the dark practice by way of default. It wasn't just what he saw as the blatant hypocrisy of Christianity; it was the overrated and misguided emphasis of forgiveness that kept him searching most of his adult life for something much more spiritually practical and satisfying. He stumbled across a dog-eared copy of *The Satanic Bible* in a halfway house about a year ago. It was one of the simplest things that he had ever read, not necessarily from an academic point of view but rather from his connectivity. The teachings appealed to the most primal aspects of human nature. One of its greatest principles and teachings was the very thing that Jelly had coveted his entire life. Number five on the list of nine declarations of Satanism was the concept of vengeance, instead of turning the other cheek.

18

Carmen Morales was on the third act of a very tough life. She was by anyone's standards a true survivor. She had survived a tough childhood in Spanish Harlem. She'd survived the incarceration of her father and the loss of her mother to a heroin overdose, all before she was sixteen. She survived a horrible marriage and the drowning death of her eleven-year-old son. Her most recent victory was the clean bill of health that she received from her oncologist, six weeks after completing her last cycle of chemo. Carmen was forty-three and filled with hope that her difficult life was finally turning around. Throughout her various challenges, people constantly reminded her that God would never give her more than she could handle. Carmen just hoped that God had finally stopped overestimating her strength, tolerance, and resolve. Her greatest victory was that through all of her obstacles and setbacks, she had miraculously found a way to remain optimistic.

As soon as she got home from her doctor's office, she rolled a joint and listened to Miles. Her father had never really given her much, but she was thankful that he had taught her and her younger brother an appreciation of great music. At forty-three years old, she was now old enough to have been exposed to the jazz greats and young enough to still appreciate the younger standouts of modern-day jazz, salsa, hiphop, R&B, pop, and even country. Despite her eclectic taste in music, today she needed a no-brainer. She needed Miles. She lit a few candles and put on his version of Monk's "Straight No Chaser." Not many things relaxed her like a good joint and the sound of his horn. Forty minutes later, after Miles put her in a better mood, she put her CD player on shuffle and gladly welcomed whatever musical surprise came her way. It wasn't until she heard Jill Scott applauding a lover who had "represented in the fashion of the truly gifted" that she was reminded of her loneliness. It had been some time since any man, or woman for that matter, had done any kind of representing in her bedroom. The chemo hadn't exactly left her feeling sexual, or even remotely attractive, but after today's news, she lamented the fact that there were no arms at home to welcome and hold her. She took a shower and ate dinner as her music continued playing in the background. By the time she made it to bed, Luther Vandross was reminding her how much a house was not a home. The joint and wine she'd had earlier failed to help her fall asleep. Just before 11:00, she reached over to her nightstand and removed her trusted rabbit vibrator.

Masturbation for her had become more of a means of helping her to sleep than true sexual gratification. After she came, she rolled over, turned the music off, and fell into a deep sleep.

Jelly sat in a chair across from her and watched her sleep. Her pale, nude body glistened under the streaks of moonlight that snuck in through the partially covered upper window. The only sound in the room was the occasional confirmation of heat rising through the old radiators of the prewar, art deco building. The apartment still smelled of baked chicken and marijuana. He sat watching her for over an hour, taking in the full details of her nudity from the moonlight and the flickering light of a nearby candle. Her body was soft and pudgy, but it still managed to arouse him. Even though his natural attraction was to small-breasted, skinny girls, Jelly still fantasized about the things he would like to do to Carmen if it were permissible or if he had been there for other reasons. Unfortunately, he wasn't there for her body. He'd come for much more.

Jelly had enjoyed killing AJ very much. Although he had often thought about it over the years, the actual act was far more rewarding than anything he'd ever imagined. It being his first kill, and him being passionately aware of all that it represented, he'd allowed himself to act much more from an emotional place than executing the ritualistic discipline required to achieve his overall goal. From an academic and spiritual point of view, he'd failed in many ways to accomplish what he'd wanted to do. On a purely primal level, though, the kill was better than he ever anticipated. He loved the hunt, the trapping, and of course the kill. Jelly was empowered as he watched AJ struggle and take his last, vanquished breath. He decided that tonight would be different though. He was determined to take his time and savor every moment and detail. He gently touched her short, thin hair and lowered his face just a few inches from hers to smell the oatmeal soap that she had showered with earlier. As Jelly woke her and she attempted to scream, he placed a firm hand over her mouth and pressed down. He pulled out a crescent-shaped dagger with an obsidian hilt and pressed the sharp tip to Carmen's throat. As she ceased to resist, he straddled her and became more and more aroused at the thick, naked body beneath him. He wondered what it might feel like to penetrate her. As turned on as he was, he remained focused and disciplined. Unlike his last kill, he repeatedly reminded himself of why he was there.

He tied and gagged her and brought her into the living room, where a large red pentagram had been painted on the floor next to a makeshift altar. More than a dozen lit candles encircled both. He had set the room up exactly the way he had been taught to do. Jelly knew how to follow instructions. His many years in prison taught him that. He was told to cut her eyelids but not to torture her unnecessarily. He was told not to rape her. His purpose for being there was singular and noble. Jelly came to take her soul. After he used a thin razor blade to cut away her eyelids he made a superficial cut to draw first blood. He voicelessly mouthed the proper chant, then raised the dagger above her. As he lowered it and cut her open, Jelly was certain that he saw her soul rise and fall at the altar.

19

Quincy arrived at the station ten minutes after his partner. Phee was much too focused on his own issues to notice any preoccupation on Quincy's part. Quincy needed the job today. He needed the investigation to direct his thoughts, even if only momentarily, away from the fears and anxiety that had kept him up all night.

Phee was already on his computer, checking out the site that Zibik recommended as Quincy approached and looked over his shoulder. Brenda taught Phee a long time ago how to smoothly navigate through cyberspace and find whatever he was looking for. He managed to pull up an old site that featured Dr. Zibik reciting the nine declarations that defined Satanism for the new age, according to Anton LaVey's *The Satanic Bible*.

She wasn't dressed in the clichéd robe or ceremonial garb as she addressed the camera. She wore a rather plain cotton blouse, with her short hair parted down the center. She spoke to the camera with ease and confidence as though she were addressing an old acquaintance.

"Our faith teaches us to practice indulgence instead of abstinence. We pursue vital existence over spiritual pipe dreams. We teach our followers to strive for undefiled wisdom, instead of hypocritical self-deceit. It is our belief that kindness should be reserved for those who deserve it, instead of wasting love on ingrates. The great master LaVey has enlightened us to the power of vengeance over passively turning the other cheek. His writings teach us that we should only practice responsibility to the responsible, instead of psychic vampires."

Zibik held up *The Satanic Bible* to the camera and said very deliberately, "This is the book of truth. And the truth is man is just another animal. He is more often worse than those that walk on all fours, and because of his divine spiritual and intellectual development, has become the most vicious animal of all. This is the book that will teach you about all of the so-called sins as they lead to physical, mental, or emotional gratification. This is the book of enlightenment. Despite some of the untruths that have been perpetrated against us, learn for yourselves how Satan is the best friend the Church has ever had as He has kept it in business all these years. These are the nine tenets of our faith. For those of you who are strong enough to embrace the truth of man's nature and the purpose of your existence, we invite you to learn firsthand who we really are as opposed to who others tell you we are."

Zibik presented herself as an everywoman. Although she had a registered IQ of 173, she came across much more as a simple and earnest woman than the intellectual elitist that she really was. She looked like a favored aunt or respected mentor. She was an effective speaker and recruiter because of her accessibility. One of her greatest assets was the deceptive perception of her plainness.

Phee watched Dr. Zibik casually espousing the values of Satanism. He couldn't understand why he was getting more and more of a queasy feeling in the pit of his stomach, the more he watched Zibik. The closest Phee came to defining his religious standing was that he had come to consider himself a liberal spiritualist. Although the general concept of God worked for him, he also supported other people's rights to believe in whatever elevated them and brought them peace as long as that didn't infringe on the rights of others. He couldn't care less what name those that chose to believe in God called Him, as long as basic goodness was manifested in them. He knew and befriended atheists and agnostics with similar qualifications, but he had never encountered a living, breathing Satanist. He had never known so little about a subject and yet had such strong preconceptions about it. Like most people, he thought of Satanism as blood sacrificing and ritualistic devil worshipping. Of course he ran into his share of that on some of the sites he visited, but he was actually surprised to find that the majority of worshippers viewed Satan much more as a philosophy than an actual being.

Zibik was right. The chat rooms were interesting, to say the least. The conversations included everything ranging from detailed rituals of initiation to heated debates from differing satanic denominations. As best Phee could tell, there were members from the Deists or Pantheists, Gnostics, the Shavians, and other names that made his head hurt. Not dissimilar to Christianity, Satanism had its share of offshoots from its most original incarnation.

"Interesting," Quincy said.

"Just your friendly Satanist next door," Phee smirked.

"To tell you the truth, she creeps me out," Quincy said as he crossed to his desk and turned on his computer.

"That's because deep down, you're a nice little Catholic boy. Hey, listen to this: It's from some guy who heads up one of these satanic churches. 'True Satanists do not believe in the supernatural, in neither God nor the Devil. To the Satanist, he is his own God. Satan is a symbol of man living as his prideful, carnal nature dictates. The reality behind Satan is the dark, evolutionary force of entropy that permeates all of nature and provides the drive for survival and propagation inherent in all living things. Satan is not a conscious entity to be worshipped, but rather a reservoir of power inside each human to be tapped at will. Thus, any concept of sacrifice is rejected as a Christian aberration. In Satanism, there's no deity to which one can sacrifice. I am my own God,'" Phee read.

"Well that about sums Zibik up. Let me ask you a question. Do you think she's telling us what she really knows?" Quincy asked.

"Of course not," Phee said.

"I got an idea last night, but it's a little out of the box."

"My favorite kind of thinking."

"Zibik's our best shot at navigating us through all of this weird shit ten times quicker than if we try to do it on our own. Plus, we both agree that she knows more than she's saying," Quincy stated.

"True," Phee said.

"If we could make a couple of good runs at her, more than likely we'd break her."

"Yeah but, I may have worn out my welcome there. Not to mention, I don't think it's necessarily the best use of our time trekking back and forth to Bedford Hills, while at the same time trying to stop whoever did the killing," Phee said.

"True, so when Mohammed couldn't go to the mountain…"

"I see where you're headed with this, but the Justice Department will never turn her over to us. We're not Feds."

"Yeah, I know, but Special Agent Maclin is. I already ran this past her. She said she would be on the first train out of DC," Quincy countered.

20

"Tickets please. Tickets," the long man in the Amtrak uniform chanted as he slowly walked the aisle of the seven a.m. express out of DC. The train was only half-full. Maclin sat quietly staring at her reflection in the window as the train raced through a dark underpass.

"Ticket please, ma'am. Ma'am, ticket please." He finally got her attention on the third try. Maclin turned in his direction but never looked at him. She offered him her ticket and not much else. As the man moved on, she reached into her pocket and removed the amber vial of pills. She popped one and chased it down with a sip of water from a half-empty Arrowhead bottle that stayed in her lap for most of the ride. As Maclin closed her eyes, she thought back to the phone call she received from Quincy just before midnight.

Special Agent Maclin owed a great debt to Phee and Quincy.

Aside from saving her life, they helped her do what she'd been unable to do on her own for the last ten years: kill Deggler. Deggler had robbed her of the things she valued most. He killed the love of her life, derailed her happiness, and all but decimated her hope for normalcy. The only constant in her life for the last decade was the deep-rooted hate that had become an undetachable shadow that led her as much as it followed her. Things had become increasingly blurry to Maclin. For the last ten years, Deggler had given her purpose. The thought of vengeance was like oxygen to her. It was her steady companion, the one thing that inspired her most. She assumed killing him would bring her peace, but unfortunately she was mistaken. Maclin couldn't remember at this point whether or not she had completely sold or merely leased her soul to the devil to catch and kill the demon that had robbed her of a meaningful life. The one thing she was certain of was how lost and alone she felt, now that her hate had been expended. Maclin had been filled with hate for so long that when she finally released it, she was left with nothing more than a shell of who she used to be. The depression started right away. Days after killing Deggler, she felt vacant and useless, like an abandoned well.

She had nothing left; Maclin felt emotionally bankrupt. She hadn't anticipated that after killing Deggler, she would be left with such an overwhelming depression. And then there was also the loneliness. She found it both relentless and reliable. Her loneliness awoke with her in the morning and waited faithfully each evening for her return. Throughout the day, it allowed her to delude herself that she temporarily escaped its grasp with the distraction of work, but it was always near, never really out of reach. When she could muster either the interest or strength, she fought back, as she did last night, with the occasional one-night stand. The feel of a stranger's warm skin was often her best defense, even if only for an hour or two. The ramification was often the greater sense of emptiness after the act. But still she took it, because it was all she had. There was nothing of value left in her, to either offer or claim.

After Maclin finished work last night, she stopped by a bar, picked up a piece of comfort, and brought him back to her place. She could tell right away that he was in great shape and more than likely spent endless hours each week in the gym. She only offered him the most perfunctory information about herself and lied about the things that she felt she needed to. She didn't ask much about him, because she really didn't want to know. As far as she was concerned, his most impressive qualification was that he was a living, breathing body of distraction. He wasn't particularly handsome, but at 6'3" and easily 230 pounds, she chose him because of his size. Maclin felt like she needed to be overpowered and manhandled. He looked like he could hurt her, like he could give her the right amount of pain to make her feel alive and connected. The bruises that he left on her body confirmed her intuition. After the stranger served his purpose and left, Maclin popped some Zoloft and Ambien. The pills helped, but not nearly enough. They allowed her to get what little sleep she could, kept her functioning, and offered her enough stability to fake her way through each day. She couldn't ignore the fact that not only did she find herself taking more than what her doctor had prescribed, but she was also developing a habit of countering the antidepressant's side effects with other prescription drugs to level her off. Her recent promotion took her out of the field and put her behind a desk. She managed to string together eight to ten hours each day of enough leadership to mask the fact that she was inching closer and closer to becoming a highly functioning addict. She medicated herself and on a daily basis hid behind the veneer of a successful agent, climbing the ladder to bigger and better things. But every day that she sat at her desk, in her cushy office with a view, she was bored out of her mind. Now that Deggler was gone, she had no idea what to do with herself. When Quincy called and said they needed her help, Maclin, without giving it a second thought, came to offer her services.

21

Maclin, Phee, and Quincy sat across from Warden Rinetti, a 53-year-old dark-skinned Italian woman with a tough but fair disposition. She listened intently to Maclin lay out the details of what the Feds and the Justice Department called their federal "Mirror Project."

"The Bureau and the Justice Department have successfully collaborated on this program in the past with your predecessor without incident," Maclin said.

"My predecessor and I have very different philosophies on how this prison should be run. For the sake of this conversation, my approach should be the only one we concern ourselves with," Rinetti said authoritatively.

"Yes, ma'am," Maclin diplomatically demurred.

"So let me make sure I fully understand this; the FBI

temporarily releases convicts to help them catch current criminals?" Rinetti asked.

"Exactly. Bottom line, Warden, we use criminals to catch criminals. If we find a con that has committed crimes with similar MOs or profiles, we use them in special cases. That's why we call it the Mirror Project. Due to the complicated nature of a current case we're investigating, we think Dr. Zibik could be of great service. We'd have her back to you in seventy-two hours or less," Maclin explained.

"How do you know she'll want to help you?" Rinetti asked.

"We make different deals depending on the con. With good behavior, she'll be considered for parole in ten years instead of fifteen, and she's been petitioning to be moved out of Bedford Hills since she got here. The Justice Department is willing to accommodate that request," Maclin responded.

"So am I being asked to sign off on this or told?"

"Definitely asked, ma'am," Maclin lied.

Maclin wasn't sure whether it was the drugs or not, but she was much more easily irritated lately. Even though it was a customary courtesy, she resented feeling like she had to jump through hoops or kowtow to the woman delaying them from catching a brutal killer. She bit her tongue and pretended to be as pleasant as possible, even though she immediately disliked the warden.

"Let me share something with you that my predecessor told me just before he retired. Three years ago, right after Zibik arrived, one of the toughest cons in this place ended up murdered, with her heart literally cut out of her. They never found it. No one talked, and he could never prove it was Zibik, but he said, 'Some of these things you just know.' Just like we all know that even though she's in here on a hit-and-run, there's a helluva lot worse in her closet. I hope you're all very clear on what you're getting yourselves into," Rinetti said as she reached over and signed the release form.

"We're clear, Warden," Quincy said.

As Maclin, Phee, and Quincy got up to leave, Rinetti couldn't help herself from offering a parting opinion on what they were doing.

"So with this 'Mirror' program, does that mean the dirt that you arrest today you'll be making deals with tomorrow? Where does it end?" When neither of the three offered a response, Rinetti added, "By the way, Detective Freeman, regardless of what I think of Zibik personally, let's make sure she's returned in one piece."

"We'll do our best, Warden," Phee said just before exiting.

Zibik looked at the two cops and the FBI agent and burst into laughter. One of the two guards that were posted inside the room suppressed the urge to smile at Zibik's contagious laughter. Zibik milked the moment. After she stopped laughing, she sat quietly for a while, fully aware that everyone in the room was hanging on for her response.

"What in the world would possibly make you think that I would even entertain the thought of helping you?"

"The Justice Department is willing to offer you earlier parole eligibility and grant your request to be moved from Bedford Hills. Of course, this is contingent on whether or not the information and assistance you provide help lead to the capture and conviction of the person, or persons, responsible for the crime we're investigating," Maclin told her.

"Special Agent Maclin, you're going to have to give me more reasons than that," Zibik responded.

"How about this, you're going to help us because if your group doesn't have anything to do with this recent murder as you claim, then you're gonna want us to find whoever it is that's trying to frame you and your people. The other reason you're gonna help us is because you're too much of a narcissist not to. The simple fact that you know we need you feeds your already overinflated sense of superiority. Besides, once your appeal is turned down, and I'll personally make sure that it is, you'll be looking at staying in here for a very long time, with no other real shot of getting out earlier. My gut tells me you're gonna want to hedge your bets," Maclin countered.

Zibik attempted to smile in the face of her seeming defeat before finally stipulating the basis of her concession. "One condition," Zibik demanded.

"What's that?" Quincy asked.

"Before we do anything, we have to stop at McDonalds. I've been craving their french fries since I've been in this hellhole."

Phee, Quincy, and Maclin formed a three-point sentry around a shackled Zibik as they walked across the prison parking lot to their car.

"Let me break down the two most important rules. You dick us around, we tell the warden you attempted to escape and have her add some time to your sentence. The second rule is if you are in fact stupid enough to try and escape, I'll be the first to kill you," Phee said, pointedly.

"Any questions?" Quincy asked.

"No, I think Detective Freeman has pretty much said it all," Zibik said, smiling.

Zibik thought it was interesting that even though she was guarded and chained and only two hundred yards removed from the prison's core, the sky looked better and the sun felt warmer. Freedom, even if only temporary and conditional, was worth dying or killing for, if given either option.

22

Phee didn't expect it, but he felt extremely uncomfortable letting Zibik examine his brother's corpse. Obviously, they all hoped that she might shed some greater light on a world they knew very little about, but still, Phee felt that her very presence was in some strange way a violation to his brother. Jeans, a sweater, and a short wool jacket replaced Zibik's prison-issued clothes. Her shackles were exchanged for regular cuffs and an ankle monitor. Kravitz sat at a nearby table in the morgue, eating his second Weight Watchers' lasagna lunch. Even though Maclin had spent much more than her fair share of time around dead bodies, and had certainly seen graphic killings, the drugs that she was on made her even less sensitive than usual. She found herself focusing on the obese coroner devouring his food.

"May I?" Zibik asked as she waited for permission to touch

the body. When Phee offered a slight nod, Zibik put on sterile gloves and casually circled the examination table as though she were inspecting a used car. She hovered over AJ's face and stared for several moments at the lidless eyes. Quincy reached out subtly and patted Phee on the shoulder as he could feel his partner growing increasingly tenser. As Zibik finally laid hands on the body, she was incredibly gentle, a bit too much. There was the weird sense that she was somehow getting off in some way on the whole experience. She ran her fingers along the edges of the body's open cavity. She felt the tips of the rib cage that had been neatly cut. She lowered her head slightly to get a better view of the empty shell and its missing organs. Phee was the only one to see it, her pride and fascination, in the details of the kill. The room was uncomfortably quiet as Zibik went about her business. Phee was certain that he saw a look of pleasure in her eyes. He unexpectedly broke from Quincy when he saw what looked like a smile on Zibik's face.

"What the hell are you doing?" Phee confronted her.

"What you brought me here to do, Detective," Zibik responded.

Quincy stepped in, pulled Phee back, and spoke to him quietly. "She's right, Phee; if she's gonna be of any use to us, we've gotta let her do her thing."

As Phee turned and walked toward the exit, Quincy's phone rang.

Phee pushed through the double doors and made his way to the men's room, where one of Kravitz' assistants was at the sink washing his hands.

"Detective Freeman, I just wanted to let you know how sorry I am for your loss. If you need anything, please don't hesitate to ask."

When Phee came into the bathroom, he vaguely remembered being greeted by a familiar face and voice. He wasn't certain whether or not he responded. Once he was alone in the bathroom, he ran hot water in the small porcelain sink. As the steam began to rise, he submerged both his hands in the rising pool of scalding water. Phee's body had gone numb, and he needed something to bring him back—anything. In the rare instances that his body shut down, physical pain had always been the quickest way for him to recalibrate. From the moment Quincy told him the news of his brother's murder, Phee worked overtime to keep his anger in check. As he stood alone in the men's room thinking of the image of AJ on the cold steel gurney, a gleeful Zibik hovering over him, he could no longer contain the fury within. He turned and punched the aluminum towel dispenser, completely caving it in. He used the bottom of his foot to repeatedly kick the metal wall of the stall. His third and fourth kick was done with such sheer force that the hinges of the stall were loosened. He punched the walls like an angry boxer. Similar to his father, Phee was the embodiment of unrestrained rage. He vandalized the bathroom, until he completely emptied himself. As he stared in the mirror, he gently rocked back and forth, until he successfully regulated his breathing. Nothing registered with him. Not the destruction that he caused, not even the hollow set of eyes that stared back at him from the cracked mirror. As his phone rang numerous times, Phee started coming back. He finally looked at the caller ID and saw that the call was from Brenda. As he let her message go to voice-mail, he noticed for the first time the blood that dripped from his injured knuckles.

Ten minutes later, Phee was in the hallway pacing, when Quincy and Maclin brought Zibik through the double doors. From the look on Quincy's face, Phee knew immediately that something was wrong. Quincy never slowed his stride as he looked over to his partner and said, "We got another one."

23

Carmen Morales was gutted in the same way as AJ. The crescent dagger rested on its side in the open cavity of her torso. Like AJ, her lidless eyes stared upward into the great unknown. There was a fresh henna tattoo of a bird on her left ankle. Candles were still burning, and music was quietly playing in the background. Phee and Quincy walked the scene for twenty minutes before Maclin brought Zibik in. Zibik studied the body with an even greater fascination and respect than she had displayed with AJ. There were as many obvious similarities between the corpses as there were glaring disparities, namely the tattoo and dagger. Zibik made her observations from a measured distance and treated the crime scene as though the killing had occurred on hallowed ground. She never got within more than three feet of Carmen. Phee saw the look on her face again. As Zibik looked down on the dissected body before her, he saw the approving smile and look of admiration in her eyes. He also detected something oddly sexual about her energy. Zibik was turned on by what she saw.

As Zibik felt Phee's hard stare, she turned and innocently smiled at him. "You're much too subjective to be impressed by how good whoever did this really is," Zibik said.

"Just tell us what you see," Quincy responded.

"Better yet, why don't you tell me what you see?"

When neither Quincy nor Phee responded to her, she turned and addressed Agent Maclin, who had started pacing in an attempt to downplay her increasing jitteriness.

"How about you, Agent Maclin? Would you mind telling me what you see, besides the obvious dead body? You can just give me the CliffsNote's version, if you prefer."

Maclin didn't like the way Zibik stared at her. It left her feeling both examined and revealed. She turned away from Zibik and directed her attention back to the crime scene.

"Body facing south, a seven-inch crescent dagger that is more than likely the murder weapon, pentagram, candles, altar—all suggesting a ritualistic murder," Maclin listed.

"I don't expect the three of you to be able to appreciate the attention to detail, but it really is a thing of beauty. Whoever did this, knows their stuff," Zibik said.

"Cut the crap and tell us what's going on here," Quincy jumped in.

"Well, to begin with, the altar is exactly three inches from the pentagram and precisely two feet in elevation with thirteen black candles, seven inches tall, each one lit at different points in the ritual. This is why there are subtle differences in their heights right now; they truly took their time and did everything to the letter, unlike the first kill. I'm sure when you check with the coroner, he'll tell you that the dissection was made from upward cutting motions and that the dagger was heated and used, not only to cut but as a cauterizing instrument as well. Everything was done to keep the victim alive as long as possible, so she could witness her own death. That's a key point in the ritual. From the look of things, I would say this was a very successful kill. Otherwise, she wouldn't have been marked," Zibik explained.

"What do you mean marked?" Phee asked.

"Agent Maclin failed to make a very important observation," Zibik informed them.

"And what was that?" Maclin asked.

"The henna tattoo," Zibik said.

"Yeah, we saw it. It's a bird. The sparrow used to be used as the mark of a Christian," Quincy said.

"I'm almost impressed, Detective Cavanaugh, but you forget that in the scheme of things Christianity is a young religion. The mark of the sparrow means different things in different cultures. Long before Christianity debuted, early Egyptians saw sparrows as soul catchers. The tattoo, the type of dagger used, and how it was left in the body tell you everything that you need to know about the two murders," Zibik said.

"And what's that?" Phee asked.

"The first one was all anger and passion, the same killer, but not nearly as disciplined. The cuts on your brother, Detective

Freeman, were more jagged and visceral. Once they got that one out of their system, they were able to be much more refined and precise the second time around. The killer was able to focus much more on the original goal."

"Which was?" Quincy jumped in.

"To take her soul," Zibik said, with unabashed admiration. "There is a bright side though. Whoever did this is so good that it may actually work to your advantage."

Zibik asked for, and was granted, access to a computer the minute they made it back to the station. There was no way for the cops to have known how many different satanic sites there were. Zibik was a kid in a candy store. She used an alias and searched different sites and cyber-trolled several chat rooms. Not the "google-friendly" crap. Zibik brought them to the hardcore stuff, where special codes were needed to gain access. She left posts on bulletin boards but spent the majority of her time talking in chat rooms.

"So, what, you expect whoever is responsible to just get online and announce it to the world?" Phee asked.

"Basically, yes," Zibik responded.

"And why would they do that?" Maclin jumped in.

"Because they accomplished what you and the rest of the world thought impossible. What good is pulling off the greatest feat known to man if you can't tell people you did it? Even though it hasn't gone public yet, trust me, people in my world already have intimate details. I hate to sound clichéd, but we actually are everywhere. Any opportunity to dispel the myths and lies that religion and society have perpetrated is the highest calling for those of us that are of the true faith. What you call narcissism, we call enlightenment."

"Do you really think that telling the world you're a murderer is all that enlightened?" Phee asked.

"Part of your problem is that you just see these as murders, when in actuality, this whole thing is much more profound."

"What's so profound about butchering people?" Phee snapped.

"Connecting to the soul as a tangible entity would be evolution of the highest order. No disrespect to your brother, but a little murder might be just a small price to pay."

Phee faked an angry response, but the truth was he refused to let himself be baited. No matter how dumb or how smart, all cons tried cops in one way or another. The balance of power was often defined by the results of those tests. Zibik assumed she knew Phee's weaknesses. As long as Zibik incorrectly thought that Phee was completely controlled by his emotions, the upper hand was in Phee's court.

"I gotta get out of here," Phee said as he looked at Quincy and gave a subtle nod. Quincy followed him to the door and out into the hall.

"Find a way to make sure Zibik gets at least five minutes alone on the computer. Let's see who she talks to when she thinks we're not looking," Phee said.

"It's a good idea," Quincy responded.

"Of course it is. I stole it from you. Three years ago, the Patterson case. I'm on my phone headed to my brother's apartment to see if there's anything there that might help."

After Phee and Quincy walked off, Agent Maclin sipped from her water bottle to quench the constant state of dry mouth and thirstiness she found herself in. She looked over Zibik's shoulder as she happily searched various sites. Zibik slowed for a beat and half turned toward Maclin, whispering as though she were sharing a secret with an old and trusted friend.

"They don't know, do they?" Zibik asked.

"Know what?" Maclin asked, confused.

"About your extracurricular indulgences."

"What the hell is that supposed to mean?" Maclin shot back.

"I'm a neuropsychologist by trade, remember? I can spot an addiction four miles away."

"I have no idea what you think you know or what the hell you're talking about. The only thing you need to be focused on right now is why we have you here in the first place."

"Have it your way, girlfriend," Zibik smirked at her before turning her attention back to the computer.

After typing in a few messages to the sites she visited, Zibik leaned back in her chair, confident and pleased with herself. "We should hear something from your killer in the next couple of hours."

"If they haven't already declared anything on any of these sites, what makes you think they will now?" Maclin demanded.

"Because the only thing worse than not taking credit for a great accomplishment is having someone else do it instead. I'm pretending to be your soul catcher."

24

Phee believed in souls. As he drove to his brother's apartment, he found himself thinking quite a bit of his own. He thought of both the possibility of its redemption and damnation. The key to redemption for him simply meant, no matter his failures or shortcomings, as long as he maintained faithfulness to the positive things he honored, then he was keeping up his part of his responsibility to the universe. Conversely, he viewed damnation as the willing betrayal of such things as love, family, fairness, and duty. It was that prevailing spirit that he saw as not only the connective force to every other human being but ultimately to whatever omnipotent entity that claimed credit for his existence. He had on occasion thought about his soul in various contexts before, but never considered it in terms of physical or tangible mass. He believed without question that it was real and ever present, even though he couldn't see it or hear it, couldn't touch it or smell it.

Phee lifted the pile of his brother's mail that was sprawled on the dining room table and thumbed through it. The name on the envelopes read AJ Delarosa. Delarosa was his mother Dolicia's maiden name. AJ stopped using his father's last name the day Clay kicked him out of the house at sixteen. As Phee placed the mail back on the table, he thought about how the history of their rejection cut both ways. Phee turned to face AJ's sniffling BFF.

"I still can't believe it. You hear and read about this shit happening all the time, but you never think it's gonna happen to someone you love."

At 6'2", the aging cross-dresser looked like a mix between Lady Gaga and Ozzy Osbourne. Timothy Bale, AJ's closest friend, had long ago been rechristened Epiphany Chevalier, shortly after moving from Arkansas and transforming into a full-fledged working girl. Mascara streaked down Epiphany's face. She'd been openly crying since the time Phee had given her the news of AJ's death, fifteen minutes earlier.

"You and AJ were roommates or…?"Phee asked uncomfortably.

"Neither," she said flatly, used to the confusion and assumptions. "I've just been staying here on and off for the last month. I was in Atlantic City for four days and just got back to the city late last night. I try to stay here as much as possible since AJ's other roommate, Shay, was killed. Did you know about that? Do you think the two murders are related?" Epiphany asked, getting more and more riled up.

"Yes, we know about Shay's murder, and, no, they don't seem to be related," Phee answered.

"So how exactly was AJ killed, Detective... I'm sorry what was your name again?" Epiphany asked.

"Detective Freeman. You'll have to excuse me, at this point, I'm really not at liberty to discuss the case in detail," Phee said, not wanting to get into it.

"The last time I saw my girl she was so happy. She had just finished making some outfits for a few of us for a ball we go to every year. I can't..." Phee stood uncomfortably by as Epiphany broke into another crying spell. After it passed, she turned back to Phee. "I don't even know what to do next. Have you found AJ's family? She never talked about them, but once or twice she said something about a younger brother. I think he was an athlete of some kind. As close as she and I were, there's still so much about her I don't know."

"We'll find the family," Phee said.

"And what about who killed her? You don't have the faintest idea who did it, do you?"

"No, but we're doing our best," Phee said curtly.

"That's exactly what the cops said when Shay was killed; and they did nothing. If it weren't for us tracking down the asshole who killed her, he would still be walking around free, hurting someone else, and we would be the only ones who cared. I guess the word 'best' means something different when it comes to people like us. But if you had ever met AJ and knew how special my girl was, then maybe your 'best' would really mean something."

Even though Phee hadn't put much thought into it before, it still caught him off guard when his brother was repeatedly referred to as a female. After a few more moments of mutual discomfiture, Epiphany went next door to a neighbor to tell them the horrible news as Phee walked the small apartment. He wasn't sure if he would actually find anything that would shed new light on the investigation, but it was his duty and instinct to look, nonetheless. On a purely personal level, he just felt a need to be in his brother's space. To get some sense of how he lived. The apartment was a five-flight walk-up in a rent-controlled building not far from the theater district. The building definitely could have used some repairs and upgrading, but once inside, AJ's space was very welcoming. It was a two bedroom with a pullout sofa. As Phee sat on the arm of the couch and looked around, he thought about AJ's ex-roommate Shay DeVane, who had been killed only a few weeks ago. They arrested the john a week later, after a group of resourceful cross-dressers tracked him down to an investment firm on Wall Street. That case was unconnected to AJ's murder but much more in line with how Phee had often suspected his brother would die. There were many times that Phee viewed his brother as a tragic blurb waiting to be written. The irony was that until his death, AJ wasn't much more than an uncomfortable afterthought, a disembodied name, with old ties to Phee and their father. Even when Phee spied on him from distant corners, he did so with an assumed indifference. It took AJ's death to bring him here. It was only after he had been violently taken away that Phee started thinking of him simply being human, and not just something garish and embarrassing. Death had reminded him that they were brothers, and not callous strangers. It took AJ's murder for Phee to realize that no matter their differences, his older brother was always there with him, connected, and a part of his soul.

Phee looked in the fridge, peeked in the closet, and opened drawers to cabinets and dressers. He was looking for things that told him more about his brother. He found a signed portfolio of fashion sketches that AJ had evidently designed: everything from women's evening gowns to elegant men's suits and blazers. Phee was by no means an expert of couture, but in his opinion, the sketches were pretty impressive. He discovered a scrapbook that was filled with famous quotes and inspirational musings. Some he'd read before, some he hadn't. He found an old family photo album in the living room credenza. He sat at the kitchen table and looked through it. The first few pictures were all baby photos of AJ. He was a beautiful baby, chubby and expressive. One was taken the day he was born being held by both his father and mother. It was strange, but Phee noticed that, unlike Dolicia, not only was his father not smiling, but there was also something sad in his eyes.

He saw a photo of his two-year-old brother being assisted by Clay as they both held Phee at the hospital on his first day in the world. Unlike AJ's first photo, all were beaming with joy. There were two pages of the album dedicated to AJ and Phee's childhood years. They were constantly hugging and hamming it up for the camera. Phee did what he hadn't done much of in the last two days. He laughed. He laughed at shared moments with his brother that he had long forgotten. He laughed at the memories of their dated clothesand skinny legs with ashy knees. He thought back fondly of the trouble they got into and the lies they told. He smiled back at the photos of the two inseparable boys with mischievous grins.

As the album narrated AJ's teenage years, Phee was aware of two things that were glaringly absent: him and his brother's smile. The last ten pages of photos were of AJ and friendships he'd made as an adult. The majority were of him with Epiphany, other flamboyantly gay men, and fellow transgender folks. He seemed happy again, surrounded by people who accepted and loved him for who he really was. Just as Phee had done with Quincy, AJ replaced his flesh and blood with adopted family. When he got to the end of the photo album, Phee flipped back to the very first page of Clay holding AJ. He couldn't help but wonder why his father looked so sad on the day AJ was born.

25

Back at the station, Quincy and Maclin brought Phee up to speed as soon as he returned. Quincy called him earlier to let him know that their plan with Zibik had paid off.

"We just put her down in holding," Quincy told Phee.

"She totally bit when she thought we weren't looking. First she gave me some bull about pretending to be the killer online, then when she thought she had our confidence, she made her real move." Maclin added.

"After we put her downstairs, we retrieved her history and caught a deleted conversation that we weren't supposed to know about. Looks like she made contact with one of her old running mates, goes by the name of Dark Crown. Zibik switched over to a different chat name, 'True Throne,'" Quincy said as he showed Phee his computer.

True Throne: "How are the Children of the Faith?"

Dark Crown: "Missing you, myself included."

True Throne: "It goes both ways. At least I left them in capable hands, with you."

Dark Crown: "We're all waiting patiently for you to come back."

True Throne: "I know. What do you know about the soul catcher? Is he real?"

Dark Crown: "Very."

True Throne: "How do you know?"

Dark Crown: "Because he contacted me."

Zibik sat in the small holding cell, counting the lines of the adjoining tiles on the floor. Quincy, Phee, and Maclin opened the cell and entered.

"You want to tell us about Dark Crown?" Quincy said.

"Who?" Zibik replied.

"Nice try," Phee said as he nodded to Maclin, who showed Zibik a printed copy of her earlier conversation.

Zibik stared incredulously at the paper as though the effort might make it disappear.

"Who is it?" Quincy asked.

Zibik handed back the paper and sat rebelliously quiet.

"Just so we're clear here, Dr. Zibik, if we throw obstruction at you, well, then you can kiss any chance of an appeal goodbye. You're not going anywhere. We'll find out who they are sooner or later, so you should just be smart and tell us now," Maclin said.

Zibik looked at the three and weighed her options. "He's a brother in the Faith."

"We want a name!" Phee demanded.

"I can't give that to you, no matter what you threaten me with. Our entire movement has been built on faith and loyalty. Nothing you say can make me destroy that."

"If you're so interested in protecting your little cult, then why won't you just have him tell us the truth, so that your movement is cleared? If you all are as innocent in this thing as you claim, then there should be no problem. Just have him talk to us. Your terms," Quincy said.

26

Zibik's man agreed to meet at a rock quarry out in Jersey. His two conditions were that he be granted immunity if he incriminated himself in anything other than the actual murders and that the meeting was with Zibik and only one cop. Quincy ran point and drove Zibik to the designated location. The quarry wasn't far from where Quincy had almost been killed by Deggler only weeks ago. As he thought back to that night, Quincy was reminded how life was never to be taken for granted.

When Quincy pulled into the main yard, he saw a man in a ski mask patiently sitting on the hood of a black F-150. The man's name was Stringer, a second-generation Satanist from Bayonne. Quincy exited the car and went around to the passenger side to assist Zibik, who was cuffed and shackled. As Quincy approached Stringer, he noticed the 9-mm handgun on the hood next to him.

"How are you Daria?" Stringer asked Zibik.

"I'm well, brother. Good to see you, even under these circumstances," Zibik responded.

"Detective, would you mind taking out your gun and putting it on the hood next to me?" Stringer said.

"Actually, I would. That wasn't part of the deal," Quincy responded.

"Well that's the beauty of holding all of the cards. You get to change the rules at will," Stringer said.

Two armed men in ski masks appeared from the rear of the truck. Thirty yards away, a man dressed in camouflage gear held Quincy in the crosshairs of a high-powered rifle. A small red laser dot canvassed Quincy's back in search of the perfect target.

"Whatever it is that you think you're doing, we don't have time for this. Dr. Zibik thinks your group is being set up. If I don't walk out of here convinced of that, I'm not the one who loses," Quincy said.

"Who says you get to walk out of here?" Stringer laughed.

Quincy had no way of knowing that the red laser dot had come to rest in the center of the back of his head. He looked at the three men and held his ground, still refusing to relinquish his weapon.

"Tell your boys to stand down, Dr. Zibik. Don't be an idiot," Quincy said.

"Is it better to be a free idiot, or an imprisoned genius?" Zibik asked.

"You might want to know that at this very second there's an

HPK 720 rifle with a laser scope warming up the hairs on the back of your neck," Stringer informed Quincy.

"Dr. Zibik, we both know that you're too smart to let them go through with this," Quincy said.

"Really? If you thought so highly of my intelligence, maybe you should have taken that into account before you made that pathetic play back at the station. Did you really think I didn't know that you all intentionally gave me enough free time so that you could track whomever I was talking to? You've been had, Detective, plain and simple."

"Okay, nice play. Ball's in your court. Now what?" Quincy asked.

"You take off the cuffs and bracelet and walk away, and we go find who's been trying to set us up," Zibik said.

"That's not going to happen. Does your man here know who's behind the killings or not?" Quincy asked.

"What we know or don't know is irrelevant. Your only concern right now should be getting these cuffs and monitor off of me." Zibik said.

"So all of this was just bullshit?" Quincy said.

"Not exactly, but we won't be telling you what we do know. Keys." Zibik ordered.

"I told you that's not going to happen."

"We're not cop killers, but don't test me. If my associate raises his hand, you'll be dead before he lowers it. Take off the cuffs," Zibik demanded.

"Fuck you and the clowns you're with," Quincy insisted.

"Have it your way," Zibik warned.

The laser dot on Quincy wavered as Stringer raised his hand. Suddenly, the dot shifted to Stringer and a bullet punctured his palm. Stringer yelled in pain, and one of the armed men pointed his gun at Quincy. The man was dropped with a gunshot to the leg by Phee, who quietly climbed out of the trunk of Quincy's car. Both men were writhing in pain as Phee kept his gun trained on the third one, whose name was Barnes.

Two years straight, Special Agent Maclin took second place in the Bureau's annual sharpshooting competition. Before arriving at the stone yard, she'd popped a Xanax to keep herself calm and maintain her focus. She was steady, with no telltale signs of compromise. After subduing Zibik's sniper, she hit her mark square in the palm thirty yards out. Being that accurate under such peculiar circumstances, she liked her chances—for first place, in next year's competition.

With Zibik's men down, Quincy pointed his gun at her and demanded, "What do you know?"

Zibik stared at Quincy, refusing to speak. Quincy raised his hand, and a red dot danced across the body of the uninjured Barnes. A second after the dot stopped on the ground, an inch from his left foot, a shot rang out, and a bullet kicked up dirt next to him. Barnes jumped back frightened. When Zibik still refused to speak, Quincy raised his hand again, and Maclin repeated the process, intentionally just missing Barnes' right foot. Although Barnes looked at Zibik completely frightened, Zibik stood quiet, still refusing to give in.

"Fine, have it your way," Quincy said as he raised his hand again.

The red dot moved across Barnes' chest and abdomen, slowly making its way downward. He completely freaked, when the red dot rested on his groin. As he tried to move away, the dot followed him, holding steady on his family jewels.

"Please, Dr. Zibik, don't let them shoot me," Barnes pleaded.

Zibik knew that the advantage had now shifted back to Quincy's court. "Okay, you've made your point. You let them go; I'll give you a name."

"Why would I let them off that easily?"

"Because I know who supplied the dagger that was used to kill the Morales woman. That information should lead you back to your killer. But only if you let them go."

"Take off the ski masks," Quincy ordered.

The three men didn't move until Zibik nodded at them to comply. As they took off the masks, Quincy used his cell phone to take pictures of the trio. "Here's the deal, you talk they walk. You try bullshitting us again, and all of you will spend the next twenty-five years talking about the day you underestimated us."

27

The wooden doorframe of the small shop split into jagged pieces as Phee and Quincy kicked their way in with guns drawn. Separating at the door, they moved in opposite directions and made their way to the back of the shop. As they slowly opened the door to a small work area, they both saw the pool of blood on the floor. The blood led back to the body of an older man who was lying faceup with two ornate daggers sticking out of his chest. Phee bent over and touched the man's face.

"Body's still warm," he said.

"How warm?" Quincy asked.

"Twenty minutes, give or take," Phee said.

Quincy pulled out his phone and called Maclin. "We got a body. Bring Zibik in."

A few minutes later Maclin walked in with Zibik. "Is this your man?" Quincy asked.

"Yeah, Arthur Tan. He was the best blade maker around. All of his pieces were one of a kind, very exclusive stuff," Zibik answered.

Agent Maclin immediately started looking around as Phee walked back out to the front of the shop.

"Was he one of your followers?" Quincy asked Zibik.

"Arthur Tan followed whoever paid the most."

Phee stuck his head back into the room. "Quincy, I'm going to take a look outside and see if any of the other storefronts have cameras that could help us out. I'll call Alvarez to get a warrant if I find anything."

Quincy nodded to Phee as Agent Maclin thumbed through half a dozen thick portfolios filled with photos of one of a kind knives, daggers, and swords. Toward the end of the fourth album, Maclin found a photo of the crescent dagger that was used to kill Carmen Morales. She matched the ID number that was next to the dagger with a name from the shop's client list.

"Quincy, take a look at this."

As Quincy approached her and looked at the name in the book, he quickly turned back to Zibik.

"You wanna take a guess whose name is registered as the owner of the dagger that killed Carmen Morales?" Quincy asked.

"The dagger was registered to me, but it's not what you think," Zibik said defensively.

"Oh really, because from where we're standing, the most logical assumption is that someone from your camp used your weapon on our murder victim," Quincy said.

"And the convenience of it all doesn't bother you?" Zibik asked.

"If you're so concerned about what bothers us, then why don't you quit with the games and lies. You or somebody in your organization knows way more than you're admitting. Who are you protecting?" Maclin added.

"I'm not protecting anyone. I know you don't believe me, but I can prove it to you," Zibik said.

"And how do you propose doing that?" Quincy asked.

Zibik responded, "The only way that you can understand, by showing you."

The storage facility looked like the Devil's lair. It was a twenty by twenty-foot space filled wall to wall with books, artifacts, and all sorts of objects related to the occult. The walls were adorned with poster-sized images of decapitations, lynchings, autopsies, barbarism, cannibalism, and blood rituals from various cultures. Witchcraft, vampirism, and, of course, devil worship were all depicted and represented in some form or another. Unlike most public storage facilities, this particular space was set up as though it were a cozy den in someone's home. The few pieces of furniture were tasteful and neatly arranged for the occupant to comfortably appreciate the morbid spectacle. Zibik sat cuffed in an easy chair as Quincy, Phee, and Maclin walked around the makeshift museum. The trio had each seen their fair share of strange and even disturbing things over the course of their careers, but none of them had ever felt such a close proximity to what was best described as pure evil. This was as close to truly seeing into Zibik's twisted soul as they would ever get. Although they each wore latex gloves, the three of them rarely actually touched anything. Their avoidance was more out of repulsion than procedure. Zibik enjoyed watching how uncomfortable they were surrounded by the objects that meant the most to her.

"I hope that you all can appreciate the fact that you're the only guests I've ever allowed in here," Zibik said.

"I guess we should feel honored," Phee said sarcastically.

"Slightly illuminated would suffice," Zibik shot back.

"You actually believe in all of this stuff?" Quincy asked.

"Not at all. I'm just fascinated by the depths of depravity that man is capable of achieving when he sets his mind to it. You wanna talk about scary, you'll find a Bible, Quran, and Torah around here some place. Unlike most people, I choose not to limit my thirst for knowledge to only the things I already believe in," Zibik said smiling.

"No matter what you try and tell yourself, Dr. Zibik, like everything in this room, you're just another freak in a freak show."

"You shouldn't insult me, Agent Maclin. I might take it personally."

"You can take it any way you want to," Maclin responded as she turned and walked away.

As Maclin circled the room, Zibik watched her every move intensely.

"Alright, so we came. Besides your little twisted souvenirs, what exactly are we supposed to be seeing?" Quincy asked.

"Agent Maclin, would you be so kind and draw back the curtain on the wall next to you?" Zibik said.

As Maclin pulled the curtain back, they all saw an impressive collection of antique guns, knives, daggers, and swords neatly hanging in a glass display on a wall rack. In the center of the blade collection was a familiar-looking crescent dagger, identical to the one used to kill Carmen Morales.

"Check his books, and you'll see that this dagger is the only one registered to me. The one used to kill the Morales woman was a replica. Someone is going through a lot of trouble to make it appear that I'm somehow connected to all of this," Zibik said.

"Or you're going through even more trouble to make it appear that you're not," Maclin retorted as she reached for the handle to open the display case. Phee kept his eyes on Zibik. He didn't like the way she was staring at Maclin. In addition to her usual smugness, he detected a sense of her anticipation. There was a subtle glint in her eye that unnerved him. He quickly looked back at Maclin, just as she was opening the door to the case. As his instincts kicked in, he dove toward Maclin and knocked her out of the way of the pendulum blade that suddenly swung from the ceiling in her direction. Phee tackled her and knocked her to the ground, just as the blade grazed the side of her neck and drew blood. In the commotion, Quincy immediately pulled his weapon and drew down on Zibik as he yelled in the direction of his fallen colleagues.

"Talk to me Phee!"

As Phee and Maclin disentangled themselves from the body pile they made on the floor, Phee stood first. "I'm good." He extended his hand and helped Maclin to her feet. "You okay?"

Phee bent back down and picked up something off the floor that his foot had brushed up against.

Maclin stood and wiped the blood from a superficial cut where the swinging blade just missed doing major damage. Although the cut didn't amount to much more than a heavy scratch, the sight of her own blood had her lunging at Zibik before being restrained by Quincy and Phee.

"You sick fuck," Maclin spit out at Zibik, who remained calmly seated, seemingly pleased with herself.

"You'll have to forgive me, Agent Maclin; it's been a while since I've been in here. You can't expect me to remember every detail. I hope you don't take it personally."

Maclin made another push toward Zibik and managed to land a blow, splitting the doctor's lower lip.

"Agent Maclin!" Quincy's voice finally slowed her as Phee positioned himself in between the two women. Quincy holstered his weapon, and Phee grabbed Maclin forcibly by the shoulders, steering her toward the exit.

"Let me take her out to get some air. You keep an eye on Zibik," Phee said as he opened the door and led Maclin out.

Phee leaned up against a red brick wall just outside of the storage facility, while Maclin paced back and forth. Even though her anger had subsided, she strategically kept moving to avert Phee's stare. She pretended to still be angry with Zibik, because it was the perfect diversion to hide her real issues. Maclin kept moving in the hopes that Phee wouldn't see her weakness and malaise. She had been successful in hiding her budding addiction from everyone else, but Phee and Quincy were much more perceptive than most. She didn't look at Phee, because now that he had reason to scrutinize her, she was afraid that he would see how far off her normal game she actually was. The more she tried to deflect his unwanted attention, the more anxious and insecure she became. The truth was Maclin was on edge and needed realignment. Already compromised, her body and mind were craving the temporary equilibrium that the drugs offered. If Phee hadn't been watching her so closely, she could manage her condition with the tiny pills in her pocket.

"You know the profile on Zibik. We gotta stay on our toes at all times with her," Phee said.

"Yeah, I know," Maclin mumbled back apologetically.

"You okay?"

"Yeah, I'll be more careful next time."

"I'm not just talking about Zibik. I mean are you okay otherwise?"

"Look, I dropped my guard for half a second. It won't happen again. Why don't we just leave it there?"

"I was only…"

Maclin was relieved when Phee was interrupted by his phone. He looked at the caller ID and answered it. The conversation was short and one-sided, in which he did all of the listening. After thirty seconds, he hung up.

"Alvarez found something on one of the security cameras."

As Maclin moved toward the door of the facility, Phee reached out and slowed her walk.

"You dropped this inside," he said as he opened his hand, revealing the small plastic bottle of Zoloft. Maclin refused to make eye contact. She took the bottle and walked back into the building.

As they looked at the video playback, they didn't have the clearest angle but were able to pick up a light-colored SUV speeding away fifteen minutes before they arrived at the knife maker's shop. The best that they could do on the plates was to get a partial read. They were able to make out the first letter to be a "Z" followed by the number 7. Alvarez compiled a list of sixty or so light-colored, late-model SUVs with the same prefixes on New York plates. If the vehicle wasn't stolen, it could prove to be their biggest break yet in the case.

28

Kravitz was having a hell of a bad day. Overslept, underate, aching bunion, nagging wife, and now a visitor from his past that he had prayed to God he would never see again. He was performing the autopsy on Carmen Morales when he got the call. There were voices and faces that some men never forgot. The voice was sonorous and confident. Even when it asked questions, it did so already knowing the response it wanted and expected to receive. Even before the voice on the other end of the phone announced his name, Kravitz knew who he was. Nearly forty years ago, the same voice had terrorized Kravitz and threatened to kill him. There were people in the world from one's childhood, mainly bullies and scary aunts, that always managed to reduce even the most confident of adults into the scared, impotent children they used to be. This was the one voice in the world that had that effect on Kravitz.

"I'll be there at two. Would it be possible for you to be the only one there?" was the last thing the voice said before the phone went dead.

The question wasn't a question but rather an understated command. Kravitz had his assistants work until 1:45 and then sent them out for a long lunch. He found himself straightening things up, as though that alone would make the morgue a more inviting place for his expected visitor. Kravitz was prone to flatulence when he was nervous. The big man waited in the hall and found himself fanning the air a few times at the SBDs that slipped through his control. At exactly 2:10 the elevator door opened. Kravitz turned to greet Clay Freeman.

"I'd like to keep my visit just between the two of us. I promised Phee that I wouldn't come here," Clay said.

Kravitz was uncertain whether or not he was being spoken to or simply spoken at. He chose to assume the latter and remained silent.

"Where is he?" Clay asked.

In preparation for Clay's arrival, Kravitz had removed AJ's body from storage and placed it back in the primary autopsy room. Kravitz didn't know how much Phee had told his father about the details of AJ's murder. He had no way to gauge Clay's level of preparation for what he was about to see. Kravitz' stomach bubbled and churned as he walked rigidly in front of Clay, desperately hoping to control the horrible case of gas he felt worsening.

"Do you have any kids, Dr. Kravitz?" Clay asked as they walked back to see AJ.

"Yes, a daughter," Kravitz nervously responded.

"What does she do?"

"She's a doctor."

"Of course she is. Whether they know it or not, all they really want to do is please us."

Kravitz was ultimately too scared to tell Clay what he hoped he already knew. Even though he had placed a sheet over AJ's torso, Clay immediately reacted in horror at the sight of his son's eyes and his missing eyelids. As he noticed that the sheet was precariously sunken in the abdomen region, he pulled it off to discover his son's hollowed torso. Clay had seen and done so many terrible things in his life that very few things penetrated the tough exterior he'd developed over the years. He had been many things to many people—ruthless, cunning, generous, and kind—but weakness had never been a viable option for him. The sight of his dead son momentarily debilitated him. The world slowed down, and everything became thick and exaggerated. All movement on his part was involuntary, especially the twitching of his hands and excessive blinking. Clay's mouth dried, and his eyes watered. His breathing was inconsistent, starting and stopping at will. When he did manage to breathe properly, the air around him smelled sour and flatulent. Clay was the most dangerous man Kravitz had ever met. In fact, the two times that proved to be without a doubt the most frightening moments in his life both happened in Clay's presence. The first, of course, was when Clay kidnapped and threatened to kill him, and now the second was as Clay stood crying over his murdered son.

"What the hell have you done to my boy?" Clay demanded.

"I, uh…nothing."

"You call this nothing? Look at his eyes. Look at how you butchered him," Clay said as he grabbed Kravitz and pulled him closer to AJ

"Please don't… I didn't do this. This is how he was murdered."

"What are you talking about?"

"I'm trying to tell you that he came in here like this," Kravitz spurted out.

"Phee said… Phee said it was a blow to the back of the head. That he never even saw it coming."

"I'm sorry, Mr. Freeman. He must have been just trying to save you the pain of seeing this for yourself."

Clay stood there, processing the butchering of one son and the betrayal of the other. He forced himself to take in every detail of AJ's corpse. The truth was unyielding and painful, but he needed to see firsthand the specifics of his son's mutilation. The first time Clay ever held AJ in his arms, there was no doubt that his son was the most amazing thing that life had ever offered him. And now he had been prematurely taken back in the most barbaric of ways. Clay's anger hadn't subsided but, more or less, just redirected itself. He swore to Dolicia and God that his life of crime and violence ended when AJ came into the world. Now that his son had been killed in such a way, he swore to whatever greater power was listening that he wouldn't rest until whoever had done this died of no less a painful death.

As Clay was heading out, he caught a glimpse of the name

Carmen Regina Morales written on a dry-erase board next to a covered corpse. He approached the body and removed the sheet, fully exposing her. He recognized her instantly. He had managed to keep her a secret from his family, but for a large part of her life, he had played the role of an unofficial godfather to her. When she was a kid, he made sure people from the neighborhood looked out for her and her younger brother. Clay paid for her to attend nursing school and periodically sent her money to help her get by. He paid for, and attended the funeral of, her son after he drowned in Far Rockaway. He helped her partly out of empathy for the overwhelming challenges life had thrown her way, but mainly he helped her out because of a convoluted sense of obligation. Although he wasn't directly responsible for what happened to her father, he still felt a sense of loyalty to the man who helped him exact his revenge against his mentor's murderers. Carmen was the oldest child of Blue Morales. Clay knew immediately that it wasn't a coincidence that his and Blue's firstborn had both been murdered in the same sadistic manner. He also knew that whoever was responsible for the killings would soon be coming for him and Blue.

29

The minute Clay left the morgue, he called his fixer. There were many questions that needed answers and work that needed to be done. If Clay was going to get to the bottom of things, he needed the services of Soloman Nangobi, AKA The African.

After getting the call from Clay, The African immediately headed up to Spanish Harlem in search of Blue Morales. It took him a few hours, and three different boroughs, but he was finally able to track down a cousin of Blue's who ran a strip club up in the Bronx. It was a neighborhood spot called Temptations, known for their variety of imported beers and local girls, who were all homegrown and sans silicone.

The African ordered a three-finger scotch and then made his way to the back office to speak with Blue's cousin, Chuchi Torres. A large bouncer stood in a nearby corner, keeping a close eye on the two men as they talked. The African sat in his chair with such authority that it was difficult to tell who was the guest and who was the host.

The African heard how Chuchi Torres used to be feared. Back in the day he was a fringe player with exaggerated ties to the mob. These days, he was content running the club and chasing young ass that was naïve enough to think that he was actually still relevant.

"What are you lookin' for my cousin for?" Chuchi asked.

The African still spoke with the singsong cadence of his native dialect, despite the fact that he had lived over thirty years in the states. He was also in the habit of replacing the letter "T" in the beginning of certain words with the letter "D."

"De person dat I work for needs to talk to him."

"What about?"

"Dat's between the two of dem," The African responded.

"Who do you work for?"

"Dat's between me and my boss."

Chuchi never did care for Africans. He found the majority of them to be too entitled for his taste. The shiny black man that sat across from him and acted like he owned the place didn't do much to change Chuchi's perception.

"De only thing you really need to know is dat dis has nothing to do with any type of ill will or violent intentions toward your cousin. My boss just needs to talk with him. You call anybody you know out in Brooklyn, I'm in Red Hook. Everyone knows me, and knows dat my word is bond." The African added.

"Yeah well, even if I did know where Blue was, I still wouldn't tell you."

"First of all, it's not a question of 'if' you know, because we both know you do. Second, I came in here with nothing but respect. Where it goes from here is entirely up to you."

The large bouncer tensed as The African slowly reached in his pocket and pulled out his wallet. He removed a single dollar bill and placed it on Chuchi's desk. Chuchi looked to the bouncer and then back at The African confused.

"What the fuck is this? You think I'm gonna tell you where my cousin is for a dollar?"

"Dat's not for you, brotha'; it is for me. It is just a little peace of mind and reminder for me dat I at least attempted to handle dis situation diplomatically, before I resorted to de unpleasant things dat I do best."

The African never really cared for Puerto Ricans. He thought they acted like life owed them something. When he left with Blue Morales' address, he was a bit disappointed that Chuchi ended up complying so easily. There were times that he actually enjoyed hurting people. Had Chuchi continued resisting, this would have certainly been one of those times.

30

The years hadn't been kind to Blue. Since the fateful night at Varelli's, he'd lost an eye and was severely disfigured. The two skin grafts that he tried were only minimally successful and still left him with a face that scared children and made adults pretend not to stare. Even some of the people who he once considered friends called him "Two-Face" behind his back. His woman left him and had long since died. He was estranged from his children, and at fifty-seven he had amounted to nothing more than an addict and petty street hustler, barely rubbing two nickels together. Six months out of prison, the best he could do was a cramped efficiency up in Inwood, which was the northernmost neighborhood on the tip of Manhattan. The small room came complete with a Murphy bed, roaches, and part-time hot water.

Jelly sat in an SUV across the street from Blue's apartment

complex. He watched The African and Blue exit the building, get in a late-model Escalade, and head downtown. Jelly followed them to the Waldorf Astoria Hotel. He exited his vehicle and followed the two men in. While Blue waited in the lobby, The African crossed to the bar, and in a few minutes returned, trailing Clay. As Clay and Blue shook hands, they were both uncomfortably aware of the polarity that existed between their stations in life. The hotel staff and passing guests looked on uncomfortably at the odd pairing of Clay in his four thousand dollar suit and his shabby-looking guest with the melted face. The two old acquaintances headed toward the elevator and up to Clay's suite as The African went back outside to move the car.

It took Jelly years to find them. All he had to go on was the fact that they were both black and one of them had been badly burned. There was nothing particularly distinguishing about the other man. All Jelly remembered was an image of the man's face that he was incapable of articulating to anyone else. Even when he started feeling that he was making even a hint of progress, he was in one way or another derailed. He lost valuable time due to his many stints in prison. There were many times that he thought they were dead or had simply vanished. Most of the private eyes he hired did nothing but take what little money he had and produce very little in the way of progress. But the last one managed to track down a couple of old-timers who were well versed on the Harlem underworld of the '70s. One name emerged that was rumored to have tangled with Antonio Varelli and one of his associates named Calvin "Honey Boy" Jones. The minute Jelly was shown a current and past photo of Clay, he knew immediately that he was one of the men he was searching for. Finding Blue Morales was considerably easier, once he had the name. His perseverance was finally paying off. Although he had fantasized about this moment for years, he was appreciative of the timing. Jelly could never kill them enough, so he started by making them suffer. He warmed up on their eldest children. Just as they had done to his brother, Jelly took the lives of their firstborn. Soon, very soon, he would take his full revenge in ways that they could never fathom. The only thing better than knowing that he would be killing them soon was the knowledge that he had learned how to take their souls and punish them for an eternity.

Jelly did his best to blend in with the holiday crowd as he slipped past security, followed the two men to the elevator, and got in behind them. A family of four from the Midwest was already in the elevator, mapping out dinner plans for the evening.

"We should probably do the steakhouse that the concierge recommended on 57th Street, BLT," the father of the clan suggested. Clay and Blue stood stoically by as the two annoying children felt compelled to give a blow-by-blow of their first visit to the Big Apple.

Jelly stood in an opposite corner, trying his hardest not to be too obvious with the glances that he stole of the two men. After all the years of searching and dreaming of finding them, they were now both at arm's length. He was close enough to smell the sweet scent of Cognac that came from Clay's direction. Once or twice Jelly's hand caressed the gun that was stuffed in his waistband. He knew he could kill them both right now and be done with it. He saw their deaths vividly in his mind. He could empty his clip into the two of them. All head shots. Blood and brain matter everywhere, a smoking gun, and terrified tourists hovering in the corner in a state of shock. Jelly wanted to do them right then and there, but he refrained because he knew that what he had in store for them would be ten times more gratifying.

Success had undoubtedly refined Clay's edge but in no way diminished it. He could easily spot a con three miles away. Even before he got into the elevator, he peeped Jelly in the lobby of the hotel. More than likely, it was just a coincidence that the large man was now in the elevator with him, but because of all that had recently happened, Clay was much more alert. As a precaution, Clay's hand rested comfortably on the handle of the 9 mm he'd surreptitiously removed from the small of his back and discreetly held under the overcoat that was draped across his arms. The elevator ride took longer than necessary because the children pressed buttons to floors that none of them were going to. Clay's focus was directed at the con in the corner, effectively shutting out everything else, even the acoustical assault of the bickering children. If anything went down, he was poised and ready. As the family reached their floor and disembarked, Clay kept a peripheral account of every move the silent man made. When they exited on the next floor, Clay was very aware of the fact that Jelly also got off but walked in the opposite direction.

As the two men looked over their shoulders at each other, Clay was staring so hard that he nearly collided into the evening maid making her rounds of turndown service. Even as Jelly rounded the corner and disappeared, Clay firmly gripped his gun until he and Blue were safely behind the locked doors of his suite.

Clay kept a suite at the Waldorf for the times that he didn't feel like going back to Greenwich. He paid over seventy grand a month for the room, even though he rarely used it. It was worth every penny to a man like Clay, to know he always had options. He chose the Waldorf over ten years ago as his home away from home, not just because of its prestigious name but more so because the hotel was very much like him. It had been renovated and upgraded, but at its heart, it was still decidedly old-school.

The suite was what one would expect it to be, its elegance and functionality befitting a man of Clay's stature.

He poured himself a scotch and handed Blue a bottle of cold beer. "So after all of these years, why all of a sudden is it so important for you to see me?" Blue asked.

"When was the last time you saw your daughter?" Clay responded as he offered Blue his beer.

"That's none of your business."

"You're no longer young and dumb, Blue, so you can't hide behind that excuse. Stop being an asshole, and answer my question."

Blue rose from his chair angry and confrontational. Clay was cool, a panther unfazed by the threat of a gazelle. He spoke with the patience of a parent clarifying things for a special needs child.

"Sit down, Blue, before you let your mouth write a check that your ass can't cash. I'm asking you nicely, so that neither one of us has to regret what comes next," Clay said as he held Blue in a hard stare. To save face, Blue walked over to the bar and grabbed another bottle of beer, then returned to his seat and sat down.

"Carmen's dead, Blue. I saw her this afternoon. She was in the morgue next to my oldest boy," Clay told him.

"What the hell are you talking about?" Blue demanded.

"Just what I said… And before you ask me, yeah, I'm positive it was her, just as sure as I am that it was my son."

"What…happened?" Blue mumbled.

"They were both murdered. Someone cut them up pretty badly."

"I don't… I don't believe you, man," Blue said desperately.

"What, you think I'd make this shit up? I saw my son, and I saw your daughter, and trust me, somebody killed them. Who did you talk to about the day we killed Honey Boy and Varelli?"

"Honey Boy and Varelli, what are you talking about?"

"That's the only thing you and I have in common that would make somebody want to come after me and my family. Who did you talk to?"

"Nobody, man," Blue said dismissively.

Without warning, Clay sprung forward, broke the beer bottle, and held the jagged edge under Blue's one good eye.

"Don't fuck with me. Who have you been talking to?" Clay demanded.

"I swear on my son's life and my daughter's soul, I never talked to nobody about that shit," Blue said sincerely.

Clay stared at him for several beats, then finally released Blue and lowered the broken bottle.

"I don't know what the hell is going on, but somehow it's connected to that day," Clay told him.

"That was a long time ago, if anybody was gonna come after us, they would'a done it by now," Blue said.

"Well it damn sure isn't just some kind of coincidence. It's got something to do with that day."

"Did Carmen know your son? Maybe this was about them and not us."

"Anything is possible, but my gut still says it's about that night. I want to be clear here: if I find out that you ran your mouth and it cost me my son, I'll kill you, Blue. So help me God, I'll kill you six ways to Sunday," Clay said as he crossed to the door and opened it for Blue to leave. Blue rose and crossed to him. As he got in the hallway, he turned to face Clay.

Blue was broken by the news of his daughter's death. By the time he walked out of the room, he was listless and looked even more pathetic than when he entered. Right or wrong, he took the news as yet another addition to the already lengthy list of accumulated blows and failures in his life. His eyes were dull and his voice was flat when he addressed Clay. There was no emotion, a man left with nothing to lose or fear. He walked into the room a hard-looking fifty-seven and walked out looking older and even more pitiful. "You ain't the only one that lost somebody here. You don't scare me no more, Clay. There ain't nothin' you can do to me that even matters anymore. All these years, you always thought you were better than all of us and bigger than the game. But you ain't. Even now, with your fancy clothes, errand boys, and penthouse rooms, you still like the rest of us, just another scared brotha' lookin' over his shoulder, waiting for your bullshit to catch up with you."

31

By the time Blue emerged from the hotel lobby, Jelly was already in his car watching him from across the street. Jelly watched him exit the hotel and decline a ride from The African. After The African slipped him some cash, Blue jumped in a taxi and headed south. Jelly cut a U-turn and followed.

Blue Morales paid twenty of the fifty bucks he got from The African to a night attendant at the morgue to let him see his daughter, even though it was after viewing hours. He started crying as soon as the sheet was lifted. He hadn't been much of a father to either of his children, but in his mind that didn't mean that he loved them any less. There were times when the mere thought of his daughter and son had lifted him from the lowest points in his life. Although his personal demons had severely defeated him, he often fantasized about being a better man for their sake, only to realize now that it was tragically too late. People often said that the hardest thing in the world was for a parent to bury a child. In Blue's mind they were only half- right, because he knew now that burying a murdered child was by far the most painful and difficult thing imaginable. In plain sight of the attendant, Blue cursed God. The already precarious bond between them was now severely broken. In general he believed in God only on occasion. In times of crisis, he looked heavenward and tossed up the habitual prayer. Even though he often thought of God as being cruel and dismissive, he humbled himself when the need arose. As he cried over the body of his slain daughter, there was no longer any need for desperate prayers that went unanswered, and certainly no need for a God that was neglectful even of the innocent.

When she was born, Carmen almost saved Blue. Her birth kept him at home and motivated him to want to go legit. For a while he did the nine to five thing, working as a dishwasher in a Chinese restaurant on the Upper West Side. The owners paid him shit and treated him even worse. For the first year of fatherhood, he struggled but did what he had to do to be the provider and the type of father he'd never had. The streets started calling him shortly after Carmen turned one. He started running errands for Slopes a couple of times a week after work. Soon, he was making more money from two or three runs than he made the entire month at the restaurant. He quit his job one night when he could no longer take his bosses' constant berating and humiliating treatment. A month after working for Slopes full-time Blue returned to the restaurant after hours. A Molotov cocktail officially ended one chapter of his life and cemented the beginning of another.

His lack of education left most people like his boss at the restaurant, summarily dismissing him as just another dumb-ass street kid from the Bronx. Slopes was one of the few that saw that there was much more to him. What he lacked in book smarts, he made up for with his street savvy and his master's degree from the school of hard knocks. His mother was a two-dollar whore, so Blue grew up in the life, front and center. From the time he was a kid, he dreamed about being a "hustla." Every hero he ever had was a gangster. Bumpy Johnson, Frank Lucas, Nicky Barnes, even Madam St. Clair, a.k.a. The Queen and her gang, The Forty Thieves. They all fascinated Blue and gave him hope that someone like him, with no education and limited means, still had a fighting chance at his piece of the American dream.

Blue was the perfect street soldier, because life had beaten into him just the right amount of brutality and ruthlessness. He made his first kill at seventeen. By the time he was twenty-one, he had close to a dozen dead bodies under his belt. He never lost sleep or knew remorse, because if he were going to make a name for himself like his idols, there was no room for weakness. Blue never let one life he took cost him anything. He clearly had no way of expecting that a murder he committed forty years ago would come back to cost him everything.

Blue left the morgue at just past midnight. He couldn't get the image of his daughter out of his head. Even though they hadn't spoken in over twelve years, Blue still held on to a sliver of hope of one day reinstating himself back into her life. Someone had viciously robbed him of that possibility, much like all the dreams and "might have beens" Blue had stolen from others during his reign of crime. He was so preoccupied with his grief that he was almost hit by a cab as he carelessly stepped off the curb. Blue was busted up inside and definitely needed something to help take him to a much less painful state. He knew one or two spots near Chinatown where he could score some oxy, meth, or crack. He just needed something to take him away. As he turned down an unoccupied one-way street, he never saw the SUV with its headlights turned off, until the vehicle struck him and knocked him to the ground. His knee hyperextended and made a horrible popping sound. He felt the bone in his shin break the minute he was hit. Lying on his back, he looked up and saw a stranger standing over him.

"Call an ambulance." Blue writhed in pain.

He wondered why the man didn't move or show the slightest hint of concern or urgency. Without warning, the stranger grabbed him roughly by the collar and punched him in the face. Blue went into a defensive fetal position as the man continued pummeling him. Blow after blow, he begged the stranger to stop but to no avail. The last thing Blue saw before everything went black was the undeniable hatred in the silent man's eyes.

Jelly looked down on Blue's crumpled body. He loved the look on Blue's disfigured face as he lay in the street before him like a wounded dog. He was almost too easy to capture. He was frail and unhealthy and looked ruined, even before Jelly ran him down. Jelly snatched Blue up off the ground and threw him in the back seat of the vehicle, as though he were a bag of dirt. He tied his hands, gagged him, and blindfolded him before getting behind the wheel and driving away. Jelly drove his prisoner out to Long Island, to the abandoned house where Blue and Clay had murdered his family. The place had been sold over half a dozen times since the murders but never lived in for long. The families that occupied it all spoke of a tangible uneasiness throughout the home. Neighborhood children designated it as a haunted house and avoided it and its occupants at all costs. It sat empty for several years in foreclosure. Jelly would on occasion drive out to the house and sleep on the same kitchen floor where his mother and brother died.

Jelly threw Blue in the basement and watched him stir, disori-ented. After chaining him to a post, Jelly stepped back and looked at him curiously, as though Blue was a captured prized animal.

"I don't know what you want, but I ain't got nothin'," Blue slurred.

Jelly watched him mouth his pleas and crossed to him and repeatedly kicked him until Blue was too weak to offer resistance. Jelly then picked up an iron bar, two inches in diameter, and began beating Blue as he cried and pleaded. Releasing his rage on Blue felt much too good. If he wasn't careful, he knew he could end up killing him prematurely. The punishment that he doled out would have to be limited to his momentary pleasure, and not his ultimate goal. Jelly stopped himself, and just stared at the heap on the floor.

The torture of Blue lifted Jelly higher than he could ever remember feeling. He was now halfway to bringing his lifelong dream to fruition. Knowing how close he was, tonight he hoped that he would sleep soundly, no longer haunted by his usual nightmares. In his dreams, Jelly could hear. Over and over again, he heard the anguished cries of his mother and brother. Deep in his heart, he was certain that the deaths of Blue and Clay would quiet the unrelenting horrors of his dreams.

32

P hee, Quincy, and Maclin took half of the names from Alvarez
and decided to each investigate ten of them before calling it a
night. They separately took a borough and knocked on doors to
interview potential owners of the SUV. The three of them called
each other when they all came up empty-handed and decided to
investigate the rest of the list first thing in the morning. As Phee
headed back to the precinct, he convinced Quincy and Maclin
to knock off for the night and get some rest. When he walked
through the front door of the station and made his way toward the
stairs, he overheard a fracas in the lobby. Phee stopped and turned
toward the commotion when he heard a somewhat familiar voice
exclaim loudly, "This is bullshit!"

As Phee walked closer, he saw four cross-dressers arguing
with the desk sergeant. The obvious leader of the motley bunch

was Epiphany Chevalier. As the argument escalated, and a couple of uniforms started approaching, he intervened as diplomatically as possible.

"What's going on, Mike?"

"I'm just trying to explain to these uh, 'ladies' here that information regarding an ongoing investigation cannot be shared with nonfamily members."

It wasn't lost on Phee, or for that matter Epiphany and her crew, the condescending tone and derogatory emphasis the officer placed on the word "ladies." His contempt was obvious, and he in no way hid the fact that he held them in such low regard. To accentuate his disdain, the desk sergeant looked down at his newspaper, impolitely dismissing the quartet. The next time he spoke, he didn't bother to look up.

"I'm sure there's a costume ball somewhere tonight in the city; why don't you all just skip along and let us do our job."

"If you knew how to do your job we wouldn't be here," Epiphany shot back.

"It's always the ones that don't know what they're talking about that have the most to say," the cop sniped.

"Exactly, those are the ones they usually stick in a monkey suit and put on a desk and give them some false sense of authority. It's also been my experience that it's always the ones with the littlest dicks that are the biggest pricks."

The streets of New York were littered with the wounded egos of fools who had dared match wits and insults with a razor-tongued cross-dresser. The desk sergeant turned red with anger and embarrassment as his colleagues snickered at him. Phee jumped in, grabbed Epiphany by the arm, and led her away before she ended up spending the night in jail on a bogus charge.

"What are you doing, Epiphany?" Phee snapped at her as they stood out of range of all the others.

"Trying to get to the bottom of who killed AJ, which is way more than what you all seem to be doing."

"You coming down here and taking shots at cops isn't going to help anybody, especially not you. I'm doing everything I can to find out who killed AJ; you gotta trust me on that."

"And I'm just supposed to believe that?"

"You believe what you need to believe, but I'm not gonna stop until I find who killed AJ."

"Well then, you're a lot different from the rest of these assholes who don't give two fucks."

"No I'm not, but that doesn't matter. What does matter is that finding AJ's killer is my job. I'm good at it, and I have every intention of continuing to do it."

Epiphany stared hard at Phee, trying to decipher whether or not he was sincere. The harder she looked, the more she was able to see, despite his efforts to hide it, a level of empathy that all the other cops lacked. She wasn't sure if she imagined it, or if it was just misplaced hope, but there was determination in Phee's voice when he spoke AJ's name. Epiphany softened a bit and dropped some of her defenses.

"It's a damn shame that we're surrounded by all these cops and you're the only one that's willing to at least give us that much."

She shook her head incredulously and smirked as she looked back toward the desk sergeant and other cops. "Fuckin' hypocrites, all of 'em."

Epiphany turned back toward Phee and let out a short laugh. "You wanna hear something funny?"

"What's that?" Phee indulged her.

"You're not gonna believe this, but from the time I was a kid, all I wanted to do was be a cop; even made it through a month at the academy."

"What happened?" Phee asked awkwardly.

"Life, shit, a dose of reality, you name it. Sometimes what you wanna be doesn't leave a whole lot of room for who you wanna be. I wasn't as lucky as you, Detective Freeman. God doesn't give us all the same choices." For the most part, Phee agreed with what Epiphany said. As he continued looking at her, he began to think more of their similarities than their differences, even if only from a philosophical point of view. It was a start.

"Do you have any siblings?" Epiphany asked, completely catching Phee off guard.

Phee's first thought was Quincy, his second was of his baby sister who died of SIDS when he was six years old. Further down the list, he thought of AJ

"No, I don't," Phee answered.

"If you did, then you'd know how I felt. AJ was deeper than blood to me. So for both her and my sake, Detective Freeman, I hope you are as good at your job as you say. It's okay for us to just be real. I know freaks like us will never be a priority to people like you, but believe it or not we love and hurt just like you do, Dah-lin. We just do it with more style."

As Epiphany smiled at her own joke, Phee saw the effort it took for her to not break down. For a split second, he saw the pain that had been temporarily hidden beneath the flamboyance. After a beat, Epiphany got herself together, confidently strolled back to her group, and left the building like a rock star with an entourage.

33

After Epiphany left, Phee went directly to lockup to go over the remaining thirty names from the earlier list with Zibik. Dr. Zibik was in her cell doing a late-night workout when Phee approached. As he watched her doing perfect military push-ups, he confirmed what he already suspected, which was that she was much stronger than she looked. Although her head was down and she couldn't see him, Phee knew that she sensed his presence and was showing off.

"I need you to take a look at something," Phee said as he extended the list through the bars and held it in midair.

Zibik stopped her workout, stood, and crossed to him. Her hair was down and there was a thin sheen of sweat on her face and neck. Phee thought it was the most serene she'd looked since he first met her. Had he not known the things he knew about her, he could have easily mistaken her for something other than the cunning psychopath that she was.

Zibik sported a tank top and was braless. As she crossed to Phee and stood two feet in front of him, he couldn't help noticing her breasts straining against the thin, damp cotton material. A bead of sweat descended her neck and disappeared in the dark parting of her cleavage. Zibik dabbed at the perspiration on her face and neck with the palm of her hand and then wiped it on her pant leg. Her nipples stood erect from a combination of exertion and the presence of a single-male audience. Although it was quick, Zibik caught Phee's furtive perusal of her body. Like most women, she appreciated being appreciated. Phee squared up to her and stood with his weight evenly distributed. Even after being surprised by the athletic curves of her body, he was careful not to linger, because he knew Zibik was an opportunist who would exploit whatever weakness she could.

"You'll have to forgive me, Detective Freeman; I hope my scent doesn't offend you."

"I've smelled worse," Phee said.

Zibik smiled at Phee and in a not so subtle way looked at him from head to toe.

"Take a look at the file," Phee commanded.

"And for a minute there, I thought you were here to enjoy the pleasure of my company."

Zibik glanced at the list that he held in front of her but made no effort to take it. "I already looked at this and told you I didn't recognize those names."

"Look again," Phee commanded.

"No, because you already know that I won't recognize them just as I know that's not the real reason you're here. This relationship won't work if you don't trust me, Detective Freeman," Zibik said flatly.

It took Phee a moment, but he finally asked Zibik what was really on his mind. "Why were the two victims killed in the same manner but left behind differently?" Phee asked.

Zibik stared at Phee for a few moments before responding. Although Phee did his best to hide his vulnerability about the subject, Zibik saw through him. "If it's any consolation, your brother's body was dumped because evidently the soul catcher wasn't successful the first time out."

"Successful? He killed him, didn't he?" Phee attempted to respond as emotionally neutral as he could.

"Anyone can kill. He was after something much less obtainable."

"It's all a big joke to you, isn't it?"

"Not at all. I take the subject of souls very seriously. Do you? Out of curiosity, what do you believe in, Detective, God, Santa, Bigfoot, what?"

Phee never took his eyes from hers. "I believe that no matter what name you put on it, if it only serves you and your needs, then it's not worth worshipping."

"I think that kind of truth is the only thing that is worth worshipping."

"Truth?"

"Absolutely. The truth is human nature is self-serving. Why

do you think the concept of God was created in the first place—
for the simple purpose of regulating that nature. Give the power
and glory to Him, and then pray and beg for him to give a small
portion back. Why not just cut out the middleman?"

Phee was very careful not to patronize her in any way.

"So if man is God, then what's the ultimate goal?" he asked.

"Just that, simply being the God that you were born to be."

"To what end?"

"Perpetual omnipotence."

"The funny thing is that you say you don't believe in God,
but your entire existence is built around trying to emulate the very
thing you try to discredit. Here's a flash for you, Dr. Zibik—all
of your self-worship, and self-delusion, you're still nothing but
human. You eat, shit, bleed, and die like the rest of us. If you really
think that man pretending to be God is the 'answer,' then you, and
all of your gullible followers, have been obviously asking the wrong
questions."

"Have we? Our questions lead to spiritual elevation; yours
just to more empty questions." She paused and looked at Phee
curiously. "If you haven't already, I'm sure you'll get around to it."

"Get around to what?"

"Asking yourself if your God was so real, then where was he
when your brother needed him most?"

Phee's anticipation of the question minimized its impact.
He resisted the urge to smirk at the minor victory. "I'm actually
surprised and disappointed that you wouldn't come up with
something more original and less predictable."

"That's the whole point. The logic of God's existence is so ludicrous and far-fetched that not much else is needed. For the record, I'm sure my disappointment in you has more of a credible foundation than yours."

"How's that?" Phee bit.

"You're an intelligent, African American man. Do you really buy into the notion of there being some larger than life white man, along with his stringy-haired, blue-eyed son, sitting on a cloud impartially supplying the needs of every living being on this planet? Because who better than your people to know how badly that load of crap has worked out."

Phee burst into laughter. "I'm sorry, it's hard to take anything you say seriously when you claim to be a God, but you're locked up in here like every other self-deluded crook that thought they were smarter than they actually are."

"I'm freer than you'll ever be. The day you realize that you'll beg someone like me to teach you how to be a God."

"No, thank you. I'm cool with the one I got."

"Blissful ignorance shouldn't be mistaken for happiness."

"No more than blind arrogance should be mistaken for enlightenment," he quickly retorted.

Phee knew immediately that he had successfully hit a nerve by the shift in her body and the sudden edge in her voice.

"You're not qualified to speak of enlightenment, because despite your misperception, you're the real prisoner, not me. When you learn the true freedom of embracing your own darkness as much as what you consider light, then you'll know. When you allow yourself to submit to the depths of your depravities as much as your imagined virtues, we can have an interesting conversation. We can talk at length the day that you know what it feels like to believe in something so much that you're willing to die and kill for it. That you're willing to personally rid the world of weak, ignorant fools to prove those beliefs. Talk to me about enlightenment when you know firsthand what it feels like to hover above someone that you decide is not worthy of living, and you control the exact moment of his or her last breath. Detective, do you have any idea how liberating it is to cut open another human being and to hold their still warm blood and beating heart in your hands? To actually cut beneath the flesh, tissue, and bone until you discover and behold the indescribable beauty of a departing soul? When you begin to comprehend that type of power, then and only then, can you talk to me about enlightenment."

Phee looked at her hard, hoping for her self-incrimination. Zibik took an even closer step, so that she was mere inches from him. She wanted him to smell her sweat and even the evidence of her arousal. Zibik stood in front of him and intentionally invaded his space in such a way that Phee was made uncomfortable by the sudden suggestion of intimacy. She spoke to him just above a whisper. "Of course, I was speaking hypothetically." She smiled coolly at him, and then turned in the opposite direction. As she walked away, she removed her tank top and stood topless with her back half turned toward him. She used the shirt to wipe her neck and under her arms. When she was done, she laid the garment on the floor in front of her. "Good night, Detective Freeman.

Enjoy the rest of your evening." Zibik knelt topless before him and resumed her workout.

As Phee turned away, he thought about two things. First, how his faith had always been a given. Regardless of whatever he chose or didn't choose to call it, he believed in God. As he looked back over his shoulder at Zibik doing her push-ups, the second thing he thought about was just as he was certain of God's existence, he also knew the Devil was real.

34

Zibik knew she was a God. The simpletons that surrounded her constantly left her feeling like a rootless island in shallow waters. None of them could fully appreciate her insatiable thirst for knowledge and progress. Her parents were the only ones. From as far back as she could remember, her father pushed her to reject the norm and challenge the status quo. Her father taught her that there were men/ Gods that were born into this world whose responsibility it was to tear down and rebuild the scientific, social, political, and religious zeitgeist that shackled man and therefore hindered him from living up to his full potential. Zibik saw Satanism as man's truest hope of salvation. As far as she was concerned, it was mankind's best chance for survival. She saw self-worship as the only legitimate means of empowerment. For Dr. Daria Zibik, self-governance was the surest road to the advancement of the entire human race.

Back in the mid-'60s Anton LaVey was such a man. What became known as LaVeyan Satanism, or simply modern-day Satanism, was founded on his beliefs of individualism, self-control, and an eye for an eye morality. As with many things new or different, there were many misconceptions about his teachings. One of the first things that Zibik learned was that "LaVeyan Satanism did not involve the literal worship of any being other than self, but rather used Satan as a symbol of carnality and earthly values." Although she appreciated and credited LaVeyans with her spiritual awakening, in time Zibik outgrew the philosophies that she felt didn't go far enough. She eventually established her own following that was based partly on LaVeyanism and partly on the literal pursuit of omniscient Godliness. She viewed the dominance of souls as the gateway to her final ascension.

Six years ago, Zibik saw her first soul. She had incorporated into her doctrines ancient Egyptian rituals and Native American practices of soul catching and even more primitive Mayan teachings on human sacrificing. Zibik studied them diligently for six years before she felt she was ready. She got it right on her first kill and was immediately rewarded with the most spectacular feeling she had ever experienced. Just as her victim closed his eyes for the final time, Zibik saw the light that hovered a foot just above him. When she caught the soul of her next victim, she began to feel her transformation. Just before her arrest, Zibik knew firsthand what it felt like to be a God.

After finishing her calisthenics for the night, Zibik lay sweating on the floor of her cell. She thought about the two bodies that she saw earlier, particularly Carmen Morales. She was beautifully cut; her wounds were clean, almost as if she had obliged her killer. Zibik knew from the detailed aftermath of the ritual that her soul had been successfully taken. Just the sight of the bodies brought back the rush she personally felt the night of her first kill. Very few people would ever even come close to comprehending that feeling. Not even her closest followers were able to achieve what Morales' killer had. Just before Zibik fell asleep on the floor, she smiled at the knowledge and pride that somewhere on the streets of New York, another God walked the earth.

35

After he left work, the last thing Quincy wanted was the peace and quiet of his apartment. He needed a diversion. He struggled all day, and on several occasions lost, in his attempt at keeping certain thoughts at bay. Now that the day's work was over, he knew he didn't stand much of a chance of having any mental peace. He hadn't slept at all last night, thinking about his brother's birthday present to him. He played out every scenario he could think of to justify Liam coming into possession of the dead priest's baseball. Because of the broken stitches and red wine stain, there was no doubt in his mind whatsoever that the baseball he played with in Father Conner's office and the present that his brother gave him were one and the same. All he needed was some logical explanation that clarified how Liam ended up with the ball. The easiest one was that somehow Deggler gave it to him, but that made no sense, because Liam was quite adamant that he'd never met Deggler. The other possibility was that Deggler gave it to someone else who gave it to Liam. But in truth, Quincy wasn't satisfied with the odds of that happening. He needed to hear it from his brother directly. He and Liam never lied to each other. They had been through too much as kids to let lies come between them. They were at times painfully honest with each other. Surely if he asked Liam, there would be some acceptable reason or coincidence to explain the whole thing. There had to be.

Just as he was thinking of his brother, Quincy's phone vibrated, and he saw a one-word text from Liam. "Confession."

When Quincy pulled up in front of Liam's church, the clock on the dashboard read 12:08. He was in the confessional booth by 12:15. Liam was already on his side waiting for him.

"Hey," Quincy greeted him from the other side of the partition.

"Hey," Liam responded. "How's Phee and his father?"

"They're both strong, but I know they're hurting. They never made peace before AJ was killed."

"I've been praying for them both. I'll do everything I can to make sure the service is special."

"I know they'll appreciate that," Quincy said.

After they spoke about Phee and the funeral, they seemed to run out of things to say. Liam was usually the talkative one, but for some reason, the responsibility seemed to have landed squarely on Quincy. Even though he had plenty to ask, he was having great difficulty segueing to the things that needed clarification. In his procrastination, Quincy talked about random things, old and new. He hoped that the conversation would somehow naturally present him with an opening to talk about what was on his mind. For the next twenty minutes, he tried but could never bring himself to ask the question he'd come to ask. He somehow managed to navigate the conversation in every direction except toward the topic he needed to discuss most. Each time they ran into bumpy pauses, Quincy overcompensated with strained laughter and a string of irrelevant subjects. It took him some time before he realized that he was doing the majority of the talking. Liam was unusually quiet. Just as Quincy was about to broach the subject of the baseball, Liam cut him off.

"Ma stopped by church today," Liam blurted out.

"Really? That's a first. Did she come for Mass?"

"No, confession."

Quincy was noticeably thrown by the information. "Did you, uh…?"

"Hear it? Of course I did. It's what I do remember? Didn't know it was her until she started speaking. By that time I didn't really have a choice. Trust me; it was the last thing I wanted to hear."

"What did she…?" Quincy cut himself off as he caught himself.

He sat there quietly, now fully understanding why Liam had been so detached.

Their mother stopped attending church when they were still children. It was shortly after the priest that Quincy and Liam accused of molesting them had been transferred to another church.

Although she never directly addressed her son's claims, Quincy later rationalized her break with the Church as some kind of silent acknowledgment of the crimes perpetrated against them. It wasn't the way Liam saw it. He viewed her self-imposed exile from the Church as an admission of her own collusion in their abuse, and as such, she finally saw herself for what she had become, an embarrassment before God.

Quincy could only imagine the things that his mother might have brought up in confession. He didn't bother to ask, because he knew his brother would never violate his vows even to him. Their mother's visit left Liam in a vulnerable state. Regardless of his original objective for coming to see Liam, Quincy now just wanted to be there as a shoulder for his brother to lean on.

An hour and a half after he arrived, Quincy exited the confessional and walked back out to his car with Liam. Although he left without getting the closure that he came for, he was comforted by the fact that he had managed to lift Liam's spirits. Quincy felt guilty over his original motives for coming, but when all was said and done, he convinced himself he didn't want to know. If his brother had lied to him in any way, it was something that he really wasn't prepared to deal with. True, things might gnaw and pull at him for a while, but his hope was that in time, such things would subside. He embraced his brother and got in his car. Just before he pulled off, Liam tapped on the driver side window. Quincy smiled as he rolled his window down.

"By the way, what did you think of the birthday present I got you?" Liam asked.

Quincy's vision and thoughts were suddenly broken and blurred. He knew he owed his brother a response, but one never came. He wasn't exactly sure how long he was gone, but the muffled echo of his brother's voice brought him back.

"Hey, you okay?" Liam pressed.

"Yeah, sorry; I loved the present, thanks."

"I found it on e-Bay a couple of months ago, thought you would like it."

There were exact moments in some people's lives when they knew their world was forever altered by a person, event, act of God, or tragedy. As Quincy looked into his brother's eyes and realized he was lying, his very foundation was turned topsy-turvy.

"Yeah, it's awesome. Thanks again," Quincy said as he rolled up the window and drove off.

Halfway down the block, Quincy pulled over and threw up.

36

After Quincy left, Liam decided to go for a drive. He couldn't stop thinking about Colette's visit. She did what she did best: she danced around the crimes she was guilty of. She held her accountability at arm's length and asked forgiveness for sins she refused to name and commit to. Colette was vague and kept her confession generic, but Liam read between the lines of what she said and didn't say. Her words eventually became white noise to him. When she finally left, he prayed. He prayed for her but mostly for himself. He asked God's forgiveness for his inability to forgive his mother.

Liam saw himself as an impostor. Two diametrically opposed beings in one body: priest and murderer. He found himself being equally pulled in two different directions. Years ago, he'd killed the priest that abused him and Quincy as children by setting fire to the man's home. That kill gave him peace and satiated his desires for many years, at least until he met Deggler. It was that encounter that had awakened certain things in Liam or, more precisely, encouraged him to embrace his true nature. He constantly questioned himself as to whether he would have to kill again in order to survive. Everyone, especially Quincy, saw only the good in Liam, but no one seemed to understand the darkness that he suppressed on a daily basis. He often wondered if the purging would save him. If he faced the evil that was in him, would he eventually be free?

Before Liam actually realized it, he had driven down to the lower '80s in Manhattan and sat in front of Pastor Edwards's home. Edwards was a Baptist preacher who'd fathered at least four children outside of his marriage with young girls in his congregation. He was one of "The Befallen" from Deggler's kill list. As he waited in his car, he wondered which method of killing Deggler would have used on Edwards. Liam neither had nor wanted a repertoire of ways to kill. Fire was the one thing that came to him naturally. Tonight, he was content to just sit in his car and visualize the act of murdering Pastor Edwards, but soon, very soon, Liam would come for him. Hopefully after killing Edwards, Liam would be able to bury his hunger as well.

37

Phee got a late-night call from his father and went to meet him at the Waldorf. Clay was already three sheets to the wind by the time Phee arrived. It was possible, but Phee couldn't remember ever seeing his father this drunk.

"What can I get you?" Clay asked as he poured another glass of scotch.

"I'm good," Phee said.

Clay walked over with two glasses and handed one to Phee.

"At least help your old man chase the Devil," Clay said as he clanked his glass with Phee's. "Somebody once told me that scotch was like a good woman. I just can't remember who it was and why they thought that."

Phee hated scotch. He actually hated all hard alcohol. He could do wine and the occasional mojito, but beyond that, he had no real tolerance for the stuff. The only time he drank the hard stuff was to appease his father. He sipped the scotch, if for no other reason than to give his father a drinking buddy.

"Hey, you know what I was thinking about the other day?"

"What's that, Pop?" Phee asked.

"Your last game up in Green Bay; you caught four interceptions and ran two back for touchdowns. Everybody used to always talk about how great Brett Favre was, but you owned him every time you played him. I never told you this, but your mother almost got into a fistfight for taunting some of the Green Bay fans."

"No way!"

"Trust me; she could talk shit with the best of them."

"Pops, you're drunk," Phee said laughing.

"That might be the case, but I still know what I'm talking about. There are a lot of things you didn't know about your mother."

"Well, since I'm not sure whether or not it's you or the alcohol talking, this might not be the best time for you to tell me."

"Smartest thing I ever did, marrying that woman. Let me ask you a question: Was I a good father?"

"Pop, you know you…"

"The truth. I don't just want some bullshit answer that you think I want to hear. I want the truth. Was I a good father?"

"You still are," Phee responded.

"…Because that's really all that matters; I may not have always done right, but I tried to always do what was right by my family," Clay slurred as he poured both of them another glass of scotch.

The wind rumbled against the partly opened window as though

it were seeking shelter from itself. Phee crossed and picked up a few scattered pieces of sheet music that had fallen from the baby grand in the center of the living room. After closing the window, he turned and sat on the sill with the wind still wailing at his back. He sipped on his scotch as though he was trying to teach himself to enjoy it.

"I think I was eight the first summer you made me and AJ spend in Harlem. Spider Harris said that we were just some stuck-up white boys. He and four others from his crew chased us back to St. Nick, to the spot where you were getting your hair cut. You just looked at me and AJ, and made us go back outside, because I'll never forget what you told us. The first thing was that, 'Freemans don't run.' The second was that, 'If a man wasn't scared of gettin' his ass whooped once in a while, he'd go far in life.' I remember being so mad at you in that moment. Because I was thinking, what kind of father intentionally puts his kids in that kind of danger? Do you remember how those kids kicked our asses that day, while you and everybody else in the barbershop just watched?"

"Yeah, they put some smoke on you and your brother," Clay laughed.

"It was worth it. That was the last day I ever ran from anybody. I'm glad you made us fight."

"That day wasn't really about making you and your brother fight. It was about making the two of you understand that you had choices. You could run the rest of your life, or you could stand up. You always got choices, no matter the situation. And at the end of the day, the choices that we make introduce us to who we really are."

"I still can't believe that after they beat us up, you ended up taking us all to Mickey D's."

"Why not? They worked up more of an appetite than you and AJ did. Takes more energy to swing than to duck," Clay said teasingly.

"Come on, I got some good blows in."

"Yeah, you did… Can't say the same for your brother. I should have known something was wrong with that boy then. He fought like he was in some kind of damn musical."

Even though Phee continued laughing with his father, he couldn't help but be bothered by what Clay said. It wasn't so much that he blamed his father for labeling AJ as "having something wrong with him." Phee was mainly affected by the culpability of his own prejudice. From the time he was old enough to comprehend the meaning of "gay," he'd bought into the generational and cultural discrimination against his brother's kind. He couldn't indict his father without owning up to his own practice of dismissing AJ as nothing more than a mistake, or perverted defect. The gay thing was most definitely an awkward and unsavory topic in the African American community. The irony wasn't lost on Phee that his father was one of the most powerful men to emerge from Harlem, and yet he had sired a homosexual son. Phee laughed at gay jokes, because he had done so the majority of his life. He spent many years hating and reject-ing his brother, because at some point, a long time ago, he lost the ability to differentiate between what he had been taught and what he truly felt and believed. Clay was right. The choices that a man made told him who he was. AJ died brotherless, because Phee had chosen conformity over love.

"They're going to release AJ from the morgue tomorrow. Are you sure you're okay with Quincy's brother doing the services at St. Augustine's?" Phee asked.

"Yeah, he called me first thing this morning," Clay answered.

"Pop, there's something I need to tell you."

"What's that? Is it the truth about how AJ died?"

"Which means you already know. I'm sorry I wasn't straight with you."

"I went to see Kravitz. I saw what they did to your brother. What if it wasn't random?"

"What are you talking about, Pop?"

"I'm just saying. I know you can take care of yourself, but I want you to be more careful than usual."

Unlike most people who looked away when they either lied or tried to be evasive, Clay looked harder at Phee and didn't blink.

"If you know something, Pop, you need to be straight with me."

"Like you were with me? I'm just telling you to watch your back until one of us finds whoever killed AJ and deals with them. By the way, don't ever accuse me of not being straight with you, when you're the one who flat-out lied."

"Pop, I…"

"There's some weird shit going on right now. I just need you to be on point. Okay?"

Phee nodded, knowing there was no point in pressing the matter further.

Once Clay was satisfied that his point was made, he sat deeper in his chair and sipped his drink.

"For the record, I know why you lied and I'm not mad at you for it, because ultimately it was your choice, and you're the one that has to deal with it," Clay said.

Regardless of how subtle Clay may have thought he was being, Phee was reduced by his words. He finished off his scotch as though it were temporary refuge from his father's disappointment. After he swallowed the last bitter drop, Phee crossed and poured himself another glass. Each sip was made more tolerable by the confidence it instilled in him to finally say the things that had gone unspoken for years.

"My whole life, I tried to do the things that I thought would make you proud. No matter what it took and even at times when being your son wasn't the easiest thing. When we were kids and people asked AJ and me what we wanted to be when we grew up, I was always the first one to say that I wanted to be you. At the time, that was the best goal I could think of. But then I got old enough to understand the rumors and whispers of things you did in the past that made people afraid of you. Shit, some of the stuff I heard even made me scared of you, but not like everybody else. I was scared that whatever that thing was that was in you was in me as well. Maybe that's ultimately why I became a cop. To try and convince myself that deep down, you and I were different. But you always knew, didn't you? You knew no matter how much I bullshitted myself and tried to run from it, I was never gonna get away from the fact that I am like you. What if you were wrong earlier, Pop, when you said we all have choices? What if some of us don't? Maybe for people like me and you, shit was mapped out for us, even before we came out the womb. You used to always say that a man wasn't a man if he wasn't willing to do whatever it took to take care of his family. So I just need you to know that no matter what it takes, I'm going to find whoever did those things to AJ. You don't have to worry about them walking away, or even spending the rest of their miserable life in prison somewhere. You have my word. I'll deal with them in the way that you of all people will understand."

Phee downed his scotch, kissed his father on the forehead, and left.

38

Brenda and Phee had three kids, two wild-haired little girls and a handsome boy who was the spitting image of his father. They traded the cold, hard city for the tranquil suburbs of New Jersey. They both taught at the same small rural college. Brenda ran the computer science department, while Phee taught a new course in criminology. He took creative writing courses in his free time, and much to Brenda's surprise and delight, showed great promise as an aspiring writer of crime novels. Though their journey had proven to be long and crooked, with unexpected detours, Brenda loved the life that they were now blessed with.

Tonight, like many nights before, this was her recurring dream, the piece of happiness that teased her with possibilities of fulfillment. No matter how real the visions felt, in the end, it was all just a dream—a dream that she kept to herself and never shared with Phee. Brenda was a woman with excellent taste albeit a bit of a minimalist. A bed, dresser, and a single swivel chair from her favorite furniture store Roche Bobois were the only items in her large by New York standards bedroom. Brenda awoke to find Phee, still dressed in his overcoat, sitting at the foot of the bed. He was hunched over and staring at the palms of his hands, with little to no movement. Brenda knew immediately through his posture and behavior that he came bearing bad news.

"Phee?" she said. As she waited for him to tell her what was wrong, Brenda pulled on the string friendship bracelet that she'd worn for years. She twisted it so tightly that she felt it dig into her skin and slow her circulation like a tourniquet.

"What's wrong, Baby?" she implored.

Phee quietly rose and crossed to the window. As he parted the curtains and looked out, the second snowfall came as a blatant reminder of winter's arrival. The city was covered in an alabaster blanket, brilliant and clean. The snow sparkled like glitter under the reflective light of the florescent streetlamps. At three a.m. the only sounds heard were the occasional whistle of the northern wind and the mechanical whir of a distant street plow. Even though Phee normally hated winter and the inclement weather that it brought, tonight he found it oddly peaceful, cathartic even. Under the white sheets of snow, the city looked deceptively chaste.

"Phee?" Brenda's voice was slightly more pleading.

Phee never turned to face her. He just continued looking out of the window. By the time he spoke, his voice was quiet but clear.

"I'm sorry we didn't make it to Nice," he said.

"I don't care about Nice. I just want to see you and your father get through this. All of us."

"When I was driving home tonight, I was thinking about the first time I met you. Every dude on campus was trying to get at you. Do you remember what you told me when I asked you what made you decide to go out with me?" Phee asked.

"Of course I do," Brenda responded. "The ones before you were too busy trying to be something that they weren't, but you were different."

"So why did you shoot me down six times before you said yes?" Phee offered a half-hearted laugh.

"I only turned you down three times." She tried to smile. "To be honest, you scared the hell out of me."

"Why?"

"Because I knew then what I know now: that you were the kind of man that I could love forever. That's a lot to deal with at eighteen."

"I think you overestimate who I really am."

"Not at all. I just think at times, I know you better than you know yourself."

"What if you were wrong then and wrong now? What if in the end I'm no better than any other man pretending to be what he's not?"

Brenda crossed to the window and put her hands on the back of Phee's shoulders.

"Just tell me what's wrong."

It took Phee a minute to speak, but the minute he turned to Brenda he blurted out, "I think we need to chill for a minute."

Brenda smelled the alcohol on his breath but ignored it. "What exactly does that mean?" she asked.

"I got a lot going on. I just can't do us right now."

"You don't get through this kind of stuff by pushing away the people who love you."

"I need to do this my way, and as fucked up as this might sound, I can't be worried about your feelings right now and whether or not I'm handling things in a way that you approve of."

Brenda checked her temper and ego and kept her focus on the greater goal. She needed Phee to communicate with her, and not shut down or get defensive. If she weren't careful, things between them would become combustible. Each time in the past when she gave into her alpha instincts, he either completely turned off or felt the need to one-up her. She took a breath and thought about what she wanted to say. "I've never seen you run from anything in your life, Phee. Don't start by trying to make this about some imagined pressure that I'm putting on you. Even as dark as things are right now, those of us that love you are going to help you and your father through this if you let us."

"I can handle this on my own."

"I didn't say you couldn't, but why would you want to?"

"I just need to do this my way, that's all."

"And your way is shutting me out?"

"That's my point, Brenda. This isn't about you."

"Phee, you gotta let me in."

Phee was feeling light-headed from the scotch. Though he pretended to be listening, he missed some of Brenda's words.

He tried to act normal under the stressful circumstances. Brenda assumed, incorrectly, that he sat back down on the edge of the bed to better engage her, but instead, he did so to lighten the load on his weakening legs.

Even though they continued talking, Brenda felt at times that she was either losing him or had already done so. There were tears and long, uncomfortable silences. Sometime around 4:30, Brenda convinced Phee to at least stay with her the rest of the night because she felt he was in no condition to drive. As the two of them lay on the bed, she was uncertain whether or not the conversation had in any way swayed Phee. She fell asleep under the welcome weight of his arms. She strategically intertwined her body with his in such a way that the broader moves of his departure would awaken her.

Brenda awoke just before six. The lazy, silver moon still hung low, like a loose coin in the sky. The night snowfall had tapered off and turned to a light rain just as the sun began to rise. The floor to ceiling window in Brenda's loft faced the east, and each morning she awoke to a magnificent view that very few New Yorkers were exposed to. As she rolled over, the beautiful loft was cold and quiet.

Phee was gone.

39

New York awoke to four inches of snow. Phee and Quincy met at seven a.m. to finish off the remaining names of SUV owners. The last three names on their list were out in Queens. Maclin decided to stay at the station to monitor any potential responses to the posts that had been left by Zibik. Neither Phee nor Quincy had slept well the night before. Both men, in their own ways, were disturbed by thoughts of their brothers. The partners stopped at a spot called Just Like Mother's, a cozy Polish spot in Forest Hills. They both preferred the mom-and-pop joints that were in dire risk of extinction, rather than the corporate coffee staples. Quincy glanced at the list as he took his first sip. "We should try Leslie Wyatt next. She's not far from here."

Ten minutes later, Phee and Quincy pulled up to a single-family house in a quiet Jewish neighborhood just off Austin Street.

They knocked on the front door but got no response. The two cops went around back and knocked on a rear door. When no one answered, they headed back toward the front. Just as they rounded the corner of the house, the SUV from the video surveillance was pulling into the driveway with two male occupants. Quincy and Phee quickly recognized the driver to be Barnes, one of the men from the rock quarry. The two cops had no way of knowing that Barnes' passenger was the killer that they were looking for. Jelly locked eyes with Phee as the four men froze for half a second, each duo, equally surprised by the other's arrival. Phee and Quincy recovered first, both reaching for their guns. Barnes responded by throwing the vehicle in reverse and fishtailing out of the driveway. Phee and Quincy bolted for their car and sped after the SUV down the narrow residential street. Phee slapped the gumball light to the roof of the car and flipped the switch for the siren, but it only cackled and burped the static sound of wires being shorted before it died altogether. Although the street had been plowed, the driving conditions were still challenging. Quincy immediately called for backup and gave the plates and vehicle description of the SUV as it ran a stoplight and nearly collided with a school bus filled with third graders. Quincy was a bit nervous, because the near collision in no way slowed or deterred Phee. Great cops like Quincy and Phee usually erred on the side of caution. Quincy was bothered by the fact that Phee was driving with a similar reckless-ness as the two men they pursued. When their car hydroplaned and narrowly missed a collision with the bus, Quincy raised his voice. "Easy, Phee."

"I got it," Phee shot back as he pressed his foot on the gas and lurched forward. The SUV turned onto Queens Boulevard and maneuvered, speeding as best it could, through the compacted snow and early morning congestion. A cab driver lost his door as he opened it, just as the SUV smashed it as it passed. Phee only fared slightly better as he sideswiped a delivery truck that nearly cut him off. It wasn't his personal safety that Quincy feared for most. He had lost that gene years ago. He was much more afraid of the unforeseen tragedy that they were in danger of causing. Just up ahead, Phee and Quincy saw an oncoming cruiser, with lights flashing and siren blaring, going against the traffic and heading directly at the SUV. Phee swerved and barely missed hitting a Mini Cooper that stopped in front of them.

"Let the cruiser cut him off. Slow it down, Phee. We'll get them," Quincy said.

Phee completely ignored him as he rode the median, almost hitting cars on both sides.

"Dammit, Phee, we got no siren. I said slow it down before you kill someone."

A block later, Phee was broadsided in an intersection by a truck that had the right-of-way. They were hit on the driver side, and Phee banged his head against the window as they spun out of control. After Quincy got out of the car, Phee slid over to the passenger side and staggered out himself. Both cops shook their cobwebs in time to see the oncoming cruiser and Barnes engaged in a dangerous game of chicken. As the two vehicles sped toward each other, neither refused to yield or turn off. When they were ten feet apart, Barnes floored the pedal, causing the two vehicles to hit head on. Barnes and the cop on the passenger side took the brunt of the impact. Barnes, who wasn't wearing a seat belt, was knocked unconscious, while the passenger side cop was severely injured. The cop on the driver side stumbled out of the car a few seconds after Jelly made it out. Jelly glanced back quickly to see Phee and Quincy, two blocks back, making their way toward him. Before the surviving cop could orient himself enough to pull out his gun, Jelly bull-rushed him and knocked him through a storefront window before taking his gun and running off. Phee was slowed by the accident but took off after Jelly nonetheless. Quincy pointed his gun at Barnes and carefully approached the unconscious man. After cuffing Barnes to the steering wheel, Quincy quickly checked on the two injured cops and called again for backup and medical assistance.

Under normal circumstances, Phee would have caught up with Jelly three blocks in, but the concussive blow hindered him. The two men ran down Queens Boulevard, terrifying shop owners and pedestrians alike with the guns they pointed in each other's direction. Jelly was the first to squeeze off a round. Queens was no different from any of the other boroughs and was not immune to the sound of gunfire. One of the rules of survival was to duck, tuck, and run. People on the boulevard ran into shops and hid behind cars as Jelly and Phee came running toward them. As they turned off the boulevard and barreled down a side street, Phee started closing in on Jelly, who hopped a fence and ran across the small backyards of private homes. The harder Phee ran, the more his head started pounding. It literally felt like it was cracking open and violently being pulled apart. After jumping the second fence, Phee could feel his body rebelling. Just as Jelly climbed the third fence, Phee aimed and squeezed off two shots. The gunfire made the ringing in his head even worse. Phee was unable to clear the third fence and stumbled awkwardly as Jelly kicked into another gear and disappeared from view. Phee staggered and needed to use the fence to keep himself from falling. Just before Phee went down, he saw the drops of blood that Jelly left behind.

40

Phee lay on a gurney in the ER. wearing a hospital gown and his black jeans. Quincy and a nurse drew back the curtain and entered. "How are you feeling?" Quincy asked.

"Like shit, but I'll be alright."

"Doctor said he thinks you have a concussion."

"I'll be alright," Phee said, with a little more irritation than he intended.

Quincy turned to the nurse and asked her to give them a moment of privacy. After she left, he turned back to Phee, who was taking off his gown and reaching for his shirt.

"What are you doing? They said they need to run some more tests."

"They always say that. What's up with Barnes?"

"Punctured a lung, might not make it."

"I hit the runner. Did you have forensics run the blood at the fence?"

"Yeah, they're on it. If we're lucky, it'll take them two to three days to find out if he's in the system. If we're lucky."

"Zibik knows more than she's saying, but it's gonna take too long to break her. We gotta talk to Barnes before he goes south," Phee said.

"I can break Zibik, but you and I need to talk first."

"About what?" Phee asked.

"I need you to let the doctors sign you off before you come back."

"I'm fine."

"Good, then just let them confirm it."

"We don't have time for me to be hanging around here while they run more bullshit tests."

"As head investigator on this case, I'm not asking you, Phee."

"You pulling rank on me?" Phee asked incredulously.

"Call it what you want, but I'm doing what's best for you and, believe it or not, this case as well."

"Don't play this bullshit. You got something on your mind, say it."

Quincy folded his arms and stared directly at Phee. "Look, I know it's hard being this close to the case, but you gotta check yourself."

"What are you talking about?" Phee said with growing agitation.

"If you're not careful, you're going to blow the very thing you want most."

"Is this about the accident? We're cops. We chase suspects. Sometimes we gotta take chances that other people wouldn't. It's what we do."

"What we do is stay in control and use our heads," Quincy snapped back. "That's what separates us from them. In any given moment, I got no idea what your next move is. If we're going to catch whoever killed AJ, we gotta get on the same page."

"Fine. When some asshole butchers your brother, then maybe, just maybe, we'll be on the same page. But until that happens, we ain't even in the same fuckin' book. Let me make this easy for you Quincy; you run this case anyway you want, just without me. Do what you gotta do, and I'll do the same."

Phee finished putting his shirt on and headed for the exit.

"Phee. Phee!" Quincy called after his partner in vain.

41

Sonia Wu pulled an all-nighter over at Queen's Memorial Hospital. After her nursing shift ended at nine in the morning, she walked to the employees' parking lot, where she was surprised to discover her boyfriend, Jelly, bleeding from a gunshot wound in the back seat of her Jeep Cherokee. She managed to stay calm as she examined his injury. Fortunately, the bullet entered and exited, without damage to any major organs or arteries, but he had still lost a decent amount of blood and was at risk of infection. She went back upstairs to get the items that she needed to better help him. The asshole in charge of the drug lockup had periodically given Sonia drugs for sex. She negotiated a future hand job for painkillers, antibiotics, and some oxy thrown in as a bonus. When he wasn't looking, she managed to put a few other goodies in her purse. Before she left, she stopped by the nurses' station and stole some gauze, saline, and anything else she thought she might need. Sonia got Jelly to her house before ten and had him resting comfortably within the hour.

Before she met Jelly, Sonia Wu lived hard. She was a small woman with big appetites. Sonia was five foot nothin' and weighed 98 pounds on a good day with a bag of sand in her pocket. She drank too much, fucked too much, and, ultimately, cared too little. She was a skinny, assimilated Asian chick who wore ocean blue contacts. She spent the majority of her life never quite fitting in. Sonia was a social outcast in the first degree, complete with self-loathing and an equal hatred of the world. Her peers started rejecting her as far back as kindergarten and, ultimately, relegated her to an invisible status by the time she made it to high school. It wasn't until she started studying Satanism a year ago that she finally found a group of people who accepted and embraced her for who she was.

She and Jelly first bumped into each other at a gathering sponsored by the Church of Satan shortly after she started studying. Being the two newest converts, they seemed to naturally gravitate toward each other. She learned sign language in just a couple of months, and the effort of communication with the mute brought them closer together. In her desperation for inclusion, Sonia had always allowed men to devalue her. Jelly was different though; he made her feel, for the first time in her life, loved. His several stints in prison in no way deterred her attraction to him; if anything, there was a part of her that was turned on by his criminal past. She viewed her life as boring. Sonia was an unpopular nurse whose patients despised her and colleagues avoided her. Such trivial things no longer bothered her, because of the two big changes in her life. She'd found a religion worth following and a man worth loving.

She watched Jelly quietly sleeping. In the six months that they were together, she had never seen him so much at peace. The drugs that she had given him seemed to quiet the nightmares she was so accustomed to him having. Shortly after they started seeing each other, he told her of his childhood and the murder of his parents and brother. He also told her of his plans for revenge. As she watched him sleeping, she relished his momentary reprieve from the demons that haunted him. She nursed him and did everything she could for him, short of bringing him to the hospital. Sonia watched over him like a mother would an endangered child. She did a great job of tending to his wound. Jelly was all that mattered to her. He slept for three hours. When he finally opened his eyes and smiled at her, she kissed him warmly and repeatedly. Jelly was not only conscious but also interacted with her with his usual ease. He signed jokes and did what he could to keep her smiling. His impressive physical and mental fortitude gave her confidence in the likelihood of his full recovery. She had correctly surmised that the injuries he'd sustained were somehow connected to his acts of vengeance. She believed, like her lover, that there was no punishment too vicious for those responsible for, or connected to, the death of his family. The two nights that Jelly killed AJ and Carmen Morales, Sonia welcomed him back as though he were an exalted hero returning from an anointed mission. She made love to him as though it were an honor. She had never been turned on so much in her life as the times she felt Jelly's hands still warm from the death of another human being. Before he left to kill them, Sonia begged him to take her with him, but he refused. She wanted to witness firsthand, not only the taking of a life but also the catching of a soul.

The weight of a bullet is measured in grains. On average, the bullet from a handgun weighs anywhere from one hundred and fifteen grains to two hundred and forty, which is the equivalent of fifteen grams. Jelly was physically too strong, and much too determined, to be stopped by a single piece of lead that carried the weight of three nickels. He refused the additional painkillers Sonia offered him, because he preferred clarity to physical comfort. Whatever pain he did feel he wanted to use to keep himself focused on how close he was to finally achieving his lifelong dream. He had too many things to do to be delayed by the inconvenience of a gunshot. Jelly tested his strength by walking around Sonia's apartment, even as she adamantly protested. The movement only made him stronger. Even after acquiescing to Sonia's pleas and getting back in bed, Jelly used his rest time to finish working out the details of abducting Clay. Blue was easy, but Clay would require more strategy than improvisation.

Jelly rested peacefully as Sonia made him soup and stayed by his side. She was pleasantly surprised at how quickly Jelly was recovering. Once she was certain that he was out of danger, her thoughts turned to how devastated she would be if anything happened to the one person in the world who had shown her true love. Nothing elevated the appreciation of life more than the very real possibility of death. Sonia hadn't cried in years. Her life had been so consistently filled with heartache and humiliation that she had long ago cried herself out. But as she saw how absolutely beautiful Jelly was lying before her, childlike and innocent, the mere thought of ever losing him made her cry. Jelly's hands were hardened by a lifetime of violence. The only adult act of tenderness they had ever shown was toward Sonia. He pressed his palm against her face in an effort to stop her from crying. After she composed herself, she chose to use the opportunity to tell him things that she felt. Sonia signed eloquently the love that Jelly had planted within her. How she absolutely adored him because he had single-handedly made her feel beautiful for the first time in her life. She told him as sincerely as she could how she had no use for life without him. Jelly never made promises. He never cared enough about the people in his life to offer such assurances. After Sonia expressed how she felt toward him, Jelly promised her that he would never leave her, that she would never have to be afraid of living without him. There were only two things in the world that truly mattered to him: retribution and Sonia's love. Both Jelly and Sonia lived the better part of their lives feeling like cursed misfits. But through all their inestimable tribulations and the endless cycles of alienation, their mutual beliefs in Satanism not only gave them both hope but also delivered them to each other.

It took some doing, but Jelly eventually convinced Sonia that he was fit enough to make his move on Clay. After imprisoning Blue in the basement of his parents' home, all he needed now to complete his dream was to capture Clay as well. Jelly needed to kill the two men together, to have them watch each other die. If perfectly timed and done right, he would kill and capture both of their souls only minutes apart from each other. Sonia's opposition lessened once Jelly mapped out his plan and explained to her the crucial role that he needed her to play. She relented under the promise of being included. Jelly gave her what she desperately wanted, the opportunity to watch him kill.

42

Blue was firmly gagged and left chained to a metal post in what appeared to him to be the basement of an old house. His pant leg rode up above his shin, partially exposing his injured leg. He grew anxious over its discoloration and the fact that it ballooned to twice its normal size. The basement that Blue lay in was dank, musty, and dark. Many of the floorboards beneath him were made soft with wood rot and years of termite infestation. Fortunately, despite the snow outside, the temperature in the house was still somewhat bearable. He lay huddled under his overcoat and a couple of lice-infested blankets that his abductor left for him. There were various scratches as well as swelling on his face and body from the combination of the wooden splinters beneath him, the aftermath of being struck by Jelly's vehicle, and the beating he sustained afterwards. Blue's entire body ached, which restricted his movement even more than the chains that restrained him.

The pain in Blue's leg was horrible. Had he been able to see an X-ray of it, he would have undoubtedly cringed at the jagged break in his tibia. He couldn't feel his toes, nothing but numbness from the ankle down. In an odd way, the pain that he did feel came with the assurance that there was still blood flow and function to his injured leg. As the numbness grew, so too did his concerns for survival. Every fifteen minutes that he was awake, he massaged his thigh in hopes that it might improve his circulation. The activity gave him purpose. He needed to figure a way out and not lose hope, because for the first time in a long time, his life had at least some meaning. Blue had a daughter to bury. If he did nothing else, he at least owed her that. His fear was not so much for himself as it was the thought of failing her in death as badly as he had in her lifetime. Even though he was still angry with God, and certainly rusty with the concept of faith, he still tried to pray and ask that he could somehow find a way to escape. As he lay on the floor, he wondered if Clay was right and whether or not the sins of their past had come full circle in unforgiving demand of delinquent debts. Slowly but surely, he accepted the fact that the violence against him wasn't a random act. His mind raced overtime as he wondered who would possibly think that he was worth kidnapping.

43

P hee was out for blood and nothing less. He and Quincy had two different agendas. Quincy wanted to arrest the killer(s), whereas Phee was determined to kill them. He wasn't about to let anything or anyone, not even his partner and best friend, stop him. Now that Phee found himself in the precarious demotion of being half cop and half civilian, one of his biggest challenges would be trying to outsmart and outdistance Quincy. Phee needed to anticipate his partner's next move, so that he could stay at least one step ahead of him. Quincy made it clear that he was going to make another run at Zibik to see what she knew. Zibik may have been the key, but she was too guileful to give up anything meaningful anytime soon. If Barnes recovered, Phee was convinced that he was the one to try and break. After he waited downstairs and saw Quincy leave the hospital, Phee jumped back in the elevator and headed up to the ICU. Fortunately, he immediately recognized the young uniform posted outside of Barnes' room.

"What's up, Diego?" Phee greeted him.

"Hey Phee, you just missed Quincy."

"Yeah, I know. How's Barnes doing?"

"They just brought him back from surgery. Doctors said he's 50/50."

"Listen Diego, I need a favor," Phee said.

"Sure, brotha', anything."

"If Barnes wakes up, I need you to call me on my cell the minute it happens."

"Of course, that goes without saying."

"That's not the favor part. I need five minutes alone with him before you let anybody else know he's awake."

Many of the younger cops idolized Phee, particularly the ones of color. Some because of his father's storied past, some because of Phee's football career, but mainly because Phee was a good cop and would do almost anything for his brothers and sisters in blue. A year ago, when Diego threw a fundraiser for his sick kid, not only was Phee one of the first to donate, but he was also one of the first to show up and support. Whatever Phee needed, Diego wanted him to know that he could be counted on.

44

As Quincy rode back to the station, he called Maclin and brought her up to speed on everything; except the part about Phee quitting.

"He's a little banged up from the accident. He might need a day or two."

Quincy felt he needed to leave the door open as best he could for his partner to come back. No matter what Phee thought because of his anger, Quincy's loyalty was unwavering.

Quincy had a huge dilemma. If he did what he was supposed to do and reported back to his captain that Phee had gone AWOL and was a potential danger to the investigation, then his partner would immediately be stripped of all official credentials and privileges and, most importantly, the sanction of the badge. On the other hand, if he didn't report it and Phee did something crazy, then Quincy would be partly responsible. He hoped that Phee was just letting off steam and would come back to where he was needed and where Quincy could keep an eye on him. If he didn't hear from Phee by first thing in the morning, then he knew he had his answer. Quincy would cover for him as best he could by using the accident to buy a little more time. He just hoped Phee's next few moves wouldn't jeopardize his game plan.

After he hung up with Maclin, Quincy's mind was in overdrive. He was trying to think of the best way to make his next run at Zibik. There was no way Zibik would break easily. Quincy needed to plot out every move before he got back to the station and started his interrogation. As he and the uniformed cop that was driving crossed over the Queensboro Bridge back into Midtown Manhattan, he regretted the fact that Phee wasn't there to strategize with him.

Quincy used the squad car computer to run the photos of Zibik's three men that he'd taken at the rock quarry to see if he got any hits from the national database. The only one that registered anything was an old petty larceny charge against Barnes back in '02. The other three men, including Stringer, were nowhere in the system. As he continued pulling up as much info as he could on Barnes, his cell phone buzzed with an incoming text. When he checked the message, he saw that it was from Elena. "Just wanted to let you know that I was thinking about you and how much I appreciate and adore you."

"Funny how you seem to know just when I need a little lifting. See you tonight," Quincy wrote back.

Elena sent her confirmation in the form of a smiley face. As Quincy went to put his phone back in his pocket, he looked at it and got an idea. He turned to the uniformed cop. "Hey Charlie, did you confiscate Andrew Barnes' phone from the hospital?"

"Yeah, it's in the back with the rest of his stuff."

Quincy leaned over and grabbed the evidence box from the back seat. He pulled out a plastic baggie that contained Barnes' wallet, jewelry, and phone. Quincy immediately pulled up Barnes' phone log and text history. He saw the name Stringer next to a number that had been called several times over the last few days. Quincy called the number only to be disappointed by the disconnection message that greeted him. He had much better luck when he listened to the voicemail. As they exited 59th Street, Quincy was much too engrossed listening to the message to notice the thin mist of snow that started to fall. It was light and drifting like confectioners' sugar from the sky. He was unaware that his mouth hung open from the surprise of hearing the details of the message. As the city around him braced itself for another snowfall, Quincy's only thought was that he could hardly believe what he was hearing on the voicemail.

45

Kravitz was wolfing down his second Egg McMuffin as he watched the video playback from security cameras that he had secretly installed to keep an eye on the night crew. He perked up and stopped chewing when he saw the tall man with the severely burned face crying over the body of Carmen Morales.

The shooter was a southpaw. Phee called Kravitz to ask him if the forensics indicated whether or not the killer was a lefty as well. After he confirmed that he was, Kravitz then asked Phee to stop by his office because there was something that he needed to show him and Quincy. Phee grabbed a cab and made it to Kravitz' office in twenty minutes. Kravitz was a bit disappointed that Phee was alone. He assumed incorrectly that Quincy would have been with him. Although Clay scared Kravitz the most, Phee certainly did his share of leaving the M.E. feeling nervous, especially when left alone with him. Quite frankly, he'd had his fill of the two Freeman men to last him a while. They both managed to leave him feeling that his welfare was easily jeopardized in their presence.

"Phee, uh, your father came to see me yesterday. Well actually, I mean, he came to see your brother. I really don't want to get in the middle of anything here, but I thought you and Quincy should know that when he was leaving, he looked at Carmen Morales' body."

"And?" Phee asked.

"Well, uh, he knew her."

"What do you mean he knew her?" Phee asked confused.

"He knew who she was. And then, when I came in this morning and saw this, I thought you should see it," Kravitz said as he pressed the playback button on the video monitor. Phee watched Blue Morales weep over the body of his murdered daughter.

"He came in after hours, paid the night staff, and didn't sign in. I ripped my guy that was on duty a new asshole, but all he said was that the man claimed to be her father but didn't leave a name or any contact info. The first time I met your father years ago, I'm pretty certain that this was the man that was with him. It was the night he got burned. That's all I know."

Phee stood still, staring at the playback, absorbing the information, and trying to figure out his father's connection when his phone rang.

"Hello?"

"Hey, Phee, this is Diego, Barnes just woke up."

"Don't let anybody in his room. I'll be there in fifteen."

"You got it," Diego said as he hung up.

"Look, Kravitz, I know you didn't have to tell me about all of this, but I appreciate the fact that you did. I owe you," Phee said as he turned and hurried out before Kravitz could respond.

Despite how much he feared both father and son, Kravitz gave them props when it came to one thing: the Freeman men knew how to pay their debts.

46

Barnes had a dream that he met the Devil. Even though he was taught not to believe in the personification of Satan, in his dream, the "The Son of Perdition" was a living, breathing being. He was tall and faceless, but Barnes knew who he was right away. He dreamed that they were in a neglected garden, and he was running as fast as he could through the thorny labyrinth. The Devil was restless and angry as he chased Barnes through the never-ending maze. Just as he was nearly caught, Barnes awoke to find Phee hovering over him. He was simultaneously aware of two things, one was the anger in Phee's eyes, and the other was the growing pain at his core, where he had been repaired. The fear of seeing Phee, and the darkness that accompanied him, gave Barnes a momentary sobering jolt of adrenaline. He was lucid enough to be afraid.

For several minutes, Phee was deathly quiet, ominously frozen, just a few inches from Barnes. He didn't seem to blink or breathe. He just stared as though he were an angry boy contemplating the fate of a captured insect. As Barnes nervously darted his eyes back and forth, he noticed for the first time the reason his pain was surging with each moment. Phee made a point of showing Barnes that he held the detached morphine drip in his hand. The pain was varied and kept finding ways to top itself. At times it was throbbing, then without warning, it turned into a searing blade. Barnes grew more and more reluctant to even breathe, because the simple effort was increasingly more painful.

"Please," Barnes pleaded as he looked at the morphine drip.

"The pain that you're feeling right now is nothing compared to what I came to offer." Phee spoke quietly and with an even delivery that bordered on monotone. Barnes could see every detail of Phee's face and, more importantly, the dangerous intent in his eyes. There was something resolute yet mechanical in his stare.

"Let's keep this real simple. You're either going to tell me what I need to know, or I'm going to kill you. How much pain you feel between those two facts is entirely up to you. You and your group believe in the whole vengeance thing over turning the other cheek, don't you? So when I tell you that I'm not here as a cop, for your sake, I truly hope you understand that. Just as I hope you understand that my brother being killed trumps any bullshit notion you might have about what I'm willing or not willing to do. Who was in the truck with you?"

Although Barnes was terrified, he still remained obstinately silent.

"Fine, now things get interesting," Phee said as he casually crossed to the tray next to the Mayo stand and picked up a large thirty-cc syringe. As Phee picked up the syringe, he continued nonchalantly talking to Barnes. "The bad news is that the doctors actually think you have a good chance of making it. The good news is that a lot of times they're wrong. I worked a case two years ago where a nurse's husband was in a car accident with a chick he was bonin' on the side. He was banged up pretty badly, just like you. The nurse went to his room with one of these irrigation syringes and filled it up with air, just like this," Phee said as he held the syringe up and pulled back the retractor to suck in air. As Barnes nervously watched him, Phee turned and disengaged the IV line running from the Mayo stand to Barnes' arm. "So when she put the air in the central line, it didn't take much time for it to get into his system and start doing its damage. As the air traveled to his heart, the guy had a couple of seizures. Then he became incontinent and started pissing and shitting on himself. By the time the air actually reached his heart, he had a pretty scary cardiac episode, but unfortunately , that didn't kill him. Now this is my favorite part. The air then traveled to his brain and cut off the oxygen supply. Poor Romeo was still conscious just before he had what they call cerebral embolisms. Basically, his brain had all of these little explosions in it. There are some pretty fucked up ways in this world to die. I'm not saying this is the worst, but it's good enough for you."

Barnes was weak but summoned what strength he had to try and dissuade Phee. "Please. His name is Varelli. Anthony Varelli."

When Phee came out of Barnes' room, Diego was pacing and waiting on him. "Did you get what you needed?" Diego asked.

"He just kept fading in and out. I don't think he's going to make it."

As Diego watched Phee hurry to the elevator banks, there was suddenly the distinct sound of an emergency alarm coming from Barnes' room. Two nurses appeared out of nowhere and rushed into the room to check the machines that were helping to keep Barnes alive. As they crossed to him and started working on him, one of the nurses quickly exited the room and frantically called for a doctor.

"What's wrong with him?" Diego barked at the nurse.

The nurse never looked directly at the cop. She just threw her response back over her shoulder.

"He's in cardiac arrest."

As Phee stepped into the elevator and pressed the down button, his nose started bleeding and his head started bothering him again. There was a hollow ringing that was followed by a strange buzzing and pain. The buzzing sounded like a wounded bee trapped somewhere in the base of his skull. His blurred vision along with the sounds in his head were the obvious results of the concussion he'd sustained. Although he adamantly denied the magnitude of his injuries to Quincy, the pain and sudden onset of vertigo momentarily buckled him just after the elevator doors closed. He wiped his nose on his sleeve, like a child with a cold, steadied himself on the steel handrail, and rode out the indeterminate seconds of pain and dizziness. As he reached the ground floor and made his way toward the exit, Phee held steadfast to the fact that nothing short of death would stop him from doing what he had sworn to do.

47

Phee got Jelly's info from Detective Alvarez. After he stopped by his place and picked up his car, he drove down to East 13th Street. When he had parked, he checked the clip on his Glock, entered the building, and walked up the four flights to Jelly's apartment. Halfway up, his phone rang. When he looked at the caller ID, he saw Quincy's name. He ignored the call and turned his phone off just before he reached Jelly's door. He didn't bother to knock; he just kicked the door in with his gun pointed before him. The sparse studio only had three pieces of furniture: a bed, a desk, and a chair. The space was a box, literally. It had no windows, and what served as the bathroom was a poorly constructed addition to the illegal apartment. The room felt like a slightly upgraded jail cell. Phee looked in the bathroom, then crossed to the pile of papers on the desk. He placed his gun down and thumbed through old newspaper clippings of the Varelli murders. After reading a few of them, he picked up a manila folder with eight by ten photos inside. He was completely caught off guard by the image of his brother staring back at him. The shot was taken when he was still alive. As he continued looking though the folder, he saw a few more surveillance shots of AJ, then of Carmen Morales, and then the disfigured man who visited her at the morgue. Phee's heart stopped when he finally got to several photos of his own father. He hunched over and leaned on the desk for support. At first, he was confused by the blood that dripped on his father's photo, until he realized that his nose was bleeding again.

As Phee heard a faint creek of the floorboard behind him, he grabbed his gun and spun around, pointing it at the sixty-some-thing-year-old Armenian woman who stood there in her bathrobe and house slippers.

"Who are you?" Phee demanded.

"I'm the landlady. Who the hell are you?" the woman said.

Phee flashed his badge, "I'm a cop. When's the last time you saw Anthony Varelli?"

"He hasn't been here in going on two weeks now. What's going on? Do you have a warrant to be here? You can't just break my door like this."

Phee grabbed the folder and pushed by the woman, who continued to complain. As he raced down the stairs, his vision grew fuzzy, and he lost his footing. He tumbled down the last four stairs, losing his phone in the process. He got up and staggered out the front door. He still heard the sound of the landlady's shrill voice ringing in his head, even as he crossed the street to his car. He got in and gunned it, trying to get to the Waldorf as fast as he possibly could.

48

Zibik was in her cell rereading the *12 Laws of Power* when Quincy and Maclin approached her.

"Good news, Dr. Zibik, you get to go back to your cozy cell at Bedford Hills," Quincy said cheerily.

"What are you talking about? Did you find the killer?" Zibik asked.

"No, but we will."

"Then you still need me."

"No, actually we don't. At the end of the day, you're a waste of time. We can't believe half the shit you say anyway. Trust me; you're much more a hindrance than help."

"Is this the part where I'm supposed to play the remorseful servant who vows to be more obedient?"

"Not at all. It's the part where you continue to play the

pompous asshole that's too arrogant to realize her uselessness. You've outgrown whatever perception of value we thought you had, Dr. Zibik. And truth be told, you're not worth the energy and effort that we would now have to spend trying to protect you while at the same time trying to solve our case."

"Okay, I'll bite. What the hell are you talking about?" Zibik asked.

"You don't get to ask questions."

"Fine. Good luck in finding whoever killed your partner's brother."

"Keep your luck; you'll need it more than we do."

"You send me back now, and you'd be making a big mistake, and we both know it."

"It couldn't be any worse than the mistake we made by actually thinking you would be straight with us," Maclin chimed in.

"I've been straight with you. You might not like what I have to say, but I've been straight."

Quincy took another step closer to the cell.

"Oh really? You said you didn't recognize any of the names on the list, and yet it turns out that the owner of the SUV was one of the clowns at the quarry," Quincy said.

"I didn't lie. The only person at the rock quarry that I knew was Stringer. Since I've been incarcerated, he's the one that's been running things and doing all of the recruiting."

"So now are you pretending that you have no idea what's going on in your little group?" Maclin asked.

"I didn't say that. It's pretty difficult to micromanage every detail. That's what Stringer is for. He runs the big things by me."

"And you trust his every decision?" Quincy casually floated the question.

"Implicitly," Zibik said with conviction.

"Unfortunately, for once I actually believe you," Quincy said, sardonically.

"So, why the disappointment?" Zibik asked, confused.

"Because the idea was that you would be of help to us, but the truth is, you're being played just as badly as we are."

"If you were to enlighten me as to what you're alluding to, I might be able to either share or disavow your skepticism."

"The thing I love most about your smug attitude, Dr. Zibik, is the challenge of crushing it."

"Did you ultimately come here to discuss my ego and attitude? That seems like a waste of both of our time."

"You're right. I came here to share something with you that I thought you might find as interesting as I did. We have Stringer's boy from the quarry in the hospital. We went through his texts and voicemail and found a few goodies. Since you probably won't believe the texts, I want you to hear this. This message was left a half hour before our meeting at the rock yard," Quincy said as he pulled out the cell phone and played back a message through the speaker.

"Hey, it's Stringer. You might already be out at the quarry. I'm on my way now. When you get this, make sure you place the shooter on the southwest mount to get the best view. Like I told you earlier, if the cop becomes a problem, tell your man to take him out. Just make sure he doesn't touch Zibik. I'm the only one that gets to kill her."

Zibik tried to hide it, but Quincy and Maclin saw it all over her face. It was one of the rare instances in her life where she neither controlled nor comprehended a situation. Gone was her accustomed hubris. Quincy didn't have the luxury of gloating because his only chance at getting something useful from Zibik was dependent on how well he played the small window of vulnerability and confusion that the good doctor was currently experiencing. Quincy had to walk the fine line of not appearing too eager or desperate for Zibik's cooperation. He resisted the urge to ask Zibik questions, because he knew the very act would have been turned into a game of wills. Quincy chose instead to play his hand close to his vest. He cuffed Zibik and brought her out to the car along with Maclin for the ride back to Bedford Hills.

Zibik hadn't said a word since hearing Stringer's voice message. She sat in the back seat of the car, quiet like a disappointed child. She seemed unaware of the periodic glances that Quincy threw in her direction from the rearview mirror, as Maclin got in the car Zibik was in her own world, shattered as it was by the revelation of Stringer's betrayal. As Quincy turned the car on, he looked again at Zibik in the rearview and tossed back what he needed Zibik to believe was his parting offer.

"Your last shot at giving us anything useful."

Zibik stared out the passenger rear window, ignoring Quincy.

"We all know how smart you are, Dr. Zibik. You gotta ask yourself whether or not, once Stringer accepts that he missed his one shot to kill you, he will get somebody to do it for him in prison. That's a hell of a long time to be looking over your shoulder," Quincy said.

When Zibik didn't respond, Quincy threw the car in drive and pulled off. Five blocks later, Zibik finally spoke.

"My father died at forty-nine."

Quincy and Maclin looked at each other, uncertain of Zibik's point. They both remained silent as Zibik continued looking out the passenger window speaking to neither one of them in particular.

"He had this horrible neurodegenerative condition called Huntington's disease that literally ate his brain away. Four years ago, doctors told me I had the same thing and would more than likely die the same way he did, and even around the same age. The last thing I wanted was to die in prison. You're a good cop, Detective Cavanaugh, but as you would say, you were played from the start. Stringer set the whole thing up."

"What exactly does that mean?" Quincy asked.

"Somehow, he found out about the new program the Feds and the Justice Department were trying, using cons to help them with current cases. He told me he had a way of getting me out and keeping me out. He knew the odds of you coming to me were great, because the crimes were so unique and similar."

"So did he orchestrate the recent murders?" Maclin asked.

"I can't say for sure, but now it looks like it," Zibik answered.

"You want us to believe that Stringer put all of this in motion, and you had no idea or knowledge of what he was doing?" Quincy added.

"You've already made it quite clear that you don't believe anything I say, so I don't expect you to start now," Zibik responded.

Quincy made a choice not to respond. He felt that he was finally figuring Zibik out. For all of her brilliance, Zibik was very much like a child. Too much attention only empowered her and left too many balls in her court. But indifference to her made her much more cooperative. Quincy pretended to be disinterested in Zibik and what she had to say. As he continued driving, Zibik became more impassioned in her protests.

"Whether you want to or not, you have to accept that you need me, because I'm the only one here that knows where he hides his secrets. So you can either waste valuable time driving me back to prison, or you can take me to Stringer's house and let me show you how to get to the bottom of all of this. Choice is yours, but I think my motivation in helping you should be pretty obvious."

49

We were under so much scrutiny that we always did pretty extensive background checks on all new members. We needed to know as much as possible about who we let in," Zibik said as she, Quincy, and Maclin entered Stringer's house and walked past the two uniformed cops that had been posted at the single-family home.

"Cops already searched this place. If there was anything here, they would have found it," Maclin said.

Zibik looked at Maclin and smiled.

"Nice to know that you have a sense of humor, Agent Maclin."

Zibik led them down to a finished basement that served as a rec room/home office. She crossed to the pool table and removed a section of felt and rubber, revealing a hidden flash drive. "We could have hidden Jimmy Hoffa and the Holy Grail down here with the same results," Zibik said sarcastically.

As Maclin took the flash drive and turned on her laptop, Quincy walked over to a nearby wall that was filled with various framed pictures of Stringer and other people. Even though many of the photos chronicled what appeared to be significant events and people in Stringer's life over the last several years, Zibik was curiously absent. Quincy spied Zibik staring at a five by seven photo of Stringer and an attractive brunette. The woman and Stringer were both beaming as they stood in front of the Ferris wheel at Coney Island. As Quincy feigned preoccupation, he caught the short wave of anger that rose in Zibik at the sight of the photo. Quincy couldn't place it, but for some strange reason, the woman looked vaguely familiar to him. Once Zibik realized that Quincy was looking at her and the photo, she turned her back and looked in the opposite direction. Quincy snuck the framed photo into his overcoat, just as Maclin called him over.

"Got something," Maclin exclaimed. As Quincy and Zibik crossed back to join her, Maclin scrolled though the various photos and profiles of Zibik's followers.

"Okay, 637 members. We've got photos, general background, medical and even financial records," Maclin explained.

"I told you we were thorough," Zibik said.

"And evidently, expensive; they require their members to tithe 20 percent of their income," Maclin said to Quincy.

"Wow, I thought Christians were bad enough at 10 percent," Quincy said.

"The truth costs more; what can I say?" Zibik added.

"That's one way of looking at it," Quincy smirked.

"And what's the other?" Zibik asked.

"That you actually make not believing in God cost twice as much as believing in Him."

"Quincy, do any of these men look like our shooter?" Maclin asked as she scrolled through all of the males' photos.

"No, he's not here," Quincy said.

"Type in the words: SACRED SERVANTS. All upper case," Zibik instructed.

As soon as Maclin input the information and pressed enter, a separate file opened with the photos of twenty men and their individual profiles.

"What is this?" Quincy asked.

"Every revolution needs soldiers," Zibik answered.

As Maclin scrolled down, Quincy recognized Jelly. "That's him."

Maclin read the details on Jelly out loud. "Anthony Varelli. Says he joined a year ago after several years in and out of prison, mostly assault and battery. Witnessed his parents and brother murdered when he was a child. Suffered some type of post-traumatic stress disorder, which left him a deaf-mute. Dates another member, by the name of Sonia Wu. Looks like four months ago Stringer hired a private eye to help track down the two men responsible for the murder of Varelli's family."

Quincy sat across from Maclin as she continued searching and reading Jelly's file.

When photos of Clay and Blue popped up, Maclin suddenly stopped reading and looked up with shock. "Quincy, you need to see this."

50

Sonia Wu went shopping earlier, per Jelly's request. It was by no means a recreational spree. He gave her very specific instructions. He even had her stop back by the hospital to pick up a couple of items. Jelly spent the last week thinking of the best way to abduct Clay, and now that he was ready to make his move, he knew it would require a well-thought-out strategy and a few helpful props. As he outlined his plans, he offered her many chances to walk away. He explained to her that after tonight, there would be no turning back. Sonia made it clear that there would be no swaying her. Her devotion to him was unconditional. No matter the dangers, she would be by his side, come what may. Before Sonia met Jelly, she greeted most days with the contemplation of suicide. He gave her love, life, and purpose. If need be, she was willing to die for him.

As she rode the elevator to Clay's floor, she played back in her mind every detail Jelly instructed her to do. He made a point of going over everything with her twice. The only thing that turned her on more than his take-charge demeanor was his inclusion of her in what would be the final chapter of his revenge. After two elderly women exited the elevator, Sonia removed her overcoat, revealing the black housekeeper's outfit that she'd purchased earlier.

Clay drank more the last three days than he had in the last three years. AJ's funeral was only a day away, and it seemed the closer it got, the more he drank. Since the news of his son's murder, he'd been in a constant state of self-medication with the finest scotch money could buy. In three days' time, he'd gone through three bottles of Macallen 1937, which went for about ten thousand dollars a bottle. When he'd run out of the high-end liquor a few hours earlier, he'd switched to the best that the hotel had to offer, which was a bottle of Johnnie Walker Blue. Although the blend wasn't quite up to his standards, it at least accomplished the task of keeping him drunk. Clay always carried two cell phones in separate pockets, one for business and one for private matters. He pulled the private one out to check the time. He was hoping to hear back from The African, whom he had dispatched earlier, to find out if any of their connections in Harlem knew anything.

No matter what he did, he couldn't escape the despair. His moments of clarity were the hardest. Thoughts and memories flooded his mind like a breached levee. No matter how he tried to reason it, there was no dismissing the fact that he played some part in his own son's death. Worst-case scenario, it was somehow connected to the murders of Honey Boy Jones and the Varelli family. Even if by some fluke it was all one great coincidence that AJ and Carmen were killed by the same person and in the same manner, Clay was still guilty of allowing his son to die as a family reject. He had broken one of the most sacred bonds of parenting: he had made his love for his children conditional. Fatherhood for him came with a price tag. It was not to be given freely, but rather negotiated and purchased by his sons. Phee willingly paid the price, with hero worship and constant adulation. Clay was ultimately better at being an exalted deity than a flesh and blood father. He was ever the philosophical drunk. The more inebriated he was, the more enlightened he became. In his drunken state, it was the first time that he ever considered the possibility that maybe all of these years he'd had it wrong. Maybe AJ was the stronger of his two boys. He thought about the strength of character required to stay faithful to one's definition of self, rather than reaping shallow rewards from the appeasement of others. Phee was who he was because of his father. AJ had been who he was in spite of him.

Clay finished the last of his scotch and stared bleary-eyed at a nature special on the murmuration of starlings. He sat hypnotized by the impossible ballet that the flock of thousands performed over the skies of Scotland. The syncopation and movement of the birds lulled him to the point that his eyelids felt like steel awnings. He started nodding off and enjoying some of the peace that had eluded him for days until a maid knocking at the door woke him.

"Turndown service," he heard the thin voice on the other side of the door.

He wobbled a bit as he stood and staggered toward the door. He threw on a nearby evening jacket, which effectively covered the gun in his waistband. As he looked through the peephole and opened the door, he found an Asian maid with unnaturally blue eyes.

"My apologies for disturbing you, Mr. Freeman, but would you like turndown?" she asked.

"Sure," Clay said, still a bit groggy. As he let her in, he turned and walked back toward the television. Sonia Wu left the door slightly ajar as she headed in the direction of the bedroom.

"You're new?" Clay asked, just before she reached the bedroom doorway.

"Yes, sir; they added a couple of us for the holidays."

"Why so early?"

"Excuse me, sir?"

"They usually don't come until seven, it's only five."

"We…uh…well, sir, I was told to start my rounds at five."

Clay wasn't sure why he made the young housekeeper so nervous, but the fact that she was sweating before him caught him off guard. He was the type of man that was hypersensitive to his environment. Sounds, sights, and smells, not to mention his ever-reliable gut feeling, always served him well. Even in his drunken state, he picked up on the vibe that there was something about the woman's energy that was definitely off.

The minute Sonia made it into the bedroom and out of Clay's sight, she sent Jelly a text that she was inside Clay's room and the door was unlocked.

After dropping Sonia off, Jelly sat in a parking spot across the street. He wore the Dickie brand white pants and shirt that Sonia rented earlier. Having scouted the hotel front and back a few days earlier, Jelly knew the truck that picked up the hotel's linens came at five each day. He waited in the alley that led to the hotel's loading dock. Just as the driver arrived on time and got out of his truck, Jelly ambushed him. The man wore a similar Dickie brand white pants and shirt uniform underneath a coat with the company's name on it. Jelly knocked the driver unconscious and stuffed him in the back of his truck amongst the piles of fresh linens. After he took the man's coat and ID badge, he entered an employees' entrance, pushing a laundry bin of linens past a posted security guard. Jelly immediately pushed his cart onto a service elevator and headed up to Clay's floor. The disposable phone that Sonia bought him vibrated shortly after he got off the elevator. Once he read that she was in Clay's room, he knew his plan was working perfectly.

Clay got a call from The African.

"You were right. It does have something to do with Varelli. A private detective was asking some of de old-timers about who had conflict with Varelli and Honey Boy Jones. Dey were specifically asking about a man with a burned face," The African explained.

"Where are you now?" Clay asked.

"Just leaving 110th Street. I should be back at de hotel in fifteen to twenty minutes."

"Make it fifteen. We need to figure this shit out," Clay said before he hung up the phone. Just as he put his phone in his pants pocket, he noticed that his door was slightly ajar. Now that he knew he was a target, he couldn't afford laxity in even the simplest of things. As he crossed to the door and reached his hand out to close it, suddenly the edge of the door slammed into his face. Clay fell back about five or six feet. His lip was busted and it spewed blood from the blow. He knocked over an entryway table, shattering the glass vase that was filled with winter orchids. As soon as he hit the ground, Clay instinctively reached for the gun in his waistband as he recognized the con from the elevator as the intruder. Before Clay could raise the gun, Jelly was on him, knocking it away. For a man in his sixties, Clay was impressively fit and agile. He took a beating from the younger, stronger man but managed to squeeze in a few blows of his own. As Jelly reared back to deliver another punch, Clay grabbed a shard of the broken vase and stuck it into his attacker's side. Jelly was winded as he was stabbed close to his previous injury. Clay managed to wrestle himself free from the wounded Jelly and crawl toward his gun, which lay four feet from him. Just as he reached it and went to pick it up, he felt a sharp prick in the back of his neck. He grabbed the gun and rolled over to find the Asian housekeeper standing above him with a syringe in her hand. Clay tried to lift the gun, but all of his motor skills completely failed him. He lost all sensation in his body as the gun tumbled to the floor. Sonia Wu watched a helpless Clay succumb to the shot of succinylcholine, a quick-acting paralyzing agent. When Jelly saw that Clay was completely incapacitated, he opened the door and wheeled in the laundry bin. He removed enough of the linens to make room for Clay's body. Jelly dug into one of

Clay's pockets, pulled his cell phone out, and tossed it on the floor. Once he placed Clay in the bin, he covered his prey and quickly exited with Sonia in tow.

Clay was fully alert. He no longer felt the pain from the blows he'd endured. All he could do was watch intently as Jelly roughly lifted him and threw him in the laundry bin. He locked eyes with Jelly just before Sonia covered him with a pile of sheets. Clay was disoriented by the darkness that surrounded him. The only visual he had was the memory of Jelly's eyes before the blackness. Clay knew death. The various lives he took over the years gave him an intimate perspective. Despite all the close encounters and narrow escapes in his lifetime, Clay now lay paralyzed and helpless with the knowledge that death had finally come for him.

51

In the winter of 1990 the Tri-state High School Athletics Commission named Phee outstanding athlete of the year. Each year, the stats of student athletes were submitted from New York, Connecticut, and New Jersey. It was the first time in the organization's forty-year history that a freshman took the honors. The awards ceremony was held in New York, in the ballroom of the Waldorf Astoria Hotel. All major sports colleges attended, along with a dozen or so current NFL players and several hungry scouts as well. Phee was presented with a four-foot high trophy and the bombardment of heavy handshakes and backslapping from ambitious recruiters. Even as he was mobbed, he never lost sight of Clay and Dolicia, who sat at a table front and center beaming with pride. It was a night that he knew he would never forget. The only damper was the reminder of his brother's absence as he stared at the empty chair beside his mother. AJ was stuck working late at the law firm where he had been interning on his Christmas and summer breaks.

As soon as the ceremony was officially over, Phee grabbed his large trophy and walked twelve blocks in the snow to AJ's job. A few holiday shoppers and strangers on the street congratulated him on his award and wished him well. By the time he made it to his brother's job, his exposed hands were nearly frostbitten, but none of it mattered to Phee because he was determined to relive and share as much of his amazing night with AJ as possible. The security guard knew Phee because Clay owned the building. After congratulating him and letting Phee warm his hands on the small space heater beneath his desk, the guard unlocked the elevator and sent Phee up to the law firm on the 33rd floor.

It was twenty past ten, and most of the lights were out on the floor. It was quiet, with no signs of life. Phee walked to the cubicle that his brother worked from, only to find it empty. Down the hall, he noticed a light shining underneath the office door of his brother's boss. When he got closer to the door, Phee heard movement and muffled cries, along with the rhythmic sound of flesh slapping flesh. Phee pushed the door open and saw his brother bent over a desk with his pants down around his ankles, while his boss, whose pants were also down, was grinding the front of his body into AJ's rear. As Phee dropped his trophy, it broke in half on the marble floor. By the time AJ's boss looked in the direction of the noise, Phee was upon him. At fourteen years old, Phee was already 6'3" with the developed body of a grown athlete. He grabbed the older man, tossed him to the floor, and began beating him viciously. AJ pulled up his pants and tried as best he could to stop his younger brother.

"Phee, stop please," AJ pleaded.

Phee was both blind and deaf with rage. It was the first time in his life that he knew he was capable of killing someone.

"What the fuck are you doing to my brother?" Phee said as he continued to pummel the bloodied face of AJ's boss.

AJ tried to stop Phee by grabbing his right arm, but Phee, who was lost in a violent zone, simply tossed his brother aside. Just as AJ's boss was losing consciousness, AJ, not knowing what else to do, hit Phee with a chair to stop him. The physical interruption was just enough to break Phee from his kill zone.

"What the hell is wrong with you?" Phee snapped at AJ.

"You're gonna kill him, Phee," AJ said hysterically.

"I don't care. He deserves to die for what he did to you."

"No, he doesn't. He didn't do anything that I didn't want him to do."

"What the hell are you talking about?"

"I asked him to."

Phee involuntarily opened his bloodied hands, letting go of AJ's barely conscious boss. He looked at his brother, deeply confused and wounded.

"You mean you're really down with this fag shit?" Phee asked.

"Phee…"

"People been saying things about you for years, but I was always the one standing up for you. Now you're telling me that it was a lie all this time?"

"I never lied to you or anybody else about who or what I am. You and Pop are the ones who lie to yourselves every day because I don't fit some convenient image that you all need me to. You're my brother, and I love you for who you are. I just wish you and Pop could do the same."

"You ain't my brother."

"Don't say that, Phee. No matter what, I'm always your blood."

"Fuck you! From this day on, you ain't shit to me. You hear me? You ain't shit to me."

Phee rose and crossed to the door, never looking back, as AJ knelt down to aid his boss.

After Phee told his father all the sordid details of what he had witnessed, Clay made the decision that his fourteen-year-old son was now old enough to be charged with the responsibility of restoring the family's honor. Phee accepted the task and made a phone call to The African that would haunt and cost him for many years to come. The next day, while AJ's boss was at home healing, he received a visit from The African. No one ever heard from or saw the attorney again.

52

The pounding in Phee's head started again as soon as he left Jelly's apartment. He sped up Madison Avenue as best he could in his desperate attempt to save his father's life. This time of year, all major avenues were congested with tourists and shoppers on the already overpopulated New York streets. After getting stuck in traffic between 48th and 49th Streets, he reached for his phone to warn Clay. When he couldn't find it, he punched the steering wheel and cursed loudly as pedestrians nervously crossed in front of him. Phee abandoned his car on 52nd Street, amidst the snaillike pace of the holiday gridlock. Cars honked furiously at him as he got out and ran as fast as his spinning head and heavy legs allowed him. By the time he made it to 56th and 5th Avenue, he found himself doubled over vomiting as disgusted passers-by gave him a wide berth. Despite his bleeding nose and the increasing buzzing sound in his head, Phee forced himself to push on.

By the time he reached his father's hotel, he looked like warmed-over bear shit. Phee drew his gun the minute he got off the elevator and saw his father's door standing wide open. He fought to control his rising panic as he noted the signs of violence in the room. He hurried past the blood and broken vase to check the bedroom. Just as he was coming back out of the bedroom, he heard a noise in the doorway. Phee quickly spun his gun in the direction of the sound and found himself pointing it at The African, who simultaneously had his gun pointed at Phee.

"Where the hell is my father?"

"I don't know. I just got here."

Phee looked through him as though he were a total stranger.

"Phee, put your gun down. It's me, Solomon," The African said as he slowly lowered his gun, hoping Phee would follow suit. The African was always quite fond of Phee. From the first time he met him, he saw in the young boy great character and an uncorrupted soul void of darkness.

It wasn't the barrel of the gun pointed in his direction that scared The African the most; in his lifetime, he'd had more than a fair share of guns trained on him. The thing that scared him was the hollowness in Phee's eyes. It was a look that The African remembered all too well from his childhood and the unconscionable things he and his fellow child soldiers were forced to do. It was a look he had seen in Clay's eyes several times when he commanded The African to kill. It was the same frigid stare that he saw every day of his life staring back at him from the reflection of a mirror.

"Phee, please put your gun down," he said calmly, hoping Phee would recognize the familiar tone of his voice. Phee blinked a few times and steadied his breathing. He slowly lowered the gun as he continued staring in The African's direction.

"I just spoke to your father fifteen minutes ago. Should I try calling him again?" The African asked.

"Absolutely not," Phee said as he crossed and picked up Clay's discarded phone and examined it. "Give me your phone." Phee insisted. He took The African's phone and immediately starting dialing.

"Hopefully my father still has his second phone on him. I can get one of my guys at the station to track him that way," Phee explained.

Phee was growing impatient, until he heard a voice pick up on the other end after five rings.

"Hey Alvarez, it's Phee. I need you to stop whatever you're doing and get a GPS track on a number for me. It's an emergency. As soon as you get the info, call me back on the number I just called you from. No, I lost my phone. No, I'm not with Quincy. Look, Alvarez, stop asking questions, and just do what the fuck I say okay?" Phee snapped.

After Phee barked the numbers to Alvarez, he hung up and quickly crossed to the hotel phone and called the manager.

"Terry, this is Phee. There's been a crime committed in my father's room. Send up security to seal it off. I need you to have your guys pull up the past thirty minutes of video surveillance of this floor. I'm on my way down now."

Phee hung up and turned toward The African.

"Gimme your car keys," Phee demanded.

"I'm going with you."

"No, you're not."

"You need me, and we don't have time to waste arguing," The African said firmly.

"Look, I don't…"

"Phee, unless you're willing to kill me right here and right now, I'm going with you."

The African clearly held the advantage because they both knew unequivocally that death was the only possible contender in keeping him from finding Clay. Phee reluctantly accepted the fact that further protest would be futile. And though there was no verbal acknowledgment, the two men reached an understanding. Phee hurried through the door with The African right behind him. Although he knew some but not all of the horrible things The African did for his father, there was never any doubt in Phee's mind that this man would, without hesitation, lay down his life for Clay. As they rode down the elevator in silence, he found himself glancing at the hands of his father's protector; they were heavily scarred, with two fingers missing. These were hands that intimately knew violence, just the sort of hands that Phee needed to help him kill Varelli.

53

Quincy looked over Maclin's shoulder at her laptop as they both read all of the googled articles pertaining to the Varellis slaying, along with surveillance photos and detailed profiles of Clay and Blue Morales. Pulling out his phone, Quincy called the station. "Alvarez, call the Greenwich police and have them send a car out to Phee's father's place and send one of our guys over to the Waldorf in case he's here in New York. We just found out he's a target," Quincy rattled off as Maclin continued pulling up info from the confiscated flash drive, while Zibik sat nearby, trolling chat rooms on Stringer's home computer.

"It's too late. Something already went down," Alvarez responded.

"What are you talking about?"

"Phee called a little while ago and told me to put a GPS track on his father's phone. I just called him back with the info and he told me his father was abducted by some guy named Varelli about twenty minutes ago," Alvarez explained.

"Oh shit! I need the locale on his father right now."

"Sure, I tracked his phone to a place out in Nassau County, 924 Lake Edge Way. Phee made me promise not to call the local cops. What's your take?"

"Phee's right. We go in with sirens and lights and Varelli will kill Phee's father for sure."

"How do you know he hasn't already?" Alvarez asked.

"If he just wanted to kill Clay, he would have done him on the spot and not taken the extra risks of abducting him. This guy has been dreaming of this night for over thirty years. He's got something special planned. Our best shot is to try and surprise him. I'm on my way now. Get there as fast as you can," Quincy said, just before hanging up and ushering Maclin and Zibik upstairs and out of the house. Maclin cuffed Zibik with her hands in front of her, so that she would have a chance of balancing herself for the turbulent ride ahead. She then jumped in the front passenger side as Quincy peeled off down the street, despite the four inches of snow and the treacherous driving conditions. It was only two days ago that Quincy admonished Phee for his reckless driving, but now that Clay's life was in imminent danger, Quincy sped down the slippery blankets of snow with more determination than caution.

"In case either of you are interested, I found Stringer," Zibik said, holding on to the back door for support.

"Why didn't you say something?" Quincy asked.

"It happened while you were on the phone."

"Where did you find him?" Maclin asked.

"In a chat room… He was boasting about being elevated tonight."

"How about we stop with all the monkey talk and you just tell us what's going on?" Quincy demanded.

"He posted an image of two nesting sparrows, which means two souls will be taken tonight. The fact that they're nesting together means that they will be taken at the same time. A dual soul catching."

"In addition to Phee's father, I'm guessing it's safe to assume that Varelli has Blue Morales," Maclin said.

"And when Varelli attempts to take their souls, trust me Stringer will be right there with him," Zibik stated.

"What makes you so sure?" Quincy asked.

"You read the file. Stringer mentored him. The father of a God is a God in his own light. It's the kind of moment that people like us live our entire lives waiting for. The killing of the woman and your partner's brother were merely warm-ups. What better way for Varelli to make them suffer than to kill their family before killing them," Zibik said.

"Sins of the father revisited on the heads of their firstborn. The ultimate revenge," Quincy added.

"Revenge is a much more limiting outlook. I wouldn't expect either one of you to understand, but it goes much deeper than that. Retribution is much more in keeping with our teachings," Zibik added.

"No matter how you try and dress it up, it's all the same thing," Maclin countered.

"Hardly, revenge is only self-serving; retribution puts us all on par with what you call God. After all, why should he have all the fun?"

Quincy slammed on the brakes at a stoplight and Zibik jerked forward face-first into the back of the front seat.

"I'm sorry, Dr. Zibik, you were saying something," Quincy said as he smirked into the rearview mirror.

Zibik collected herself and held on tighter to the door. "My point exactly, Detective."

"What role does the girl play in all of this?" Quincy casually asked.

"I'm afraid I'm not following you."

"The brunette, back at the house in the picture... I couldn't place her when I first saw her, but I knew she looked familiar. Of course, she looked a lot different from the first photo I saw of her when she was dead. Samantha Vick isn't it? A bank teller, one of the three people you were accused of killing, or soul catching, or whatever the hell you call it."

"Accused, but never proven," Zibik clarified.

"Save it. So at least now we know why Stringer wants you dead. What was it, some kind of lover's triangle gone bad? Did Stringer leave you for her?"

Even though the very subject angered her and brought back feelings of jealousy and rejection, she tried to mask her state as best she could. "I have no idea what you're talking about."

"Of course not. Let me ask you a question. What good is it to think of yourself as a God when you're still plagued by the same petty bullshit as the rest of us? I guess even Gods get jilted too," Quincy said as the car raced down the snowy street.

54

How many men have you killed?" Phee asked as The African sped toward Long Island.

"Why?" The African responded.

"Just curious."

"In de end, does it make a difference?"

"To the ones you've killed and their loved ones, I would imagine so."

"But in de eyes of God, it's all de same, whether I've killed one or one thousand, and therefore not worth counting."

"So you actually believe in God?"

"Only in times of weakness."

It dawned on The African that no one had ever bothered to ask him such a question.

Phee pressed for more, "Then how do you...?"

"What? Do the things I do? I said dere are times I believe in God. I never said anything about ever fearing Him. Only de man with a soul fears God. I gave up such inconveniences a long time ago."

"Do you really think someone giving up their soul is an easy choice?"

The African shot Phee a look that told him that he was either offended by the question or disappointed in him for asking it.

"What is it dat you think you know about me, Phee? I mean besides de things you've heard."

Phee just looked at him quietly, knowing that The African was right, that although they had been in each other's lives for years, there was very little Phee actually knew about his father's protector.

"Did you know dat when I was seven, Idi Amin's soldiers came to my village, put a gun in my hand, and made me choose between killing either my mother or my father? I chose to kill my mother, because children born during de madness of war know de horrible things dat animals do to unprotected women. My father then begged me to kill him, so dat de rebels wouldn't have the pleasure of torturing and making sport of him, and so I did. For the next four years de soldiers made me do things dat…you weren't born to understand. By de time I was eight, I lost count of de people I tortured, killed, and maimed. My superiors used to laugh and call me one of deir most perfect weapons. For four years I stayed with de same twenty soldiers dat abducted me and forced me to kill my parents. At age eleven, on de four-year anniversary of deir death, I killed my entire unit while they lay drunk and high after a raid on a tiny village in de Acholi region. So to answer your question, I never said giving up one's soul was easy, or always by choice. I just think dat when necessity and choice are de same thing, it doesn't always leave a lot of room for things like God and souls."

Phee stared at The African ashamed of himself that he'd known this man the majority of his life and yet, not only did he not know anything of importance about him, but this was the longest and most in-depth conversation they'd ever had.

Phee was troubled by a distant memory.

The beelike buzzing was still bothering him, but the exchanges with The African gave him better things to focus on. Phee looked out of his window and then suddenly started the conversation that he had wanted to have for years.

"Do you remember when I was fourteen and found my brother with his boss? Me and my father sat in his office and decided what to do to them for dishonoring the Freeman name. He disowned my brother and then told me it was time for me to be a man, and he made me decide right then and there what should be done to my brother's boss. I called you and told you to 'handle' it. We never talked about it again, and that was the last anybody ever heard of him. But tonight I think I got a right to know how a man was murdered because of me. I'm not a kid anymore, Solomon."

"No you're not, Phee. Your father saved my life shortly after I came to this country. I've never disobeyed him directly or even indirectly, except for one time. When you told me to handle AJ's boss, I asked you dat night on the phone if you knew what dat meant. And even though you said you did, I knew you really had no idea what it truly meant to kill or have a man killed. How dat simple choice brands you and defines you for de rest of your life. When I went to AJ's boss, I made sure dat he knew what his fate was and what would happen to his entire family if he didn't leave de country forever and completely disappear."

Phee stared at the man incredulously.

"You know if my father had ever found out, he would have killed you."

"Yes, I know."

"Then why did you risk it?"

"Because had I killed him, it would have ultimately cost you much more than it could have ever cost me."

"But in all this time, why did you never tell me?"

"Because, Phee, you don't need anyone to tell you who you really are."

55

Sonia and Jelly went to work as soon as they got back to the house. Candles were lit, and two pentagrams were drawn in the large kitchen that had previously been transformed into two makeshift altars by Jelly in anticipation of this night. After tying Clay to four posts on one of the altars, Jelly brought Blue Morales up from the basement and secured him in the same way. Although Blue was pale and sickly, he still had enough life left in him to satisfy Jelly's needs. Blue's eyes perked up ever so slightly at the sight of Clay. Clay's paralysis had worn off ten minutes ago, and he was able to turn his head and face Blue. Jelly had given Sonia specific instructions to make sure the drugs' effect only lasted long enough to transport Clay from the hotel to the house. He wanted both of his victims to feel every cut. He wanted them to know the sensation of their skin and muscle being separated in preparation for their souls being expelled from their bodies. Sonia washed a paring knife and two crescent-shaped daggers in distilled water and placed each one on the small table that sat between Clay and Blue. She did everything that Jelly instructed her to do, handling every detail with great delicacy. She was aware of the fact that he could have done everything by himself in half the time, and yet, because he loved her, he made sure she was an integral part of his night of retribution and his full ascension as a God.

Stringer arrived with three of his men. He posted two outside as guards and only allowed one in to witness the ceremony. He stood by quietly and watched as Jelly and Sonia made the final preparations. Stringer thought about how Zibik had mentored him and how he had, in return, found an amazing protégé in Jelly. Because of the hate that motivated him, Jelly was malleable mentally, philosophically, and most importantly spiritually. Stringer had proven to be a much better teacher than student. He failed miserably when Zibik presented him with the opportunity to put his faith to the ultimate test. He was certainly no soul catcher. Not that he was above killing, but he lacked the fortitude to actually cut open another human being in hopes of capturing the unseen. Before he met Zibik, Stringer was best described as a recreational Satanist. He was a part-time follower who privately viewed the religion as a passing fad but publicly proclaimed his membership, because it made him feel original in certain circles. Zibik was the one that educated him on the ways of the true religion and eventually the hybrid version that they currently practiced. It was Zibik who introduced him to the concept of soul catching. Even though

Stringer often felt that his faith left him feeling battered and that his religion sometimes took more than it gave, he continued to believe in the possibilities of greatness that Satanism presented to him. He watched Jelly prepare with one part envy and two parts pride. The night was supposed to have been a night of retribution for both men, but Stringer allowed himself to be outsmarted by the cops and lost his shot at killing Zibik personally. There were contacts he had in prison that he could hire to finish the job that he failed. Although he hated the fact that he now had to revert to his backup plan, he comforted himself with the assurance that no matter what it took, or how long, Stringer would still be the one responsible for the death of Dr. Daria Zibik.

56

Watching Jelly meticulously prepare his two victims, Stringer thought back to the night he witnessed Zibik capture her first soul. It was a retired college professor from Canada who had discredited Zibik's father and led the witch-hunt against him back in his teaching days.

Stringer remembered the night vividly.

"Wash the dagger in distilled water," Zibik commanded.

Stringer's hands trembled ever so slightly as he did what he was told. He caught eyes with the terrified professor, who was bound on an altar, still pleading for his life. As Stringer tried to turn away, Zibik forced him to stare at the helpless man.

"Owning another man's fear is the first part of owning his soul," Zibik said calmly.

As Zibik lifted the dagger and began chanting an ancient

Mayan prayer, Stringer looked in the direction of Samantha Vick, who stood quietly in a nearby corner. Stringer and Samantha were the two followers that Zibik felt showed the most promise. She chose Stringer to be her assistant and allowed Samantha to serve as an observer. Although the three of them had talked for weeks about what would happen to the professor, the discussion of killing a man and the actual act proved to be as vast as it was difficult for Stringer. As he struggled with his role in the ceremony, Samantha tried as best she could to encourage him with the assuring smiles she threw his way anytime he looked in her direction.

"If the two of you focused more on the things that you're supposed to, you might actually convince me that what I saw in you was real potential, and not just my own misguided sense of favoritism," Zibik chastised them both.

"I'm sorry, Dr. Zibik. It won't happen again," Stringer said sheepishly.

He forced himself to focus on the tasks at hand as best he could and fought to remain indifferent to the deafening cries of Zibik's victim. Zibik refused to gag the professor, because she wanted to hear every sound that the dying man could offer. Stringer held it together for the first few incisions. Pretending that the blood that oozed from the cut man's skin was actually something other than what it was. Zibik covered parts of herself in the victim's blood and proceeded. She was a master cutter. Somehow she managed to keep the professor alive for a few seconds, even after opening him and severing the first organ. They each knew the exact moment the man died. The frozen look of agony etched across the professor's face was the most horrible thing Stringer had ever seen. Even though he was eventually able to turn away, the one thing that Stringer wasn't able to ignore was the smell. The combination of fear and fresh blood coupled with urine, vomit, and bodily gasses made Stringer swoon. Just as Zibik finished gutting the professor and completing the last stanza of the prayer, Stringer lost his lunch. He bent to his knees and vomited what looked like a week's worth of food. Even though Zibik was both disappointed and irritated with Stringer's pitiful bout of weakness, she worked much faster because of the crucial window of opportunity while the soul was at its most vulnerable. Because both Stringer and Samantha were looking down and otherwise preoccupied with Stringer's collapse, neither one of them actually saw the precise moment that Zibik intercepted the professor's soul. They each thought they saw a flicker of light brighten the room followed by a short breeze that blew in opposite directions. What they were sure of was the difference in Zibik by the time they each looked at her again. It was a look that Stringer would never forget. He couldn't find the exact words to accurately describe how his mentor looked. The best that he could come up with was that Zibik looked illuminated.

As Stringer drove Zibik back home, no one spoke about what had just happened. And though he had a thousand questions, he knew his act of weakness in the moment of truth had forfeited his right to ask anything. When they pulled up to Zibik's house, she sat frozen for several uncomfortable moments.

"Dr. Zibik, I'm so sorry for letting you down," Stringer said.

"We all have our roles to play. At some point you'll have to decide what yours is. Not all men were born to be Gods," Zibik said as she exited the car.

Stringer needed Jelly to be successful tonight. He needed him to accomplish things that he himself had been unable to. Just like parents who came up short on their own dreams, the redemptive shot of greatness was often cast upon the shoulders of their children. He needed to prove to himself that Zibik was wrong about him and the role that life had assigned him. Even if only by association or inheritance, Stringer was determined to be illuminated.

57

The African turned down the street that Jelly's house was on. They drove past two crows feasting on the carcass of a smashed squirrel. As the car neared, the birds hopped on the curb as if they were in a sack race. Just as he and Phee got to the end of the cul-de-sac, they both noticed the guard posted in front of the house. As the guard looked in the direction of their vehicle, they both caught a glint of metal in his right hand. The African calmly made a U-turn and headed back up the street.

"What are you doing?" Phee demanded.

"Easy Phee, we don't know what de situation is in dere; no need to announce our arrival."

The African cut off the lights and pulled over half a block up the street. He reached under the seat of his car, pulled out a handgun, and attached a silencer. He handed the weapon to

Phee with an extra clip, and then grabbed a gym bag from the back seat.

"What about you?" Phee asked referencing the gun.

"Don't worry about me; I've got what I need. You take de front I'll go in through de back."

Even though Phee had his own gun, he took the offered weapon and turned to exit, until The African stopped him with a firm hand on his shoulder.

"Dere are things dat I'm gonna have to do when we're in dere Phee, and I can't be worried about you being a cop," The African said.

"You don't have to worry; I'm not a cop tonight. Just do what you do," Phee said as he exited the car and made his way back toward the house.

Phee made a quick jog through neighboring yards. His vision blurred a couple of times from the burst of energy. He hid behind a bank of snow-covered hedges, taking a second to clear his head. The last ten feet to the house was completely open terrain. The crunchy, thick snow beneath him made the thought of an unannounced arrival impossible. He burst from behind the bushes and ran as fast as he could toward the guard. As the guard turned and raised a nickel-plated .38, Phee popped the man twice before he could get off a shot. Pffft, pffft, the two bullets knocked the guard off the porch and deposited him with a thud in a mound of snow. The imaginary bees that Phee heard in his head returned, seemingly angry at having been awakened.

The African was a living myth. A fantastical legend that was embellished upon each time tales of his exploits were told. There were those that labeled him a ghost. A man killed at least a hundred times or so who repeatedly refused to stay dead. Some said that he sold his soul to the devil at the tender age of eleven. Others said that he was the devil. However blurred the lines of fact and fiction, there was one indisputable truth: The African was the purest of killers. The guard at the back door had probably never heard the urban mantra that proclaimed, "Bad boys moved in silence and violence." He never saw death coming. One second the guard was standing and sucking on a cigarette; the next he was facedown in bloodied snow. He looked like he was lying on a bed of cherry-flavored snow cones. The man died terribly confused.

58

For all of his hatred, for all of the years that he begged for this moment, Jelly performed his duties in a very calm manner. He took his time, obviously relishing every second. When all preparations were complete, Jelly made the first cuts. He positioned Clay and Blue in such a way that they could easily see each other and everything that was being done to them. Jelly wanted them to witness the methodic torture that both men would endure. Knowing that Blue was the weaker of the two, he decided to use him to help break Clay and prolong tormenting him. Jelly started on Blue, then moved over to Clay. As was the practice, the initial cuts were simple and clean. He made surface wounds that were only meant to serve as an introduction of the victim's blood. It was a bloodletting with the added advantage of inducing great terror. Jelly had been taught by Stringer that the first step to owning a man's soul was owning his fear. Nothing scared a man more than the sight of his own blood. Jelly heated the paring knife in the flame of a nearby candle. As he ran the hot blade across Blue's chest and the blood began to run, he saw the panic that he was after. Clay on the other hand was much more of a disappointment. He never showed fear. Loathing, indignation, even resignation, but never fear. Jelly wondered how Clay's resolve would fare when the gutting began.

After he finished the first phase of the ceremony, Jelly instructed Sonia to stand a few feet away in the corner, which was near the back door. He wasn't sure how she would handle what came next. Even though she was fiercely dedicated to his cause, and even though he had told her in detail what he had done to the others, the actual act of seeing another human being disemboweled was a traumatic undertaking even for the strongest of wills. He placed her in a position where she could see as much, or as little, as she could handle. Even though Stringer stood front and center, Jelly noticed that the guard was off to the opposite side of the kitchen, where he intentionally had a much more limited line of vision. Jelly grabbed one of the daggers and stood over Blue and mouthed the words of the Mayan chant that Stringer taught him. Next he reached for a razor blade and cut both of Blue's eyelids.

"Wait a minute, please. It wasn't me. Clay was the one. I mean he made me come here. I tried to talk him out of it, but he said he had to kill Varelli. Please don't do this to me. It was Clay, not me," Blue pleaded and lied as blood rolled down both sides of his face like red teardrops.

Blue yelled and struggled in vain as he watched Jelly raise the dagger above him. He cried and continued begging. He vehemently placed all the blame on Clay and said that he was solely responsible for the death of Jelly's family. Every incision that Jelly made only served to heighten Blue's desperate thrashing about. He was eventually weakened by his injuries and blood loss. The closer he got to his death, the more his body succumbed to the dreaded calm of his own defeat. Blue was simply too weak to continue protesting. Unfortunately for him, he never went into full shock. He was conscious and aware of the things Jelly did to him. Blue was still alive when Jelly cut him open. As the blade exposed his innards, his head fell to the side facing Clay. He wasn't certain, but he thought he heard Clay's voice above his torture. He couldn't tell what he said, but he thought he heard it nonetheless. Even though Blue was in a fog and fading, he saw Clay staring at him, offering himself as the last piece of familiarity Blue would see before dying. Just before the light left his eyes, Blue had flashes of the first time he and Clay met and other key moments of his life. His first love, his mother dying, Slopes taking him under his wing, and other highlights he hadn't thought about in years. The very last thought that Blue had before he died was of his daughter Carmen and how on the day she was born her beauty and helplessness alone had almost saved him from a life of crime…almost.

After opening him, Jelly literally saw Blue's lungs take in their last breath and the second they stopped moving. Jelly continued cutting and removing organs until Blue's torso was empty. He then covered himself with Blue's blood so that the detached soul could recognize him as its rightful owner. Jelly was the first to see it rise. A translucent mass of energy that was as real and as beautiful as anything he'd ever seen. It was even clearer than the soul he had taken from Carmen Morales. Sonia, Stringer, and the guard felt the presence more than actually seeing concrete evidence of the soul's extrication. They felt its presence solely on the power of their faith. What they did see was a noticeable change in Jelly. Each of them at different times was convinced that they saw a faint ring of light surrounding him. They saw what their faith had taught them to see. Clay simply saw a madman, covered in blood, surrounded by candles. After successfully catching the first of the two souls, Jelly checked once or twice to see how Sonia was holding up through the ceremony. Although he could tell that she was overwhelmed and queasy, he saw her determination to see it through. He saw in her the type of resolve and unconditional faith in him that made him love her even more. Stringer's guard was not as strong as Sonia. Jelly saw him throwing up in a corner. Stringer stood fifteen feet away, willing himself to stay engaged. He refused to be defeated, as he had been the first time. Jelly even looked at Clay to see his reaction. The older man's face was still a mask of contempt. He still refused to give Jelly what he wanted. Clay may have been terrified, but he refused to show his fear. The two men were locked in a battle of wills, but Jelly was convinced that Clay would break long before he was separated from his soul. Now that he was finished with Blue, he wanted to see how much longer Clay could shelter his fear.

59

Clay no longer believed in souls. It was a privilege and responsibility that he'd relinquished years ago in what he eventually defined as the spring of his emancipation. It was an awakening when he no longer felt that he was imprisoned by the delusion of salvation. He reasoned that the burden of belief only compromised ambitious men like him and decided the night he killed the Varelli family that he was no longer bound by the precepts of virtue and morality. Not that he could ever be mistaken for a righteous man, but that night marked a dark turning point in his descent. From that night forward, he never had occasion to question the ramifications of his moral turpitude. The few times in his life he had actually worried about death were based more on the toll it would take on his family than his own dread of loss. Clay was much too pragmatic to fear death and thought only a coward or fool feared the inevitable. Just as he had taken many lives, he accepted the likelihood that he would also be killed. The only surprise in the equation was that it took so long for fate to finally catch him.

He was not intimidated by Jelly and stared back at his captor defiantly, as though he held some powerful secret that gave him the upper hand. Even as Jelly stood over him mouthing the Mayan chant and holding the dagger, Clay smiled, having found victory in defeat because he knew whatever Jelly was looking for underneath the flesh, whatever spiritual delusion he was under, he would only be disappointed in what he would find or, more specifically, what he wouldn't.

When Jelly reached for the razor blade to cut Clay's eyelids, he felt a draft of cold air, saw a quick flash of movement, and turned to see The African holding Sonia from behind with a large serrated Bowie knife at her throat.

The African recognized Sonia from the video surveillance at the hotel. After she and Jelly abducted Clay, they were recorded kissing in the freight elevator on the ride down. Jelly was standing too close to Clay with a dagger in his hand for The African to risk a direct attack. Sonia was the bargaining chip. Jelly froze with the dagger in his hand not certain what to do. The African had him in a position where he had to decide whether or not to sacrifice the one person in the world who he loved the most in order to kill the person he most hated. They were at a momentary standstill, both threatening to kill what the other held most sacred.

As Stringer's man reached for his gun, Phee came in firing. Stringer crouched behind a counter and pulled out his own gun.

In the process of firing at Stringer and his guard and dodging their return, Phee managed to squeeze off two shots in Jelly's direction. One of Phee's shots whizzed just a few inches in front of Jelly's face, kicking out plaster dust from the wall behind him. When Jelly ducked, he fell backward and ended up two feet or so farther from Clay. It was just the separation The African needed. He knew the one thing that would redirect Jelly's focus and fury. The African locked eyes with Jelly, stuck four inches of his Bowie knife into Sonia's stomach, and cut her gut to gill with the same indifference he would have used in cleaning a fish. She died on her feet staring at Jelly as though she somehow still expected him to save her. Jelly made the sound of a wailing boar, as The African tossed her body aside and advanced toward him. The two men collided like wrecking balls even as gunfire continued around them.

Phee reloaded as Stringer and his guard attempted to flank him from both sides. A burst of adrenaline brought back the warring bees in his head, but the bigger problem was that his vision began to distort. As he held Stringer in his sights, he started seeing double. He fired at the image on the left, but Stringer kept advancing. Phee adjusted his aim, focused on the image to the right, and squeezed off another shot, which wounded Stringer and dropped him to the floor. Stringer's gun slid across the room as he fell over a piece of abandoned furniture. Phee turned his attention to the guard who was coming at him from the left. Once again his eyes played tricks on him, and he saw double images of the man. This time, Phee aimed at the image to the right, fired, and hit the guard in his thigh, putting him down for good with a second shot square in the chest.

As Phee crossed to his father, Jelly and The African were still pitched in their fight to the death. Both men bled profusely from the knife wounds that they inflicted on each other. They were equal in strength, intention, and hate. Armed with the ceremonial dagger, Jelly did as much damage to The African as The African did to him. They stabbed each other half a dozen times, but both refused to die and continued to stab each other repeatedly until their momentum carried them crashing through a bay window and out onto the chaste snow below. Phee untied Clay and covered him with his overcoat.

"You okay?" Phee asked as he hugged and kissed his father.

"Yeah," Clay responded.

When Phee crossed to the broken window and looked down, he saw the crimson circle where the two men had fallen. Jelly was faceup, submerged in a few inches of blood and snow, both knife and dagger firmly planted in his chest. He looked like a perverted art project, some over-the-top thesis on violence and winter.

Just before he died, Jelly was convinced he saw a warm light two feet above him. He thought it was beautiful, and for some reason it reminded him of his mother. He wanted to touch it, but his entire body was numb and unresponsive. He watched the light churn and dance above him like leaves being chased down a street by a playful wind and let go of the various things that held him captive to the world. In the end, his only thoughts were of his love for Sonia and the beautiful light that hovered above him. His final conscious thought was of the sensation of weightlessness he felt as the light carried him and dispersed in the dark, frigid air.

As Phee looked closer, he was puzzled that The African was nowhere to be found. A few fading footprints in the snow accompanied by a warm blood trail that disappeared into the night was all that remained of him.

When Phee crossed back to Clay, he saw movement in the adjoining room where he shot Stringer and his guard. He raised his gun and moved toward the source. Stringer was bleeding and crawling in the direction of his fallen gun. Phee moved in quickly and kicked the gun back toward the kitchen. As Phee pointed the gun down on Stringer, he heard Clay in the background say, "Go ahead and finish him."

60

Quincy pulled up and parked a few homes away from Jelly's house, checked his gun, and turned to Agent Maclin. "I need you to sit on Zibik. If I don't call you in five, that means we don't control the situation. Call Captain Bellamore; she runs homicide outta the two-nine. Have her send some cars for backup."

"But shouldn't we…"

"You gotta trust me on this one. More than likely Phee is already inside. That's either gonna help us or hurt us." Quincy cut Maclin off.

"It's rude to bring a girl to the prom and then expect her to stay in the car, Detective Cavanaugh. Surely you're not going to deprive me the satisfaction of coming in," Zibik said from the back seat.

"Afraid so, Dr. Zibik. Not sure what I would do with myself if, somehow, something horrible happened to you in there," Quincy said sardonically as he opened his door and bolted toward the house.

Zibik looked out the window of the car and watched Quincy disappear. She then turned her attention to Maclin's every move, waiting for the perfect time to strike. Agent Maclin jumped on the phone and called Captain Bellamore at the 29th precinct and requested backup. As she hung up the phone, she looked back toward the house. Maclin hated waiting. The more anxious she grew, the more her body craved the steadying effects of the pills. The second she put her hand in her pocket and reached for them, Zibik made her move. She threw both hands over Maclin's head and started strangling her with the links of her handcuffs. Zibik kept her knee planted firmly in the back of Maclin's seat for optimal leverage. Maclin desperately grabbed at Zibik's hands and tried to free herself, but unfortunately, Zibik was deceptively strong. Agent Maclin thought about her gun and tried to calculate exactly how much time it would take her to reach and unholster it. In the time she released one of her hands, she knew she would be giving Zibik yet another advantage. On the other hand, with each passing second, she could feel her larynx closing and her breathing becoming more and more restricted under the heavy pressure of the cold metal around her neck. Maclin waited a second too late. By the time she released one hand and tried to reach for her gun, Zibik leaned back in such a way that she nearly lifted Maclin over the seat. Maclin fumbled for the gun but was ultimately too weakened to pull it out once she put her hand on it. Her eyes watered and bulged, and saliva escaped through the corner of her mouth. Zibik kept pulling until she felt Agent Maclin's body go limp and there was no more resistance.

61

When Quincy entered the house and walked past the second dead guard, there was little doubt in his mind that Phee was inside. As he quietly came around the corner with his weapon drawn, he saw Phee standing over an unarmed Stringer, pointing his gun at him.

"Go ahead and finish him," Quincy heard Clay tell Phee.

"Phee," Quincy said quietly as he attempted to divert his partner's attention.

Phee quickly pointed his gun at Quincy and looked at his partner as though they had never met. He was dark and distant. There was coldness in his foreboding stare. Phee was wild-eyed, and his nose was bleeding as he kept his gun pointed at Quincy. Quincy stepped out of the shadows, holstered his gun, and opened his arms to show that he was in no way a threat.

"Phee it's me, Quincy. Put your gun down, okay?" he gently implored. "Where's Varelli? Phee, where's Varelli?"

Ironically it was the mention of Varelli's name that got a response from Phee. He looked at Quincy with more recognition. "He's out back. He's dead."

"Okay, then it's over. We got him and your father's fine. Now put your gun down."

"It ain't over yet," Phee said as he took his gun off Quincy and pointed it back down on the wounded Stringer.

"Yes it is," Quincy quickly retorted.

"It's not over, Phee, until you finish it," Clay said from the background.

"Listen to me, Phee; it's over," Quincy said more pointedly. "Varelli's dead and Stringer will spend the rest of his life in prison."

"You and I both know it doesn't always play out that way," Phee said flatly.

"Maybe, but the law is still all we got."

"Yeah, well, sometimes that ain't enough, Quincy."

"The next move you make you'll end up carrying with you the rest of your life."

"You're right. Could you live with yourself, knowing that you let someone who was responsible for your brother's murder just walk away? Before you lie and pop off some self-righteous bullshit, make sure you look me in the eye and tell me man-to-man."

Quincy took a couple of steps closer, so that Phee could see him better.

"The truth is, I don't know what I would do if someone killed

Liam. I've come close to crossing lines over lesser things. Maybe I would kill that person in cold blood, but since we're talking truthfully, you gotta hold yourself to a greater standard than me, because you're better than I am, always have been. You're better than your father, and you're certainly better than that piece of trash lying at your feet. You're what keeps me from crossing those lines, so I'm begging you, Phee, for both our sakes, don't do this."

Phee looked back at his father, who stared at him blankly. As he turned back to Stringer with his gun still leveled at him, two shots rang out. Stringer died instantly from gunshots to the gut. Quincy quickly reached for his gun as it took a second to register that Phee hadn't fired his weapon. Both cops turned to find Zibik standing in the doorway, both hands raised above her head, dropping Maclin's gun to the floor. Quincy, who was the closest to her, rushed her and kicked the gun away as he threw Zibik to the ground. Both cops kept their guns trained on their prisoner.

"What the hell did you do to Agent Maclin?" Quincy demanded.

"Don't worry; I didn't kill her. I just put her out and borrowed her weapon," Zibik said smugly as Quincy turned her around and cuffed her.

Quincy pulled his phone out and hit redial. "Alvarez, what's your location?"

"Just turning on the block now," Alvarez answered.

"We've got the scene secured. Check my car for Agent Maclin. She's down. Call for an ambulance." Quincy hung up and turned back to Zibik.

"I told you she was fine. I had no reason to kill her. You should be thanking me, Detective Freeman; I actually did you and your father a favor by killing Stringer," Zibik boasted.

In the background the sound of distant sirens could be heard.

"You with all of your retribution bullshit can spend the rest of your pathetic life telling yourself it was worth it," Quincy added.

"Sorry to disappoint you and your sense of justice, but more than likely I'll be dead within the year. So yes, it was definitely worth it," Zibik gloated.

"I'm in the dark here. What went down between her and Stringer?" Phee asked.

"The rock quarry was a setup. Stringer was gonna kill her," Quincy said.

"It's funny how nature weeds out the weak. I tried to teach him how to be a God, but he was ultimately too hung up on a simple woman to appreciate what I was offering," Zibik said bitterly.

"Is that why you killed Samantha Vick?" Quincy asked.

"No single person can ever be greater than a belief. She was holding him back, preventing him from living up to his full potential. At least everything I taught him wasn't in vain. He showed Varelli how to be the God he himself wasn't able to be."

"So then ultimately you're just as much responsible for all of this as Varelli and Stringer," Clay said as he walked closer.

"That's subjective. I'm no more responsible than you are. We all have…"

BAM, BAM, BAM! Three gunshot wounds to the face, neck and chest stopped Zibik from talking forever. Even though she was already three times dead, Clay continued shooting her with Stringer's gun until the loud boom of gunfire was replaced with the repeated sound of metal striking metal. When he knew he was done, he dropped the emptied gun as Phee finally recovered from the shock and subdued him. As the sirens got closer, Phee held his father and looked at Quincy.

62

Phee sat in the holding cell with Clay and listened to him give painful details about the night he and Blue killed Varelli and his family. Clay started slowly, hesitating, and at times, seemingly allowing himself the needed respite in the long pauses between his thoughts. At some point the more he told Phee, the easier it got for him. He talked about his life beyond the night at Varelli's. Clay told Phee things about himself that were even more incredulous than the hyped whispers and rumors that Phee had heard his entire life. He was calm and direct, neither boasting nor apologizing about his past. Phee noticed how his father's entire demeanor changed with the unburdening. It dawned on him that he was hearing things that Clay had never told anyone. Although neither one considered themselves to be religious men, they were each in their own way lifted by the power of confession. Phee's job exposed him on a daily basis to murderers, robbers, drug dealers, and more, but he had never met anyone whose life had proven to be as criminally fascinating as his father's. From the time he was a child, he worshipped Clay and revered him as nothing less than a God. Clay's confession in no way lessened Phee's love for him, but under the dim lights of the holding cell, he finally saw his father for what he really was, an amazingly flawed human being imprisoned within himself.

When he ran out of things to say, Clay sat quietly with his son.

Clay's attorney knew which judge to wake. It took a couple of hours, but Clay was released on his own recognizance. As a formality, he surrendered his passport. In total, it was just over four hours after Clay gunned down Zibik that he was back home in Connecticut, resting peacefully in his own bed. Clay owned the DA and half the prosecutors in New York. He and his lawyer liked the odds of him getting off for killing Zibik.

63

After his father left, Phee lay on the bed in the holding cell. His nose started bleeding again, and the pain in his head came back. The pounding slowed and was more manageable if he didn't move at all. All he could do was lie there and think. He thought about the case, his father, Brenda, and inevitably his brother. The thoughts of AJ were what ended up calming and soothing him the most. The vivid replay of childhood memories from years long gone played over and over again in his mind. He kept thinking of the summer of '82, when he and AJ were eight and ten, respectively. June 8th was the specific date that came to mind. It was the day that Clay arranged for Phee and AJ and their cousins to go to a special screening of the movie *E.T.* It was the same day that Satchel Paige died, one of the greatest Negro league baseball players ever. Phee remembered the day well, for both the good and bad. It was the day AJ became his hero, and it was also the first time Phee saw someone murdered.

Nineteen eighty-two was called the "summer of crack" up in Harlem. The cheap drug debuted earlier in inner cities throughout America, but this was the summer that the effects of its proliferation, and the consequent stranglehold, became more and more apparent. Increasing numbers of dealers and corner-boys set up shop in the streets and abandoned buildings from 110th all the way up to Washington Heights. Thousands and thousands of tiny plastic vials with different colored caps littered the gutters, schoolyards, and parks. Young brothas started dropping like rain from the constant turf wars and violent conflicts.

When AJ and Phee got back from the matinee, they headed over to the Rucker's basketball courts on 155th Street. AJ may have disappointed his father by not liking football, but there was no questioning his skills with a basketball. AJ was a finesse player, with unbelievable ball handles. From the time he could walk, his father used to take him to watch the Rucker's summer league, which boasted the best street players in all of New York, and arguably the country. Rucker's was the place that legends came to be born. Players with names like Earl "The Goat" Manigault, who was 6'1" and was said to have over a fifty-two-inch vertical leap and was able to snatch a dollar from the top of backboards and leave change before hitting the ground. There was Joe "The Destroyer" Hammond, who on one occasion dropped fifty points in one half on Dr. Julius Erving. And then of course there was Pee Wee Kirkland, who scored 100 points in one game and then 135 points in another. There was a short frame of time that AJ aspired to be a Rucker legend. Clay was much too busy being impressed with Phee's achievements on the football field to really notice the skills that AJ was developing at ten years old. AJ and his crew consisted of his earlier rival, Spider Harris and Spider's cousin Dookie. They ran three-on-three pickup games against fourteen-year-olds from other boroughs. The boys from Harlem would intentionally drop the first game and then go double or nothing on the second, which they always won. AJ and company were engaged in a do-or-die with three roughnecks from Bed-Stuy. The game was much more contentious than their usual encounters. AJ was the only one who was able to inject an impressive degree of athleticism into the muted slugfest. His basketball IQ was far superior to anyone else on the court. His many years of constantly trying to prove himself to his father served him on the courts much more than in his father's eyes. AJ did a shake and bake on his man, pulled up in a jumper, and drained the bottom of the nets. Eight-year-old Phee stood on the sideline, cheering his brother and new friends on as Spider immediately called a time-out and huddled up his teammates.

"AJ, what the hell are you doin'?" Spider demanded.

"Just tryin' to teach these suckas that they can't come to our house talkin' all that shit," AJ said defensively.

"You keep shootin' like Dr. J. and ain't nobody gonna wanna bet us no more. Let 'em win this one, and we'll be able to take 'em for twice as much next game," Dookie added.

"Okay, whatever," AJ relented.

As the three broke huddle, AJ inbounded the ball to Spider, who was immediately double-teamed. Trying to avoid a turnover, Spider quickly passed the ball back to AJ, who was now guarded by a big fourteen-year-old named Loc. Loc was an inmate in training, a junior thug before thuggin' became chic.

"Whatchu got boy? Don't piss yourself, you got a man on you now," Loc said teasingly.

"I'm shakin'. We only need one; y'all are down by two," AJ responded.

"Don't worry about us. We can handle a bunch of faggots from Harlem," Loc said.

Spider and Dookie both stopped playing and sighed heavily simultaneously, both knowing and regretting what would come next. After their initial fight, they had only been friends with AJ for a couple of weeks but already knew how he responded to taunting, particularly when the word "faggot" was used. AJ put on a dribbling clinic at Loc's expense. Incredible crossovers, stutter steps, and even a bounce pass, alley-oop to himself that he finished with a pretty finger roll layup. Strictly highlight reel material.

"Handle that punk," AJ said condescendingly.

Just as the two crews came to blows, a gunshot rang out. Everyone except Phee stopped and ducked to see a crackhead running from two pursuers who each fired shots in his direction. The crackhead was running at Phee, putting him directly in the line of fire. Phee stood frozen with fear as one of the bullets whizzed by, barely missing him. AJ got off the ground and ran quickly toward his younger brother. He tackled him and lay on top of him, putting his own body between Phee and harm's way. Less than five feet away from the two brothers, the crackhead fell to the ground from a bullet to his leg.

"Dre, I'm sorry, man. I'll get you your money tomorrow. I swear to God," the crackhead said as he tried to crawl away from the duo with guns pointed at him.

"I told you when you started slinging for me that if you ever fucked with my paper I'd bust a cap in yo' ass," Dre said as he continued pointing the gun at the pleading man.

"I know. This crack shit had me twisted for a minute, but I'm good now, man. I'm gonna make back your money for you. Every penny."

"Niggas just don't learn. You don't get high on your own supply," Dre said as he pumped two bullets into the man's body.

While all of the other kids had scattered and disappeared after the second shot, AJ continued protecting Phee, just a few feet from the dead man. As he looked up and saw Dre coming toward him, AJ instinctively attempted to shield his little brother. Dre kicked the bottom of AJ's foot and waved the two of them up with his gun.

"Y'all little motherfuckers get outta here. You don't keep you mouths shut I'll track y'all down and kill the both of you and your family, you feel me?" Dre said menacingly.

AJ nodded nervously, but Phee stared frozen at the scary man pointing a gun at him. When Phee didn't answer, AJ stood between Dre and his brother and spoke for him.

"He understands."

After Dre and his sidekick left, Phee started to cry. AJ grabbed him and hugged him.

"You ain't gotta cry, Phee. Nothin's gonna happen to you. I'm not ever gonna let anything bad happen to you, you understand me? One day when you grow up, you're gonna be big and bad just like Daddy, and you won't ever worry about anybody messin' with you. But I got you until then, okay?" Phee nodded weakly, trying his hardest to stop crying as AJ continued in his attempts to calm and assure him. "We can deal with anything, 'cause we're the Freeman brothers. We're gonna make a mark in this world and do big things, and ain't nobody gonna stop us," AJ declared. "Don't cry okay? 'Cause everything is cool. You trust me, right? Right?"

When Phee looked at his brother, he stopped crying because in that moment, he believed everything AJ told him. He felt there was nothing he couldn't do as long as AJ had his back. The two things Phee never forgot about that day were the details of the dead man beside him and the degree of courage and love that AJ showed him.

Not much happened in Harlem that Clay didn't hear about, especially when it concerned his sons. He had plenty of lackeys to deal with the things that he no longer sullied himself with. Punishing the men responsible for threatening and endangering his children was the first assignment that he gave to a young foreigner he had recently recruited. The young Ugandan henchman went by the name of "The African." The day after the shooting, both Dre and his accomplice were found murdered by the Hudson River, with their shooting hands cut off.

64

The doctor examining Maclin was tall with dark eyes and a noticeable Eastern European accent. The blue embroidery on his lab coat identified him as Dr. L. Saum. Maclin found him to be conventionally handsome, not particularly her type, but handsome nonetheless. His face was four inches from hers as he held her head in his hands and gently moved it back and forth and side to side. She could smell the fresh Altoid that she noticed him secretly popping into his mouth shortly after meeting her. Maclin was very aware of how he took his time with her, as though there weren't a million other patients for him to attend to.

"Agent Maclin, do you know if you bumped your head or not before you lost consciousness?" he asked.

Maclin's voice was hoarse when she spoke.

"Can't say for certain, but I don't think so. It happened in a car. I was choked out."

"Okay, open up," Dr. Saum said as he flattened her tongue with a suppressor and used his penlight to see down her throat. "Say ahhh."

"Ahhh."

Maclin was very aware of not only how close the two were physically but of how much he seemed to linger in her space.

"Looks like you've got a slightly bruised and swollen larynx. Until it goes down, you'll just have to deal with the sexy, raspy voice thing," he said trying to make a joke. He was happy when he succeeded in getting her to at least smile.

"If I were you, I would drink a lot of tea with lemon and maybe even gargle with warm water and salt to help the swelling go down. Try not to raise your voice or talk too much for the next twelve hours and see how you feel. Even though I don't really think it's necessary, I'm still going to want to run a CAT scan. I don't want to take any chances on anything bad happening to you."

Maclin tried not to show it, but she liked the attention. She had almost forgotten what it felt like to have a man show genuine interest and concern for her. She relinquished long ago the possibility of another man taking Willington's place. Maclin convinced herself that the extent of her need for a man in her personal life was rough, anonymous sex that at least reminded her that she was still alive. The more she looked at Dr. Saum, the more she appreciated the details of his smile and his attempt at subtle flirtation. Even though he appeared to be done with his examination, he made no attempt to leave her. They were interrupted when a nurse stuck her head in the door and beckoned him.

"Dr. Saum, we've got a motorcycle accident coming in. Paramedics are two minutes out."

"I'll be right there."

As the nurse disappeared, Dr. Saum turned his attention back toward Maclin and smiled.

"Well, duty calls. You'll probably be stiff and sore for the next couple of days, but if you take it easy, you'll be fine in no time. I'll write you a prescription for some Vicodin, in case the pain gets worse before it gets better. Are you currently on any other medication?"

"No," Maclin lied.

She wasn't ready to admit to him what she wasn't even ready to admit to herself. Her increasing dependency on medication was something that she kept telling herself she could control and even stop whenever she wanted to. The lie compromised her and almost cost her life at least twice with Zibik. On the other hand, she felt the drugs were the only thing that got her through the unbearable days and sleepless nights. Every day, Maclin felt guilty over what she was afraid of becoming and the true sense of powerlessness to stop it.

Dr. Saum wrote out a prescription and handed her the slip of paper with a smile.

"Would you mind if I asked you a question?"

"I guess that would largely depend on the question."

"Nothing too earth shattering, I promise," he said with a disarming smile.

"Shoot."

"So is there a Mr. Agent Maclin?"

Maclin couldn't help but laugh, "No, there isn't, and for the record my first name is Janet, Dr. Saum."

"Wow! That sounds so much better than Agent Maclin. And for the record, my first name is Losher."

"That's an interesting name. I've never heard it before."

Dr. Saum wrote his cell number on another prescription sheet and handed it to her. "Hopefully, I'll be able to see you again under less professional circumstances, and I'll explain the history of my name and try to come up with a few more interesting facts about myself."

"How 'interesting' are we talking?"

"You'll never know, unless you take a chance and call me." He walked to the door and turned back. "I'll send an orderly in to take you up for the CAT scan. I really enjoyed meeting you, Janet."

After he left, Maclin just sat there, quiet, thinking. She looked down at the two small prescription sheets in her hands as though she were trying to decide which one was needed most. As an orderly entered the room to take her for further examination, Maclin put one of the pieces of paper in her pocket and balled up the other one and threw it in the wastepaper basket on her way out.

65

Quincy was sitting at his desk writing his report, when Alvarez approached him.

"How's Agent Maclin?" Quincy asked.

"She's fine. I just checked in on her. They should be cutting her loose in about an hour. Listen Quincy, Asif and Bernie caught a case that you're gonna wanna look at."

"I finish this report, and I don't want to look at cases for at least the next month," Quincy responded.

"Trust me, you're gonna wanna look at this one. You remember the name Alvin Edwards? One of the Baptist preachers on Deggler's list?"

"Yeah, what about him?" Quincy asked.

"Two hours ago, he was chained to a cross and burned alive. Looks like somebody might be trying to finish what Deggler started," Alvarez said.

After the initial shock sunk in, Quincy grunted some unintelligible response. A look of surprise and confusion was the most he could muster.

"Yeah, that's exactly what I thought when I heard," Alvarez said.

"Where's Asif at now?" Quincy asked urgently.

"They just got back from the murder scene. They're down in files, going through the stuff we logged on the Deggler case."

Quincy abandoned his report and headed toward the stairwell.

Asif was an East Indian from Mumbai. He was a good homicide detective but certainly not on the level of Quincy and Phee. By the time Quincy met him and his partner, Bernie, down in the file room, the younger detectives already looked overwhelmed. They brought Quincy up to speed on the murder scene. After listening to them describe the details of the murder, the body placement, and specifics of the method of execution, Quincy knew that they weren't dealing with a random copycat killing.

"Shit!" Quincy exclaimed.

"What did we miss the first time around, Quincy?" Asif asked earnestly.

"I wish to hell I knew. You two focus on the current kill, I'll start with the files first thing in the morning, before the funeral," Quincy told them.

"Thanks, Quincy, we'll take all the help we can get on this one," Asif responded.

By the time Quincy made it back to his desk, he had the worst gut feeling he ever remembered having. He tried finishing his report, but he was so distracted that the simplest sentences took him forever to write. He picked up the phone and called a friend of his that worked at the Port Authority. Quincy had a hunch but didn't have time to go through the proper channels, so he called Lamar Adai directly. For twenty-seven years, Lamar worked for the Port Authority of New York and New Jersey, which policed and governed all modes of transport within the two states.

"Jesus, Quincy, you got any idea what it's gonna take to get you that?" Lamar bitched.

"I wouldn't ask if it wasn't important," Quincy pleaded. "I'll tell you what, Rangers make the playoffs, you got a pair of floor seats for the first two home games."

"I'll have something for you as soon as I can. No miracles, but soon," Lamar told Quincy just before hanging up.

If Quincy's hunch was right, which he prayed it wasn't, he was going to need irrefutable evidence. There was much too much at stake for him to make any major moves without it. At this point, as difficult as it was, all he could do was wait. He refocused his attention back on his report and somehow pushed himself through to finish it.

It was just past 10, and Phee was still lying in the cell with his eyes closed. Quincy approached, stayed outside the cell, and watched his partner for a few minutes without saying anything. When Phee stirred, Quincy finally spoke.

"You thinking about switching professions?"

"Hey. I just needed to chill for a little bit," Phee said, a little groggy as he slowly sat up.

"How's your father?"

"He's cool. His lawyer got him freed on his own recog."

"Yeah, I heard," Quincy said as he entered the cell and leaned with his back up against the bars. "He holding up okay?" he asked.

"You know my father always lands on his feet. Don't be surprised if by the time he and his lawyer are done, the mayor isn't pinning a medal on him and giving him a key to city."

"Yeah, well short of lying, I did the best I could for him in my report."

"Thanks. What's the word on Maclin?" Phee asked.

"Alvarez says they're releasing her soon."

There was a clumsy silence between the two, as though the conversation they were having was just a convenient distraction from the one they really needed.

"Listen, Quincy, I uh…well, I just needed to tell you…"

"You don't need to tell me anything, Phee. You and me, we're cool. Always have been, always will be—no matter what."

"Yeah, you're right," Phee paused and smiled. "So does this mean the next time you have to apologize to me for anything, I gotta make it easy on you?"

"Absolutely. What good is forgiving if I don't get something out of it?" Quincy smiled.

"Do me a favor. Give me a ride over to the hospital. Might as well get those tests done and over with."

"You apologize and volunteer to go to the hospital all in the same conversation. Should I be worried?"

"No, with the funeral tomorrow and then having to deal with my father's situation, I figure I might as well get it out of the way now."

"Sure thing. Just let me grab my coat."

66

On the ride to the hospital, Quincy and Phee talked as though they were trying to make up for lost time—as though they were two friends who hadn't seen each other in a while. Phee shared with Quincy some of the stories Clay told him. He talked a little about The African and even the made-up story he told Barnes to scare him into giving up Varelli's info.

"You actually used the bit about the vindictive nurse injecting air into her husband's heart?" Quincy asked, laughing.

"Shit, he started singing like the fat lady in an opera. Didn't know the asshole was gonna go into full cardiac arrest though."

"Well, unfortunately for him, he didn't die. I still can't believe you stole one of my oldest bits."

"If you're gonna steal, steal from the best," Phee said.

Quincy purposely avoided Asif's new case and didn't mention

the preacher that was burned. He wanted to wait, at least until after the funeral when Phee had one less thing on his plate. There were also conversations and hypotheses about the case that Quincy was just not ready to discuss with his partner.

Fortunately, when they got to the hospital, Phee didn't have to wait long to be seen. Sick and injured cops and firemen were treated better than the average Joe. While Phee was being evaluated, Quincy called Elena to tell her where he was and what time he expected to be home. The minute she heard Phee was in the hospital, she started getting upset, even though Quincy tried to assure her that he was not in any real danger. Twenty-five minutes after Quincy hung up with her, she and Brenda were at the hospital. Phee was diagnosed with a severe enough concussion that it was recommended that he spend the night at the hospital just to be safe. Phee looked at Quincy admonishingly as Brenda came into the room, upset that Phee hadn't bothered to call her personally. As she asked Quincy and Elena to give them some privacy to talk, Quincy smiled and discreetly pulled Elena out into the hallway.

"If Brenda doesn't kill him, he'll be fine," Quincy laughed.

"It's not funny, Quincy; you don't know how hard it is to be in love with a cop," Elena responded.

Elena's simple words reminded him that there were things that he and Phee took for granted, that would now have to be reevaluated and handled with much more discretion, now that both men had loves in their lives.

"You're right, and I apologize," Quincy said sincerely. "Look, why don't we just go home and take a long, hot bath. I'll do my best to show you how much I miss you when I'm not with you."

Quincy kissed her just the way she liked, long, wet, and hard. He kissed her like he was still trying to prove to her what a blessing he thought she was in his life. When he finished, she hugged him and smiled as they stood in the middle of the hallway, oblivious to all that passed by them. Elena slipped her fingers between his and headed toward the door, hand in hand, like a happy teenager.

Phee knew Brenda was pissed and tried to preempt the lecture that was forthcoming. "Look, Brenda, I know you're upset. I get it. I didn't tell you I was here because I didn't want you freaking out and worrying."

"No, Phee, you don't get it, because if you did, you wouldn't be patronizing me right now. And for the record, it's not just about you deciding that I don't deserve to know what's going on with you."

"Is this about the other night?"

"The other night and tonight are the same thing. You don't love someone, or choose to let them love you, only when it's convenient. I don't know how to turn things on and off like you, and the truth is, I don't want to learn. I've been in love with you since I was eighteen years old, and in all that time, the only thing I ever hoped for was the day that you would put me above whatever it is you fear most, but that's just not going to happen, is it?"

"I don't know what you're talking about," Phee said confused.

"The sad thing is that you know exactly what I'm talking about. You just pretend you don't. It's okay, though, because I no longer expect that kind of honesty from you. You should get some rest. You've got a big day tomorrow," Brenda said as she turned and walked toward the door. She put her hand on the doorknob and stopped. "I'll see you at the funeral. I'll even be at your side if you need me, but after that, I agree with what you said the other night. We definitely need to chill, but this time for good." Brenda didn't bother to turn around and look at Phee. She was gone while he was still trying to figure out the conversation.

67

By the time Elena walked into the café, Brenda was already seated, wearing Tom Ford shades and a simple but elegant black knit dress. Elena, also dressed in black, crossed over to her, kissed Brenda on the cheek, and slid into the booth directly across from her. There was a half-eaten omelet on Brenda's plate.

"Thanks for meeting me so early," Brenda said.

"Of course. So sorry I'm late, I had to take my father for a walk before I left," Elena said.

"It's okay. I was starving, so I started without you. How's your father doing?"

"Great, he's recovering a lot faster than the doctors thought he would. He's started this cute little habit of writing me letters and leaving them around the apartment for me to find."

"That's really sweet." Brenda smiled.

It took a while before Brenda finally removed her sunglasses. When she did, Elena wasn't sure, but she thought Brenda's eyes looked a little puffy, possibly from crying. Elena counted Brenda as her only female friend in New York. They genuinely liked each other, not because of the closeness of their men but rather because each woman saw in the other sincere kindness and truth. The friendship was new and still slowly defining itself as a potential long-term bond. Elena fought her natural instinct to immediately ask Brenda what was wrong, because it was important that her new friend not feel that she was pushy. Elena stole glances at Brenda, who was absentmindedly staring at her cup of tea.

"Are you ready to order?" the waiter interrupted them.

Elena had been so preoccupied trying to read Brenda that she hadn't properly studied the menu. She tried to quickly take in all of her options.

"You might wanna try the mushroom and brie omelet. It's pretty good," Brenda suggested.

"Sure, I'll take that," Elena said to the waiter.

As the waiter turned to leave, Brenda got his attention. "Can you also bring an order of the chocolate waffles with bananas, and some strawberries on the side?" she added. The waiter acknowledged her with a smile as he turned away.

"Is it okay if I catch a ride with you and Quincy to the funeral? I'm just not in the best shape to drive by myself."

"Of course, what's going on?" Elena asked.

"Everything and nothing, just feels like stuff is so off and out of whack."

Elena was caught off guard by how quickly and unexpectedly Brenda was near tears.

"Shit, I'm sorry, Elena, I just…" Brenda muttered, genuinely embarrassed. "I can't believe this."

"What are you talking about? You don't have to apologize to me. I just wanna know why you're so upset. Is it what's going on with Phee?"

"I really wish I knew what the hell is going on with Phee. All he does is shut me out and keep me on the sidelines with everybody else."

"A horrible tragedy like this does something to a person, but trust me, in time he'll find his way through," Elena offered.

"It's not just this situation; he's been this way since I've known him. He's only going to let a person in so much, and to tell you the truth, I can't just keep letting him make me feel like a stranger."

Brenda stopped speaking when she found herself getting emotional again. She sat quietly for a few minutes, avoiding direct eye contact with Elena. The silence was broken when the waiter returned with their orders. Elena smiled courteously at him as he placed the omelet in front of her. As soon as the waiter placed the plate with the waffle on the table, Brenda snapped at him.

"I specifically asked you to put the strawberries on the side, and yet you put them on top. Would you take this plate and bring me what I ordered? Is that too much to ask?"

"No, ma'am," the waiter said sheepishly as he picked up the plate and headed back to the kitchen.

Once he was gone, Brenda looked at Elena and was

immediately remorseful. "You must think I'm horrible," Brenda said, apologetically.

"Of course I don't. I just think you've got a lot on your mind."

"I don't even know what I'm doing anymore, Elena. I'm trying to be there for Phee, but sometimes it feels the more I try to love him, the more it makes him resent me."

"Phee doesn't resent you, Brenda. He loves you; I guarantee you that."

"What makes you so sure?"

"For starters, that man looks at you the way every woman in the world wished her man looked at her. Maybe I can't speak on some things, but as to whether or not he loves you, that's an obvious one."

"Well then, maybe I asked you the wrong question."

"What do you mean?"

"What if what you're calling love isn't enough anymore?"

The waiter returned with the amended order. "Here we go, strawberries on the side. My apologies, ma'am."

"I'm the one that owes you an apology. I'm just having one of those days; I didn't mean to take it out on you."

The waiter smiled at her before turning and leaving.

Elena reached across the table and held both of Brenda's hands. "I'm one of those believers that true love is always enough. I'm corny that way. And I think you are too; otherwise, you wouldn't have hung around as long as you have."

"Yeah, well things are different now, and I can't spend the rest of my life waiting for Phee to change," Brenda said sadly.

When she found herself getting emotional yet again, she gently removed her hands from Elena's, turned her attention toward her plate, and started attacking her food. Elena left her own plate untouched and watched Brenda more curiously.

"He doesn't know, does he?" Elena asked.

"Know what?"

"That you're pregnant."

"How did you…?"

"I had a child, remember? The other day at brunch I didn't think much of it, but your glass of champagne was the only one that went untouched. Just now, the thing with the waiter, not to mention you're eating like a fat man on vacation."

Brenda laughed and cried simultaneously. The simple act of sharing the news was, on one hand, a much needed release and, on the other, frightening to her. She was faced with the reality of having what she always wanted, but not in the way that she had dreamed.

"I thought it would be romantic to tell him in Nice. Now I don't even want to tell him at all."

"What are you talking about?" Elena asked, confused.

"Even after this thing with his brother dies down, I don't want to guilt Plhee into being a father and spending the rest of his life with me. That's something that he has to want for himself, not something he feels forced into. I'm not doing that to myself and sure as hell not doing that to my child."

68

St. Augustine's was a large church. It was built back in the late 1800s, and refurbished twelve years ago. Its architectural attention to detail and its intricate craftsmanship distinguished it as a jewel of the city. New Yorkers came out in droves for the funeral, a veritable who's who in entertainment, sports, politics, and industry. Democrats and Republicans, drug dealers and cops sat side by side, while upstarts and legends shared the same pews. They didn't come out for the departed, but rather for the living. The vast majority of those who turned out had never met AJ or even known he existed. They came because Clay was one of the most powerful men in New York. They came because Phee was a celebrity in his own right. Some came for the scandal, some to pay debts or curry favor, while others came as opportunistic lookie-loos and for the chance of rubbing elbows with people they only read about on Page Six of the *Post*.

The difference between the father and son was that Clay expected people to pay their respects to him, whereas Phee appreciated the cops and friends that came to lend him their support. He was surprised to see some of the faces in the crowd. There was a strong showing of cops in their blues, those he knew and didn't know. Diego, the policeman from the hospital, sat in the center of uniformed cops, young and old alike. All of the detectives from Phee's squad were there, including Captain Whedon, Alvarez, Asif, and Bernie. Phee saw Kravitz and his wife sitting in the row in front of Spider Harris and his cousin Dookie from his childhood. Agent Nyguen was there with his wife and daughter and even his mother and father, whom Phee had only met once. Agent Maclin sat across the aisle from Phee. When she caught his eye, she nodded at him and offered an empathetic smile. Even though he knew it was highly unlikely, when he looked up toward the balcony section, he thought for a second that he saw The African. Phee took in the various faces of strangers and friends as he sat next to his father, who simply stared ahead. They were in the first of two rows designated as the family section even though Clay and Phee were technically the only family AJ had left. Just as she promised, Brenda sat next to Phee, supportive and warm, but noticeably less affectionate than usual; next to her sat Quincy and Elena.

Phee saw heads turning as the guests responded to some type of commotion coming from the rear of the church. Even Clay turned around, just in time to see four six-foot-plus cross-dressers, dressed to the nines, marching down the aisle over the protestations of an overwhelmed usher. Epiphany Chevalier led the decked out divas. It took a minute, but Phee realized that they were all wearing outfits that were designs from AJ's book—faux furs over brightly colored sequined gowns. People whispered and laughed, and even some of the older, blue-haired women started clutching pearls and gasping at the sight of the rowdy clique. Epiphany didn't walk, but rather sashayed down the aisle and attempted to sit in the same row as the mayor before being cut off by a bodyguard.

"What do you mean we can't sit there? The seats are empty aren't they?" Epiphany said defiantly. "By the way, Mr. Mayor, me and all of my girls voted for you, Dah-lin, so I know you ain't gonna sit up there and dis some of your loyal constituents."

The mayor smiled weakly, embarrassed by the attention. He gave a very subtle look to his bodyguard, who tried his best to discreetly diffuse the escalating scene.

"Unfortunately these seats are reserved for members of the mayor's staff that are on their way. Perhaps I could help you find another section that you all would be comfortable in," the guard said as he gently tried to lead Epiphany away.

"If you don't take your hands off of me, they are going to have to have two funerals up in here today," Epiphany said as she snatched her arm away from the guard.

"Jesus Christ," Clay said under his breath as he saw the situation potentially spiraling out of control.

"Don't worry about it, Pop; I'll handle it," Phee said as he rose and crossed over to the confrontation. "Epiphany," Phee said as he approached.

Epiphany turned and recognized Phee immediately. "Detective

Freeman, can you please tell them that I am AJ's best friend, and we have just as much right to be here as anyone else does?"

"Nobody is denying your right to be here. We just need to find you other seats, because those are unavailable," Phee responded.

"So you came over here to tell us to go sit in the back somewhere where nobody can see us, and y'all can pretend we don't exist, right?" Epiphany said defensively.

"No, not at all; I came over here to help you. Also, I wanted to apologize to you for the other day, because I didn't tell you then that I'm actually AJ's younger brother." It took a few beats for Epiphany to take in what Phee said. In a strange way, she felt betrayed. Phee saw it all in her face and actually felt bad for his prior deception. In front of the entire church, he extended his hand to her, "It would mean a lot to me if you all came and sat in the family section with us, where you belong."

Epiphany and the rest of the divas were so used to fighting for even the smallest semblance of respect from strangers that when Phee gave it so readily, the group was stumped and momentarily left speechless. Clay was too far away to hear the conversation, but once he saw the ringleader silenced he knew Phee had effectively handled the situation. He was completely dumbfounded, though, when he saw Phee turn back in his direction and lead the group of cross-dressers back toward their section. Phee sat the group in the row right behind them and then returned to his seat next to his father.

"What the hell are you doing?" Clay quietly demanded.

"I told you I would handle it," Phee responded.

Brenda couldn't help but smile. Quincy lowered his head in an attempt to hide his laughter as Elena looked around completely confused. Clay sat fuming, while the divas in all of their glory were front and center, beaming like royalty amongst New York's elite.

69

The last time Phee saw his father step foot into a church was when Dolicia died. Due in large part to her Dominican upbringing, the only religion she ever claimed was Catholicism. As a technicality, she had both of her sons baptized when they were little. Even though she had attended Mass on a semiregular basis, she defined herself at most as a "casual Catholic." Aside from the baptism, which Clay saw as a compromise, he made it clear that his sons were not to be forced into one religious direction or another—whatever belief or lack thereof they adopted would be of their own volition. Clay raised his boys to view God as an option, and not an obligation. As Phee's focus drifted in and out of the service, he realized that he had no idea whatsoever whether or not his brother even believed in God. What if he hated God? He certainly had earned a lifetime of reasons to. For all Phee knew, AJ could have believed the same as Zibik and Varelli.

Phee had been to more than his fair share of Catholic funerals. Between the Irish, Italian, and Latino cops he saw laid to rest, he lost count of the services he attended. He found Liam to be very different from the majority of Catholic priests, who in the past he never really connected to. Liam wasn't as staid, and his service wasn't as monotonous as some of the earlier ones he was forced to endure. He was accessible and charismatic in his delivery. Phee had often heard the Bible passage that Liam quoted, but for some reason, it was the first time he really heard it.

Liam stood before the assembled crowd and read the third chapter from the Book of Ecclesiastes.

"There is an appointed time for everything. And there is a time for every event under heaven. A time to give birth, and a time to die. A time to plant, and a time to uproot what is planted. A time to kill, and a time to heal. A time to tear down, and a time to build up. A time to weep, and a time to laugh. A time to mourn, and a time to dance. A time to throw stones, and a time to gather stones. A time to embrace, and a time to shun embracing. A time to search, and a time to give up as lost. A time to keep, and a time to throw away. A time to tear apart, and a time to sew together. A time to be silent, and a time to speak. A time to love, and a time to hate. A time for war, and a time for peace."

As Phee listened to Liam, he thought about the various seasons suggested in the Bible verse and how the passage related to the seasons of his own life. He thought about his successes and failures; he thought about the accomplishments that lifted him with pride and regrets that submerged him in shame. He thought about his brother, his father, his mother, his bond with Quincy, and his relationship with Brenda. He thought about the one sentence in Liam's verse that spoke to him the most: "A time to tear down and a time to build up." It was that very thought that carried him to the podium when Liam offered the opportunity for family members to say a few words. Although Phee hated public speaking, for some reason that he didn't even understand, he suddenly found himself standing in front of the crowd speaking on behalf of a brother he no longer knew.

"Very few of you actually knew my brother. Unfortunately, neither did I. I knew him when we were kids, when he taught me how to play B-ball, spending hours after school helping me with my jump shot. He was the reason that I started playing football; because I knew no matter how hard I practiced, I would never be as good as him on the basketball court. And we were always trying to outdo each other to impress my father. AJ taught me how to smoke one day and then lectured me on all the reasons I shouldn't the next. Ironically, he was even the one that taught me about girls."

There was laughter throughout the church as Phee recounted the things about his brother that he remembered most. As his speech continued, the content and delivery gradually became more serious.

"He taught me how to stand up for the things that I believed in and told me to never apologize to anybody for dreaming. One day when I was eight years old, he promised me that we were both going to make a big mark on the world. He said, 'the Freeman brothers were going to do big things.' As long as we had each other's backs, he believed we could do anything. Those are some of the memories I have of AJ and our childhood. I'm not standing here trying to paint some perfect picture of AJ, because he had his demons just like the rest of us. I was going through some of his stuff the other day and came across a quote that was written in one of his books. It said, 'We're all in the same game, just on different levels. We're all in the same hell, just fighting different devils.' Like older brothers should, he taught me things that I'll never forget. I think if there is one lesson that he tried to teach that I failed to learn, it was that he never wanted me to be afraid to love, because I think in his mind that was the worst kind of coward." Phee couldn't help but look in Brenda's direction. After a beat, he shifted his focus to the row behind her to AJ's friends. "I want to thank Epiphany and her friends for loving my brother when I didn't have the courage to. Thank you for being the family to him that somehow I forgot how to be. Today, as I stand here before all of you, I just want to publicly apologize to my brother and tell him how sorry I am for not living up to my end of the bargain, for being too much of a coward to have his back the way he had mine. I'm sorry that I wasn't smart or strong enough to learn the lessons that he tried to teach me. I'm not sure whether or not my brother ultimately believed in souls, but selfishly, I pray that he did. I pray that somehow he's still here, because there are so many things I still need to learn from him."

It became increasingly more difficult for him to continue speaking. As he struggled to press on, Phee found himself crying in front of the assembled crowd. He cried for his brother and the lost opportunities between them. He cried over the wasted years of separation brought on by his own prejudice. He cried for things that were said and even worse things that had been done that could never be taken back. Most of all, Phee cried over the death of one of his earliest heroes, who was unsuccessful in his efforts to teach his younger brother the power of unconditional love. Brenda, Elena, Epiphany, and the divas, along with others throughout the crowd, cried openly as they watched Phee struggle and fail in his attempts to hold it together. The next time he tried to speak, it took much more effort. "Epiphany, since you're the most qualified person here, I was wondering if you would come up and say a few things about my brother and tell us all who he really was."

A true diva never passed up an open mic and a captive audience. Epiphany wiped the mascara that had run down her face, got herself together, and wowed the crowd. She told funny stories about AJ one moment, then poignant ones the next. She playfully reprimanded the mayor. "Dah-lin, since today is all about forgiveness, I forgive you for 'dissin' us earlier. And don't worry, I'm still gonna vote for you in the next elections just because AJ used to always say that you were the sexiest Republican she had ever seen." Epiphany even had the divas stand and show the crowd the outfits that AJ designed. There had never been a funeral at St. Augustine's the likes of AJ's. As Phee sat between Clay and Brenda, he smiled and thought it fitting that his brother's send-off was very much in keeping with how AJ had lived: unconventional and unapologetic. By the time Epiphany stepped away from the mic, New York knew who AJ was and the marks she'd made.

70

After the actual burial ceremony, invited guests ended up back at the Waldorf, where wine and food flowed freely in the ballroom. There was plenty of networking, schmoozing, and ass kissing. Epiphany and the divas held court as the unofficial hostesses. The gathering felt much more like a social event than a solemn occasion. It was, after all, a Clay Freeman production. Quincy was catching up with Agent Nyguen, when Maclin approached.

"Hello, Agent Maclin, good to see you again. How've you been?" Nyguen greeted her.

"You know from experience it's never a dull moment when you work with Quincy and Phee," she smiled. Her voice had improved some but was still a bit heavier than usual.

"How are you feeling?" Quincy asked Maclin.

"Besides the sore neck and bruised ego, I'm fine," she responded.

"Maybe a nice long vacation would do you a world of good right about now," Quincy suggested.

"Maybe you're right, but I need to be back to work first thing Monday. If anything, this case has brought me more clarity on why I wanted to be an agent in the first place," Maclin said.

"How's that?" Quincy asked.

"Because case after case, we see the kind of evil that most people can't even imagine. I don't delude myself that we're ever gonna stop it all, but last night when I fell asleep, I did so feeling that people like us make a difference because, just like the Zibiks, Varellis, and Degglers of the world, we're actually willing to die for the things we live for the most."

The three continued talking until Lamar Adai, Quincy's contact at Port Authority, approached.

"Hey Quincy, can I talk to you for a sec?"

"Sure," Quincy responded as he excused himself from the two agents and walked off to the side with Lamar.

"Took me most of the night, but you said it was important," Lamar said as he handed Quincy a thick envelope.

"This is great. I really appreciate it," Quincy said surprised.

"Nothing like playoff tickets for motivation. I didn't exactly follow protocol getting you this stuff, so let's just make sure it stays between the two of us," Lamar said.

"You got it, and thanks again," Quincy said as he patted Lamar on the shoulder and walked away.

Elena gently reached out her hand and intercepted Quincy as he walked by. She and Brenda were midconversation with Liam.

"We were just telling your brother how beautiful the service was. Definitely different, but beautiful nonetheless," Elena said.

"I was thinking of letting Epiphany lead Mass tomorrow, just to shake things up," Liam joked.

"I would pay good money to see that one. Might even be a good way to get Phee to start going to church," Brenda added.

"By the way, where is Phee? He told me his father wanted to see me," Liam said as he scanned the room.

"I saw them a few minutes ago, going into one of the little rooms in the back next to the bathroom," Elena said.

"Quincy, do me a favor: stop by tomorrow. I need to talk to you about something," Liam requested.

"Sure, I'll swing through around noon."

"You all take care," Liam said before moving off.

As Quincy watched his brother walk off, the uncomfortable thought of Liam somehow being involved with Deggler and the murders was all he could think about. For just once, he hoped that the same gut feelings that never misled him were somehow off. He quietly prayed to God that he was wrong. Dead wrong.

71

I t was a good service," Phee said.

"You think so? For a minute there I thought it was turning into a circus," Clay responded.

"We sent AJ off the way she would have wanted to go. Can't ask for more than that." As Clay quietly nursed his ever-present scotch, he looked pointedly at Phee, referring to AJ as a woman. Phee stared back and made no attempt to either correct himself or apologize. When Clay turned away and looked out the window, Phee studied his father. "How are you feeling?" Phee asked.

"Like a man who just buried his son."

"We buried AJ a long time ago, Pop. Both of us. The funny thing is, today was the first time in years that we allowed her to live the way she wanted to. I need you to know that I wasn't trying to embarrass you or anything. I just…"

"You didn't embarrass me, Phee. You honored your brother.

And in honoring him, you did the one thing that I forgot how to do a long time ago."

"What's that?" Phee asked.

"Love hi—the way family is supposed to be loved."

Clay sipped his scotch and was quiet for a beat. When he finally looked up at Phee, his eyes were wet with remorse. "I know I was always hard on you, Phee, always pushing you. I was thinking about the other night when you said that as a kid all you wanted to do was be like me when you grew up. That wasn't why I pushed you though. I pushed you so that you would be better than me. And Quincy was right: you are. You are the greater standard. Out of all of the things that I've done wrong in this world, you're the proof and reminder of what I've done right. The day that you have this conversation with your son, you'll know exactly what it feels like to have done the one thing in this world that matters the most."

The two continued talking until Liam knocked on the door and interrupted them. Clay hugged his son, and then asked to speak to Liam alone. Just before Phee closed the door behind him, Clay called after him: "Sol Rosen told me you called him at six a.m. Must have been important," Clay said smiling.

"Yeah it was. Very," Phee responded.

"For what it's worth, I'm really glad you made the call."

"Yeah, me too. Good night, Pop."

Phee stood in the doorway for a beat and watched Clay speaking quietly to Liam. Even though he couldn't hear anything that was being said, he couldn't help but wonder if his father was finally seeking penance.

72

Just outside of the ballroom, Phee almost collided with Brenda as she came around the corner.

"Sorry," she said surprised.

"No, it was my fault; I wasn't looking where I was going," Phee responded. The two were alone for the first time since Brenda left him at the hospital, and they both were immediately aware of how awkward they were now in each other's company. Brenda looked back toward the ballroom doors as loud laughter spilled out.

"I think a full-fledged party may be getting ready to break out in there."

"Well, you know it's not officially a party until the cops come knocking. Since it seems like half the force is already here, looks like we're ahead of the game."

"It was a beautiful service, Phee. I was so proud of how you handled everything."

"Look, Brenda, I…"

"I really gotta get going. I was just coming to say goodbye."

"What if I asked you not to?" Phee said.

"I've got a ton of work I've gotta do, and…"

"No, I meant what if I asked you to never say goodbye to me again? What if you were right…and I am the man that you're supposed to love the rest of your life? And I'm supposed to love you the same way? Do we really want to say goodbye to that?"

"Maybe I was wrong. You know one of the hardest things in the world, Phee, is loving someone that doesn't believe they deserve to be loved. All I've ever wanted to do was make you happy, but now, after all these years, I'm not sure you even know how to be happy. I mean really happy, down in your soul. I know this is a very difficult time for you, but I can't be, won't be, some kind of knee-jerk reaction for you that only lasts until the next time you feel afraid—or the need to run and hide from yourself."

"That's what I'm trying to tell you: I'm not running anymore, Brenda. And for the record, the only thing I've ever been afraid of was disappointing you, by not being the man you thought I was."

"And that's the very thing you ended up doing," she said.

The very thought of him disappointing her was bad enough; hearing her confirm it was a blow to Phee. He leaned against the wall trying to regroup and find the words to redeem himself. As he sunk his hand into his pocket, it rested against the small ring box that he'd been carrying around all day. Even though he was tempted, he decided not to take it out. The last thing he wanted was for his proposal to be misinterpreted as a theatrical act of desperation.

He had woken his father's jeweler, Sol Rosen, at six a.m. and picked out a beautiful three-karat canary diamond in a princess cut setting. He rebooked the hotel and got two tickets to Nice, leaving on the red-eye. He had a very clear picture of how special he wanted the moment to be. He tried to think of every detail, so that when he asked her to marry him, everything would be as she deserved: perfect. But he knew now more than anything that he first had to prove himself. If he couldn't win her on the merits of what his heart told him to say and do, then he truly wasn't worthy of her.

"Brenda, you gotta ask yourself how much forgiveness goes into loving someone for the rest of your life. Maybe you really don't think it's worth it anymore. I don't know. Maybe I've slowly taken everything from you, and now you got nothing left for me. The thing that I do know is that I'm ready to do any and everything to prove to you that I am worthy of your love. I'm not going anywhere ever again, and I'm never putting anything before you. I'm guilty of a lot of things, but the one thing I've never done was lie to you, and you know that. Whether I'm deserving of it or not, I'm asking you to believe me when I say I'm never leaving."

Phee tentatively stepped closer and reached for her hand. Even though she neither resisted nor encouraged him, Brenda was acutely aware of how present and vulnerable he was. It was the first time she ever felt that there were no parts of him that were off-limits to her. He kissed her with the intention of showing her what his words couldn't convey. Phee kissed Brenda the way she always wanted him to, as though the process of pressing his lips to hers was not just a simple act of pleasure, but rather one of great necessity.

By the time he stepped back and allowed her to breathe again, Brenda was left physically weak and emotional. She tried not to cry, but Phee didn't make it easy on her. As they continued to talk, he told her things that she had all but given up hope of ever hearing. In all the years she'd loved him, she had never felt him as exposed as he was now. He let her know the things that he was most afraid of. The things that he feared might reduce him in her eyes. Phee shared his insecurities with her, at least the ones he had identified and claimed. He told her all about The African, and AJ's boss, and the choices that he made as a fourteen-year-old boy that filled him with corrosive regrets throughout his adult life—regrets that slowly but constantly ate away at his core. When he realized that the possibility of losing her was not only real but also likely, he held very little back. Brenda stood in shock when he told her of the dream he had in the hospital. Although she never bothered telling him about her recurring dream, she was left speechless when he shared with her the details of his most recent vision. He told her in his dream that they had left the city for a quieter life. He told her of the three children he saw, two curly-haired little girls that looked like her and a son that was the spitting image of him. As he continued holding her hand, he told her the thing he remembered most about the dream was that they were happy. And complete.

EPILOGUE

After Quincy dropped Elena off at her father's, he went and sat on a bench in Battery Park. He'd spent the last two hours distracting himself and attempting to talk himself out of opening the envelope that Lamar gave him. There was a queasy feeling in the pit of his stomach that seemed to only get worse with each passing moment. As he looked at the envelope in his lap, he felt conflicted by both needing and not wanting to know the contents within. Unfortunately for Quincy, there was nothing blissful in ignorance; not knowing was torturous. He had to open it, because he was so troubled by the fact that no matter how hard he tried, he couldn't reasonably justify how Liam lied to him about how he had innocently come into possession of Father Conner's baseball. He had to open it, because the night Deggler was killed, there were too many questions left unanswered.

Deggler definitely had help transporting his victims, and everyone assumed, Quincy included, that Deggler's brother was that help. But shortly after Quincy killed Deggler's brother, something started gnawing at his gut that there was more to the case than everyone thought. Liam gifting him the baseball only exacerbated his doubts and concerns, and now the most recent killing of the priest made it urgently clear that he could no longer ignore the horrible possibility that he knew who the killer was.

When Quincy called Lamar, he'd asked him to forward footage of photos from tollbooths leading in and out of Jersey on the night Deggler was killed. He wanted to see photos of every driver in vehicles matching the description of the van used in transporting Deggler's victims. Quincy narrowed the timeline down to two hours before Deggler kidnapped his victims and two hours after he was killed. In the four-hour span, there were eighty-four dark cargo vans entering and exiting bridges and tunnels between Manhattan and New Jersey.

Quincy loved his brother more than anything; he had no idea what he would do if his darkest suspicions were confirmed. After a few aborted attempts, he finally opened the envelope and began nervously thumbing through the eighty-four photos that Lamar had printed out. Three-quarters of the way through the pile, Quincy was gut-punched by what he saw. The quality of the photos was surprisingly good. The resolution, angle, and time stamp were the irrefutable evidence that Quincy would have given any and everything to change. He started shaking as he looked at the picture taken at the George Washington Bridge toll booth and saw clearly that it was Liam driving a van. As Quincy looked closer, he noticed the van had the same license plate as the one that was abandoned by Deggler's accomplice. The brutal facts winded Quincy and weighed him down like a sunken anchor. It was information that he wanted to give back and pretend never existed. His hand cramped as though the photo were a thousand times heavier than it was. Every time he blinked, there was hope that the image would change to a much less painful confirmation. Thick snow fell and swirled around him as he sat on the bench blurred by the information, without the faintest idea of what he would do next.

Liam sat quietly in a chair in a darkened corner playing with the gold band on his ring finger. It was a channel-set single tanzanite stone that Quincy gave to him several years ago shortly after his confirmation. A priest wearing a ring often did so as a representation of his eternal marriage and fidelity to God. In times of stress Liam rotated it repeatedly, but before this night, under no circumstances had he ever completely removed the ring.

He watched the silhouette of a sleeping body comfortably nestled beneath a slightly tattered secondhand comforter. The only sound in the room was the unsteady pitch of someone snoring in the background. Liam stared at the covered mound and thought long and hard about his purpose for being there. He thought of the various reasons he came; the most pressing was his need to kill. The night before, when he killed Reverend Edwards, he did so in the hope of quieting the urges that started consuming him shortly after Deggler's death. It was his hope that killing the fallen Baptist would satiate him enough to repress the growing obsession and save him from becoming what he feared most. He was wrong. The killing gave him two things that he never expected: strength and corroboration. For the first time since he was a child before the molestation, Liam felt liberated. He regained power that he had ceded long ago. When he set Reverend Edwards on fire and watched him burn, he no longer felt like the victim but rather the victor. For reasons he couldn't understand, he didn't know why his recent kill was so much different from the first. Years ago when he killed, he was immediately filled with remorse and shame before God. He knew that it was that sense of accountability to God that had helped him in the past to resist killing again. Now that he had finally given in to the part of his nature that he had disowned for years, he felt whole and empowered, beholden to no one. Not even God.

As was the case with Deggler, last night's kill was intended as a public statement and outward condemnation against what both killers viewed as the most blatant acts of religious hypocrisy. Killing the fallen clergy was nothing more than an extraction of cancerous cells that threatened the entire body of the Church. Their death was a necessary extermination. The crimes committed by the men had all in one way or another breached the very spiritual tenets that they were supposed to fortify. He saw them all as traitors of the highest order. Now that Deggler was dead, it was up to Liam to punish those who betrayed their most sacred duties. The only difference between the protégé and mentor was that Liam believed that such justice should not just be limited to the fallen men of the cloth. There were certainly others in the secular world that were equally deserving of such acts of reckoning. The poisonous well ran much deeper than the Church. There were others whose spiritual crimes infected generations and left countless victims in the wake of their various offenses. He thought all those guilty should be equally punished. The onus rested not just on the shoulders of the primary perpetrators but also upon their coauthors by way of their laxity, indifference, and complicity. Liam saw the tolerance of evil as an endorsement of it. He saw parts of his new mission as righting some of those wrongs. Now that he had finally embraced who he really was, not only was he ready to take up where Deggler left off, but he was determined to go even further. Immediately after killing Reverend Edwards, Liam felt not just reinvented but reborn. There was still one final thing to do to complete the metamorphosis. If he had hopes of success in his new role then he knew he had to start with the most important kill of all.

Liam walked closer to the bed and studied the sleeping form more closely. He bent over and shook the body until it stirred and the snoring stopped. He turned on a nearby lamp and threw the covers off of Colette, who was slowly awakening from a heavy sleep. He shook her again, this time more forcefully.

"Ma, wake up."

ACKNOWLEDGMENTS

First and foremost thanks to God, the Author of all authors

I can't recall exactly how old I was the first time I heard the old saying—"Your talent is God's gift to you, what you do with it is your gift back to God."

It is something that has always stuck with me and made me feel incredibly blessed to have been born an artist who has always wanted to tell the kind of stories either as an actor, director or writer that truly resonated with people

Though the vast majority of authors face an incredible accumulation of rejections the one bright beam of encouragement is that all it really takes to completely turn the tide is one publisher to believe in your voice and potential. Fortunately for me it was Dominique Raccah who has built a great career and reputation by taking chances and thinking outside of the box. I am so proud and appreciative for the opportunity to work with you. Thank you.

Lavaille Lavette—without you none of this would have happened. You have quickly proven yourself to be just the type of game changer I've always dreamed of finding. It's incredible to me how your vision of the book series is so intrinsically aligned with mine. We speak the same language and dream similar dreams. Thank you for simply "getting me."

My agent Rockelle Henderson—you've been the amazing architect who created the path that led to me finding the right publishing situation. Not once have you wavered in your support of this series. Instead you've consistently doubled down in your efforts when the road seemed the most bleak. You truly are the rock.

Mandy Chahal—From our first panel event that you set up at Comi-Con I knew that it would be a fun and enlightening ride learning from you. Working closely with you on the marketing of the books has simply been awesome.

Thank you to the readers for your support. You really are the buoys that keep authors afloat amidst the sea of rejections and self-doubt.

—E—

About the Author

Actor/director Eriq La Salle is best known to worldwide television audiences for his award-winning portrayal of the commanding Dr. Peter Benton on the critically acclaimed and history-making medical drama *ER*. Educated at Juilliard and NYU's Tisch School of

the Arts, his credits range from Broadway to film roles opposite Eddie Murphy in *Coming to America* and Robin Williams in *One Hour Photo*. La Salle has maintained a prolific acting career while at the same time working steadily as a director, taking the helm for HBO and Showtime in addition to episodics such as *Law & Order, CSI: NY,* and *Under the Dome,* to name a few. He lives in Los Angeles, California.

🐦 EriqLaSalle23
f EriqLaSalle
🌐 IAmEriqLaSalle.com